Fatal Opinions

STEPHEN MURRAY

Fatal Opinions

St. Martin's Press
New York

Library of Congress Cataloging-in-Publication Data

Murray, Stephen.
    Fatal opinions / Stephen Murray.
        p.   cm.
      ISBN 0-312-08193-6
      I. Title.
    PR6063.U76F38   1992
    823'.914—dc20   92-28379
                                                     CIP

First published in Great Britain by HarperCollins Publishers.

First U.S. Edition: December 1992
10 9 8 7 6 5 4 3 2 1

Fatal Opinions

CHAPTER 1

'I never dreamed you would settle on such a godforsaken place,' Tina Blake burst out. 'Why on earth couldn't you have chosen a university town? Cambridge, say; or York? Even Milton Keynes would have been better than this dump!'

'You really do hate it, don't you?' Darby observed, amused by her vehemence. The Tyneside accent he had never cared to lose turned 'hate' into 'heat'.

'It's so *dead*. There is nothing whatsover to *do*. Unless one wants to join some tedious lot of busybodies. I never imagined that there could still be people in the world whose idea of a bright night out is tenpin bowling followed by a takeaway Chinese meal! God, I mean, and that's the *adults*!'

He smiled 'Who cares? Anyway, I shouldn't have thought it would worry you. With your ... outside interests.'

Tina Blake looked at her husband's business partner speculatively, as if he was himself not wholly innocent of tedium. Sometimes it seemed that his accent and his laid-back attitude to life were all that separated him from the unremarkable multitude of men; but then she looked again at his handsome, lazy features and the dark amused eyes glinting in their web of laugh-lines; and his sardonic tolerance and his gentle teasing of her were strangely compelling. And his body was broad and healthy, the skin all but concealed by a dark pelt of hair, which fascinated her.

All the time she had been talking they had been taking off their clothes, since time was limited. A gesture in the direction of romance would have been enjoyable, but in this as in all of her life Tina was a realist, and experience had taught her to make do with the possible. A thoroughgoing, swept-off-one's-feet romance would offer a more effective relief from her paralysing boredom; all the affair with

Anthony Darby offered her was periodic physical satiety and a scratch at her itch for danger; nevertheless, it was better than nothing.

Tina Blake had slipped into cynicism via marriage. A promising—some said brilliant—career in research had received a severe setback when she fell in love during her post-graduate year with a colleague more forceful, though less clever, than herself, and had never recovered. Now it was *his* research laboratory that was in question, with Anthony Darby as his partner; and Tina's own post as research assistant was dangerously close to an expedient designed to keep her occupied. Sometimes at dinner parties Tina outfaced covert pity by proclaiming that it was John's ploy for keeping her off the streets. The smile which greeted this remark had come to be stretched rather thin.

Did John know that this was how she took her amusement? Were his long nights at the lab a way of abdicating from the need to be aware of—as they simultaneously gave her the opportunity for—her unfaithfulness? Did John know, she wondered, as she surveyed Darby hungrily from his cheerful, bearded face to the tight-curled hairs on his long, strong legs that her current lover was his co-director and Medisearch's brilliant geneticist Anthony Darby, who so often *didn't* work late?

Now they stood naked on opposite sides of the bed like boxers waiting for the bell, each wondering what was passing through the other's mind; and then Tina said, 'Shall we get on with it, then?' and her expression softened as Darby knelt on the bed and reached over to pull her roughly to him.

In the front room of a detached house on the newest of the estates on the outskirts of Crawley, Kate Randall sat back in her chair, slipped the cap on her pen, and nodded to Andrew Mackenzie. Andrew looked round the room with a satisfied air and asked, 'Who's for coffee?'

Clive Morris, with a cheerful creased face and almost bald head though he was still in his thirties, crossed his short plump legs and nodded. 'Thanks, coffee, yes.' He watched Kate fold her shorthand pad and ease her cramped fingers. She looked tired, he thought. Her blue eyes beneath the halo of fair hair were less sharp than usual, and weariness had fined the flesh from her small, spare features. He could see how she would look in middle age. He let his eyes fall with swift regret to her guernsey jumper. Her frame, like her features, was slight and the jersey hung loosely, all but expunging her breasts. Baggy cord trousers were tucked cossack-style into her short boots; and here it was still January, Clive lamented, and summer's fresh, light fashions a long weary time away.

Andrew went on round the room, ticking off the numbers on his fingers. Someone asked for his coffee black. Ginnie, GP's wife and a doctor herself, and Judy glanced up and smiled their thanks before returning to their conversation, Ginnie's plain, high-boned face with its frame of mousey hair leaning closely towards Judy's small, energetic features—like an imp on a mediæval carving, Clive Morris thought whimsically, with her cap of close, curling dark hair. Someone declined coffee; someone asked if they could have orange instead; someone reminded Andrew that her husband took sugar.

Out in the kitchen, filling the percolator and spooning in the coffee, Mackenzie decided the evening had been quite satisfactory; as efficient as meetings led by Kate Randall always were. Her single-mindedness was so genuine that despite her well-known ruthlessness with irrelevant small-talk, red herrings, and gossip about mutual acquaintances, the meeting had been generally good-humoured. Things were coming to a head, with a vital bill coming up for debate in Parliament, and CAMEX, the Campaign Against Medical Experimentation, had to take its task seriously. Possibly some of them had failed to appreciate that, when a year or so ago they had first daringly formed this local branch of the national pressure group. Now, with Kate working fulltime on the campaign since she lost her job, they had all come to acknowledge that there really was no

option other than dedicated and hard work; unless it was
to give up altogether. In the last two months the committee
had been increasingly active, culminating in the organization of last Saturday's simultaneous protest marches
through the centres of five local towns. As Kate had said
baldly tonight, if anyone had joined CAMEX merely as a
token gesture, they should never have joined at all. They
did not exist merely to register dissent; they existed to
oppose, with every means that could be found, medical
experimentation with human embryos.

Andrew switched on the percolator and waited until it
started to squawk and bubble, then reached a packet of
biscuits out of a cupboard and began to arrange them on
plates. The empty packet he disposed of carefully in the
pedal bin, sweeping the crumbs up with his hand too, so
that Alison when she returned should find her kitchen in
its usual pristine splendour, then carried the plates through
to the living-room.

Twenty minutes later the front door of the Mackenzies'
house shut behind the last to leave, Judy Baker and Ginnie
Kemp. They stood by Judy's Renault for a few minutes,
chatting. A car turned into the road and drove into the
Mackenzies' drive: Alison, back from her pottery class.
They chatted on a while longer, then Judy unlocked the
door, climbed in and drove away. Ginnie walked along to
where her own car stood twenty yards away in the shadows
at the end of the cul-de-sac. Once inside, she started the
engine, buckled her seat-belt and put the car into gear. It
felt strangely reluctant to move. Unbuckling her seat-belt
again, she climbed out. The tail-lights of Judy's car were
receding, and as the engine note faded the cul-de-sac fell
silent. There was not much light, but enough to show
Ginnie that she had a flat tyre. As she opened the boot to
fetch out the spare, she noticed something else, and as a
result walked right round the car.

She had not one, but three flat tyres.

'Oh no!'

Ginnie looked back at the Mackenzies' house. There was

one light on, upstairs, and even as she watched it flicked off. Two streets away at the entrance to the estate she knew there was a telephone-box. Feeling in her jacket pocket for change, she locked the car, turned up her collar, and trudged off to find it.

A dozen miles away, Miles Wetherby was taking his leave of his father in the hallway of another new house on another small estate, on the outskirts of Uckfield. It was a tedious drive to his chic terraced house in Wandsworth (Miles considered the combination of an address which still had a proletarian ring and a reality of rock-solid property values—if you chose your neighbourhood carefully—tailor-made for a man in his position), and as he shrugged himself into his motoring coat his mind was already considering whether it would be quicker at this time of night to cut across to the M23 or stick on the A22 and risk being stuck in a queue at Purley.

'Mind how you go, lad,' Dan cautioned. He tended to avoid the use of his son's name these days; perhaps because the boy had been christened Leslie, and Dan had no sooner schooled himself to use the diminutive 'Les', at his son's insistence, than 'Les' was unaccountably dropped and 'Miles', his middle name, became *de rigueur*. The idea of changing one's name to suit one's current image was alien to a man of Dan Wetherby's background—precision engineering—and age.

Miles smiled fleetingly in acknowledgement of his father's ritual expression of concern, and looked past him to Carro. Carro had been Dan's last secretary, before the works was sold and Dan retired; and though it had been no real surprise that Dan, a widower, should try his luck there, and even ask her to marry him, it had been considerably more difficult to understand why Carro should have accepted. She had been thirty-five—just her stepson's age—a strong, well-muscled woman who carried an air of suppressed energy which stood her in stead of conventional good looks. From the marriage she had gained a protective, modestly prosperous husband, who was of an age where he was unlikely to give her sleepless nights about his extra-mural activities, a comfortable home, the wherewithal to dress well, and the security which a woman of thirty-five begins to appreciate the value of.

A woman of thirty-five also frequently begins to appreci-ate the value of a family—or at least to feel the ephemerality of her ability to create one. Whether Dan Wetherby's appearance of vigour had proved a delusion, or whether she found too late that she herself had been short-changed when it came to fertility, the children for which perhaps she had partly married Dan never came, and the houses they lived in came to have that showpiece cleanliness and order which tell of the absence of small feet and reaching hands.

Now she was forty-five, still strong and athletic but a little dried-up. In the last year she had investigated the possibility of adoption; but it was too late: they were con-sidered too old. Though she behaved as a woman in the prime of her life who has merely postponed the starting of a family, Miles knew that in reality the opportunity was past.

'Kind of you to come down, Miles—' she smiled at him, placing a hand on her husband's shoulder—'when you're so busy.'

'Old Billy can't hold out much longer,' Miles said confi-dently. 'With the spadework I've done—let's say I'm in with a good chance.'

'Why you want to get into that beargarden is beyond me,' Dan Wetherby grumbled. Billy was an elderly MP, whose East End constituency was one of the country's safest Labour seats. His strokes had been getting progressively more severe, and it was only a matter of time until one more proved fatal. 'And it doesn't do to build up your hopes, lad. If you don't get it, you've a harder fall.'

'I'll get it,' Miles said, with the easy certainty of a man whose whole life has been devoted to being in the right place at the right time and with the right credentials.

'I hope then you'll divorce that wretched woman,' Carro

said, as he drew on his driving gloves and sorted out his keys.

'We'll see. Been seeing anything of her?' The question was aimed at his father; Carro's antipathy to Miles's estranged wife Judy was such that she could rarely bear to be in the same room with her, but Dan saw her from time to time, doting as he did on his grandson Thomas who lived with her, and thereby a sort of channel of communication was kept open between her and Miles. He also, to Miles's advantage, took over most of the responsibilities of Miles's access, by proxy as it were. Miles did not see himself as particularly cut out for fatherhood, and was happy to let his own father perform most of his duties for him. Besides, the Wetherbys senior were much more on the spot here in Uckfield than he was in Wandsworth.

Carro's words none the less stayed in his mind as he unlocked the car, waved and drove away. He turned out of the estate. Down in the cutting a late train rattled its way the last few hundred yards to the station. He negotiated the mini-roundabouts and the traffic lights and made his way out to the bypass to join the main road. There was no doubt that Judy was a problem, but so long as they lived apart and Judy maintained herself off her inheritance (thank God for that inheritance!) it was a problem in abeyance. A divorce now would be fatal to his plans: pity he had not insisted on it years ago, but then she had been tied up in all sorts of unpleasantness and he had rightly feared some of the mud rubbing off on to himself . . . Perhaps the simplest thing was just to be content with the status quo; but could he trust Judy not to involve herself in some scandal? Already that night Carro had informed him that 'that woman' had got herself tangled up with those CAMEX nutcases . . .

He put his driving into automatic pilot and gave his mind properly to the problem.

CHAPTER 2

Driving home through the winter darkness, the wind-screen-wipers flicking intermittently at a chill drizzle, Tina Blake wondered how she was going to cope. There had been a certain interest and excitement in the months it had taken to set up the laboratory and get things running smoothly; but now Medisearch was functioning, all she had left was her untaxing routine. John she rarely saw, for he worked all hours, attending to the administration when he wasn't engaged in the laboratory. She and John had a daughter, Sophy; but Sophy was sixteen and might have spoken a different language for all the communication that they had. Certainly there was not much left of Tina's duties as a mother, apart from loading the washing-machine every night and seeing that there was always something in the freezer. She had never thought she was much cut out for motherhood anyway, but now that role was being taken from her she felt its loss keenly. Perhaps that had something to do with why she was tied up in this silly affair with Tony Darby.

It's all very well for him, she thought viciously, content with his scrubby little flat and utterly absorbed in his work. But me: I'm like an engine tearing itself to pieces because it's not coupled to any useful work. The unoriginal simile pleased her, and she let it float around her mind while she negotiated the roundabouts and the short stretch of dual carriageway which took her round the town centre. That was the trouble with life, she decided: there was not enough excitement. Once, science had provided it, when she was being talked of as the best research student of her year. Marriage had slammed the door on that. Then twelve years ago when Sophy had just started at school and Tina had time on her hands the first taste of adultery had been heady. Subsequent episodes had been spiced with the possibility of being found out, or the risk to her job (she was by then working part-time for a pharmaceutical company; her lover was a senior man in another department). After that, excitement and risk had receded leaving only the satisfying of the sexual itch. What spice had there been to this evening's little episode?

Tina's own work at Medisearch was mere scientific drudgery. It was John, the biochemist, and Tony Darby, the geneticist, who lived with the stimulus of genuine pioneering. Sixteen years of scientific advancement had passed by while Tina changed Sophy's nappies and sewed nametapes into her first school uniform and packed her sandwiches, and worked part time persuading bored doctors to prescribe one brand of painkiller rather than another, and Tina had been left behind, fit only to execute other people's ideas.

Still, the research they carried out at the laboratory was technically interesting, and there was the additional boost of knowing that they were working on the coming thing. If all went well and research led to practical applications it would, additionally, make them all extremely well-off.

On the other hand, the whole thing could collapse. Medisearch had borrowed heavily on its prospects, but those prospects were dependent not only on the outcome of the research but on the outcome of the current debate on the ethical issues involved, and the system of checks, licences and permissions which would be decided by Parliament. In the very worst case, all research of the type they were pursuing would be embargoed, though Tina considered that unlikely, Parliaments being normally adept at jumping on bandwagons which had already gathered speed and unwilling to bow to loony luddite pressure groups. Meanwhile, they were dangerously exposed financially—and that was one of the few kinds of danger for which Tina hadn't developed a taste.

Once they had a product to show all would be roses— *then* investment would be forthcoming by the million; but they needed some of that investment now. It was all rather like a juggling act. Turning into the avenue where they lived, Tina reflected that she was not totally confident in her husband's juggling abilities. He always had been a clumsy man.

It was time, she considered as she parked the car in the drive, that she took a hand.

Kate Randall pushed Clive Morris's hand away. 'Thanks for the lift, Clive,' she said firmly.

'My pleasure.'

'Love to Betty, now!'

'Yes.'

She climbed out and turned away, rummaging for her door key, and was relieved when she heard Clive Morris drive away. One of the things a campaign like CAMEX taught you was tolerance of your fellow humans, she reflected wryly, slipping the key into the lock. You thought those who felt as you did on the one big issue would share your tastes and habits and interests in other respects too; but you found with a bump that you were in harness with those from whom you would normally run a mile—and that they were as serious as you, and as honest in their convictions.

Kate had been lucky: she had gained good friends through CAMEX. Ginnie Kemp was one; Judy Baker was growing to be another, though her reticence about her private life made the process slower and more problematical. But on the other score were those who affected Kate like fingernails scratching on a blackboard—and Clive.

Clive had been no problem until recently. She rather liked him—he was a science teacher, with a good mind used to the concrete and quantifiable, an asset in a group only too happy to conceptualize until the cows came home. He was shrewd, too, in gauging public reaction to CAMEX, guiding them into courses of action which would have a memorable impact and increase popular support.

However, when a month or so ago Kate had lost her job, and with it her company car, she had learnt another side of

Clive which was more awkward to deal with. The CAMEX committee meeting invariably took place in the Mackenzies' house in Crawley, and Kate gladly accepted Clive's offer to collect her from her flat in Felbridge and run her back there afterwards on his way home to Betty and his two young girls in Blindley Heath.

Kate was not in the market for an affair with a married man, but she would have been a good deal happier if that was what was offered: simple to recognize, simple to reject. Instead, Clive turned out to be one of those men who made you uncomfortable, without giving you anything concrete to complain of. The first time his hand had strayed to her knee after changing gear, she had supposed it a preliminary to a definite assault in the car park outside the flat, but no assault came. It seemed to be enough for him to read intimacy into their very presence in the car together, so that the journeys were oppressive with unspoken meaning; but he ventured no further physically than the hand on the thigh. The whole effect was smothering, and more unpleasant so far as Kate was concerned than if he had been physically more presumptuous.

She wondered if Clive knew about Charlie, to whom she was more or less engaged, or whether he didn't care. It seemed that in Clive's mind there was a strange equation by which behaviour which went that far but no further preserved his faithfulness to Betty; but to Kate's mind, that was a strange way of judging faithfulness.

Judy Baker could see the livid glow of the television through the imperfectly drawn living-room curtains as she turned the car into the drive, but by the time she entered the room the screen was blank and Sophy's tangled locks were bent devoutly over the school books which surrounded her.

'How has he been?'

'Fine, Mrs Baker. Not a peep since he went to bed. He wouldn't let me watch him have his bath, so I made him promise to scrub all over with the flannel while I waited outside. He *sounded* as if he was washing.'

Judy laughed, and paid her the money she owed her.

'Did you have a good evening?' the girl asked, transaction complete.

Judy said: 'You ought to come along to one of our public meetings: see for yourself.'

'No, thanks. I mean, if you believe in it, I suppose you have to go, don't you, but I don't see what all the fuss is about, myself,' Sophy replied dispassionately.

Sophy left shortly afterwards, her current temporary boy-friend collecting her in his mother's car to run her back home.

Judy pottered about, climbing the stairs to listen outside her son's door. His breathing was regular, with the slightly snuffly wheeze which meant he was lying on his back. His real name was Thomas, but between themselves Judy called him Trooper. It was a nickname she considered he had certainly earned.

Downstairs Judy made a hot drink, flicked through the *Radio Times*, but in the end just sat contentedly in the little sitting-room listening to the silence. It was two years since she had come here, to the semi-detached cottage with its tile-hung upper storey and white-painted porch. The pair of cottages belonged to Heather Campbell; or, perhaps, to her husband; nobody had much bothered, just as nobody had much bothered with a formal lease or strict accounting when Judy first came here as a bolt-hole. Only now was she beginning to realize just what a selfless, even foolhardy, gesture it had been on the Campbells' part to offer their newly-vacant cottage to the drunken, layabout, dishonest one-parent-family Judy had then been.

An elderly man, retired from working on the farm before the Campbells bought it, lived in the adjoining cottage, where he cooked on a range in the winter and a Baby Belling in the summer, bathed in a zinc bath, and content-edly tended his spotless vegetable garden while the jumbo jets from Gatwick thundered overhead. The Campbells, thoughtfully, had left her alone, except for offering the most casual and unburdensome occasional company, and it had been the old man, Harry Weeding, who had watched over her as she set about swimming first against, and then out of, the tide. He had brought her early peas when her sobs and curses had crossed the hedge between them, feigning oblivion to her swollen eyes and red cheeks and grumbling about his deafness. He had brought her asparagus, and spent a morning showing her what to do with it, and marvelling at her electric cooker. Once, he had called the ambulance; often he had set himself to tidy her garden where he could stay within sight and sound of her wasted, despairing days, on hand in case of need. He had taught Trooper to use tools in his wooden lean-to shed, and how to put them away afterwards so that they would always be bright and serviceable; and the beginnings of the male lore which Trooper had hitherto had to pick up as best he could from very different role models.

Judy had learnt from Harry Weeding that there was a life worth living even at eighty-five; and that the contentment which informed his every day was neither the jealous property of extreme old age nor owing to luck, but a matter of hard-won choice. Gradually, she had learned to taste a little of it for herself. It had been sweet.

Judy unashamedly lived off the income which her shares in her father's biscuit manufactory still brought her; that money had served worse purposes in the past, she thought, than buying breathing-space for her and a future for Trooper.

It had been one of the sharpest revelations of her return to sanity (as she considered it) to find that she loved Trooper so much. She had always thought of herself as a woman without maternal feeling; and during what she thought of as the dead years, first in Brixton and then in Cheam, she had certainly behaved as one. She was ashamed now to think of it, and looked back with a shudder on what Trooper had had to undergo. Last year, when she had unaccountably fallen once more into a three-day drinking spree (it was the time when Harry Weeding had had to call the ambulance) Trooper's grandfather, Dan Wetherby, and his wife Carro had given the boy a home for a fortnight. At the end of that time Judy had had a struggle to get him back, in the face of the Wetherbys' possessive attachment to the boy and Carro's fierce denunciation of Judy as a dangerous and irresponsible mother.

That had opened Judy's eyes to the depth of her own love for Trooper, and frightened her, too. She realized, with a sense of perilous escape, that she could so easily have lost her son for good, and her reaction was to resist fiercely everything which she interpreted as an attempt to separate Trooper from her. Just recently Trooper's father had taken to exercising his right to see the child at weekends, and Judy had been surprised by the depth of jealousy this aroused in her. Miles had paid little enough attention to Trooper when he most needed it; now she supposed it suited him to play the role of the responsible father. He had even, to Judy's fury, taken to turning up occasionally to parents' events at Trooper's school—the school which she, Judy, paid for Trooper to attend. Judy was scrupulous in ensuring Trooper saw his father's side of the family; but she sometimes wondered why.

And now there was CAMEX, something Judy had become caught up in after attending one of their public meetings, and now enjoyed beyond measure. That in itself, she realized, marked her down as an outsider, for to those at the centre CAMEX was intensely serious, painfully important. Judy believed CAMEX was right to fight against what she thought of as the Orwellian drift of medical science but she recognized that she was not at heart a crusader.

No, what Judy valued was the company, and the responsibility she had increasingly won—and the fact that it was something she had done by herself, not the result of anyone else's efforts to 'draw her out of herself'. Andrew Mackenzie and Ginnie Kemp and the rest accepted her as they found her. They knew nothing of her history beyond the obvious fact that she and Trooper lived by themselves; or perhaps they did—either way they treated her with casual good nature. In their company Judy herself could not quite forget that she had so recently lived the life of a lonely drunk; but she could consign the fact to its place in history.

Only Kate Randall knew her story: Kate whom Judy still found enigmatic; Kate who was so frighteningly efficient and dedicated, who had withstood the loss of her job and used it as a spring-board to greater work for the campaign. Kate whom Judy admired and, just occasionally, feared.

CHAPTER 3

Judy was firm when over the telephone Clive Morris's name came up and Kate hinted how uncomfortable her trips home with him were.

'No problem: I'll give you a lift instead.'

'But it's miles out of your way. He comes past my flat anyway.'

'So what? It's only twenty minutes.'

'That's kind of you. Poor Clive! I feel guilty now. He's bound to be hurt, but it's his own fault.'

'Of course it is. It's just a pain for you that it's you he's got a crush on.'

After she had put the phone down, Judy began to wonder how Kate coped in the normal way. Of course there were buses, and trains not far away; but it wasn't like it had been in London, where there was almost always a tube station within walking distance, and buses down every High Street. She turned it over in her mind during the afternoon, and when she set out on the school run she fancied she had come up with the answer to Kate's problem.

If there had been nothing else to show that The Pines was no longer the Edwardian country house of a prosperous City shipping magnate, the traffic pattern in the lanes that converged on it through the shallow wooded valley would have been sufficient.

In that corner of south-east England where the Kent, Surrey and Sussex borders converge, a tidal flow of commuter traffic affected even the smallest lanes when office workers from Croydon, Sevenoaks, Redhill and Bromley followed their daily course to and from work. But after the morning rush had died down, and again before the evening one began, there was a secondary tide of traffic which was more selective and composed not of company saloons each carrying one man in solitary splendour, but of estate cars and 'hot hatches' driven exclusively by women, bearing cargoes of children.

This was the school run; the daily double highpoint of the lives of innumerable wives who, out of maternal conscientiousness or because insufficient opportunities to help out in socially acceptable posts (antique shops, charity shops, vets' surgeries) were available, lived a life of easy tedium in their timbered farmhouses, barn conversions, private estates and ranch-style bungalows. For the children who attended The Pines and many another private school the school run was no more than a means of getting there; for the women it was an end in itself, and a lifeline.

And I am one of them, Judy Baker reflected as she negotiated the roundabout by the Mormon church. I drive fifteen miles each way, twice a day—probably passing half a dozen perfectly good schools on the way—and I should contend fiercely with anyone who suggested that it was all really unnecessary. I could walk with Trooper to the school in the village, and we would be able to spot wild flowers, look for the first lambs, feel the change of the season; but no, I pack us both into the car and we whizz past everything of that sort, registering only the length of the queue at the roundabout, the increasing congestion, the bad tempers and worse manners of other drivers.

But I enjoy it. I enjoy meeting the other mums when we drop our kids off, and even more so while we wait for the end of afternoon school. I enjoy the shared feeling that we are doing the best we can for our children in bringing them all this way to a school as well-thought-of as The Pines. I enjoy the fact that our cars are chic and have new registrations; that some of the youngest women are not mums, but nannies or au pairs (whom we greet democratically nevertheless, as they stand a little apart in a huddle of their own).

Oh God, Judy thought with the keenness of one who has been near the brink, to think how nearly . . .

The awareness of her good fortune reminded her of her idea for solving Kate's transport problem, and she made a mental note to call in at the car showrooms on the way home. Trooper would enjoy that; and Judy had had it in mind to change the car while prices were so favourable. If all went well, when she got home with Trooper she would be able to give Kate a ring and offer her the use of the old car as long as she needed it.

Her face clouded. She had suddenly remembered that she couldn't call at the showroom this afternoon; because today was the day the woman from the Social Services was due to call. Instantly the afternoon which had looked so sunny and optimistic became black and sour. Judy's hands trembled on the steering-wheel of the car, and she gripped it more tightly, until the skin on her knuckles hurt. She felt physically sick.

It was not the police who were the ultimate bogeymen in Judy's life, despite her past occasional brushes with them: it was the social workers. She had lied, manœuvred, schemed and fought to stay clear of them, even through the worst of her troubles, because the social workers could do something to her from which she knew she would never recover: they could take Trooper away.

Black anger pulsed through her veins at the thought that now, when everything else was set so fair, this cruel threat could be raised again. The letter she had received gave no details: merely advised her that a Mrs Kelso would call at half past four; but Judy's mind would not content itself with any innocent explanation. Indeed, how could there be one? But what had happened to trigger their nosey interest in her now?

At any rate, Judy was confident that this Mrs Kelso

would have no reason to go away dissatisfied. She would see a clean, neat house, a model mother and a contented, articulate boy in the uniform of an expensive prep school. Let her try and make something out of that!

'How was your day, darling?' Tina Blake asked absently, reading the microwave instructions on a carton.

Sophy looked up from her copy of *Elle* and stared at her mother's back. 'Pretty bloody,' she said deliberately.

Tina turned sharply. 'Don't swear, sweetheart.' But Sophy's head was bent over her magazine once more, and Tina couldn't see whether her expression was mutinous or contrite.

This was the only sort of contact they seemed to have these days, Tina told herself bitterly, setting the timer. She had worked hard to be a good mother; to excel at that, after she had had to reconcile herself to the second best in everything else. Now they only conversed in these haphazard spurts, preoccupied on her own part, laconic on Sophy's, like ships signalling. And the girl's father saw even less of her, coming home late in the evening when Sophy was out with friends, or babysitting, or upstairs in her room doing her homework. If she turns out like me, Tina thought fearfully . . . And it'll be my own fault if she does! And she resolved to give up Tony Darby forthwith.

But if she gave up Darby, the itch would still be with her. It would be with her when she no longer had the means to gratify it, a day, she thought emptily, which couldn't be so very far off.

But then, they were poised to become much better off. In a year or two her life might not be so empty, and they could lavish more care on Sophy too, to demonstrate that they did love her, really.

Provided CAMEX didn't put their spanner in the works, she thought bitterly.

After supper Sophy took refuge in her room. The impossibility of any sort of communication with her parents oppressed her blackly. She did not think she was naturally inclined to be rude, but somehow she found herself being so whenever her mother made any attempt to converse. The whole situation seemed out of control: she and her mum circled each other like sparring cats, and her father she hardly saw, and when she did he made ineffectual attempts to smooth the troubled waters.

In addition, Sophy found the nature of her parents' work disturbing. The whole area of fertility, conception, embryos, what is a person and what is only a little lump of tissue, was disconcerting; a bit too close for comfort; and it also made her schoolfriends look at her askance. Their parents were accountants, sales executives, teachers, owners of shops and garden centres. Sophy's parents were scientists: and she felt marked out.

At the same time she carried an additional burden of guilt. CAMEX was not a popular organization in the Blake household. She had never told either of her parents that the one place where, these days, she felt fully accepted and treated as a human being was in the house of a CAMEX member.

Judy Baker shut the door as if it was made of porcelain, and then turned and sagged back against it, bitter tears burning her eyes. Dimly she heard a car start up and move off as Mrs Kelso drove away. After a while she looked up, and saw that Trooper was watching her anxiously from the living-room. She tried to smile at him, but somewhere along the line the smile turned into a strangled sob, and that opened the gate to tears of rage and frustration.

To be told that she was suspected of sexually abusing her own son!

It was obscene. Obscene that the woman could come uninvited into Judy's house and tell her that as a result of 'information that had come to her notice' she had arranged for Thomas to visit a children's unit for assessment; obscene that the neat house, the well-behaved child seemed only to make Mrs Kelso's mouth purse even more tightly, as if they were somehow stigmata of obsessionality; obscene that her own single state was twisted into proof of deviance!

And *how* had the bitch known of last year's drinking episode? *How* had she known of Judy's rocky past into which, she had had the nerve to say, she would 'have to do some research'?

Judy looked round her memory for anyone who might hate her so much as to set this remorseless council Big Sister on her trail.

She knew one thing. If she lost Trooper, and ever found out who had been behind it, she would kill them.

CHAPTER 4

Sophy and her friend Hannah left school in the usual gaggle of friends: three or four girls and half a dozen boys. Hannah was quieter than usual, and Sophy was not surprised when she hung back and let the rest of the crowd outdistance them.

'We won't take the bus today,' Hannah said. 'We'll walk. I want to lose two pounds before the Easter holidays.'

They turned down a side road to cut through the housing estates towards home. After a while they came to a corner shop, and Hannah went in to spend her bus fare on sweets.

'No point taking it home with me, is there?' she asserted.

'Oh yes! And who said she wanted to lose weight, then!' Sophy scoffed.

Hannah shrugged. 'My mum reckons I'm anorexic as it is.'

Sophy, casting around for possible explanations of her friend's low spirits, said, 'That Cathy Spencer's got her eye on Damon.'

'She can have him,' Hannah said.

Sophy said nothing, conscious of thin ice, and the two girls walked on in silence side by side.

'Morris put his hand up my skirt today,' Hannah said off-handedly.

Sophy thought she must have misheard. 'Morris?'

'Morris. You know—chemistry. *Mr* Morris.'

'Hannah, he never!' She looked at her friend in startled astonishment. 'Hannah, he *couldn't* have!'

'Think I'm lying?' Hannah retorted. 'I asked him about the magnesium experiment, right, you know when yours worked and mine didn't, so he did it again, the experiment, I mean, so then there was just him and me there, wasn't there? And I was sort of leaning over the bench, wasn't I, with my bum stuck out, and he came up behind me and put his hand up my skirt. He went all pink.'

Both girls had stopped, Sophy gaping at her friend in astonishment. Now Hannah walked on, and Sophy had to run a few steps to catch her up.

'Did he . . . where did he put it? What did you do? I'd have *died*!'

Hannah settled down to be factual. 'Well, he sort of felt up my leg. I mean, I was just stood there like a lemon. When I felt him feeling my knickers I sort of realized I'd better do something, so I told him I'd scream if he didn't take his hand away. I would've, too, and he knew it!'

'And did he?'

'Yes.'

'But what did he *say*? He must have said something.'

'Just said, "I'm sorry, it won't happen again." I said it had better not. I mean, I was thinking all the time he was about to take his thing out.'

'I thought you were a bit quiet.'

'Sophy Blake the great psychologist.'

'Poor you!'

'Yeah. You know the way he looks at you, right? He *looks* like a groper, I mean, doesn't he?'

Sophy wasn't sure what a groper should look like, and thought about that for a while. It was true, Mr Morris did look at you rather funnily, in a way which made you uncomfortable; but in other respects he always behaved

very nicely. Having got her confession off her chest, Hannah
perked up, and they discussed the matter with detachment
the rest of the way home.

'Now if it had been Andy Hughes . . .' Hannah sighed.
Andrew Hughes taught history and was by common con-
sent the dishiest man on the staff.

'You should be so lucky!'

'I'd have dragged him into a dark corner.'

'I'd have been down on the floor with my skirt up before
he knew what hit him.'

'I'd have raped him.'

'You're shameless, woman!'

By the time they reached Hannah's house what Clive
Morris had done in the chemistry lab was somehow happily
relegated to the same sort of unreality as their fantasies
about Andy Hughes.

Hannah turned, her hand on the front gate, and warned
her friend, 'You're not to tell anyone, Soph. Promise?'

'Oughtn't you to tell your social tutor?'

'And lose Morris his job? Promise!'

Sophy shrugged. 'Of course.' She hesitated. 'You're sure
he didn't . . I mean, it was just . . .'

Hannah grinned. 'No, we had it off on the chemistry
bench and I've got the marks of the bunsen burner on my
bum to prove it. See you!' And she slammed the gate behind
her and walked jauntily down the path, her school bag
swinging from her hand.

Sophy walked on thoughtfully.

Something had gone wrong with the weather. Maybe the
scaremongers were right for once and the greenhouse effect
was to blame; but the new month came in more like May
than December. Within two days the tight-rolled buds on
the honeysuckle trained up Frances Walker's porch were
showing tiny green tips.

I shouldn't if I were you, Frances warned them as she
pulled on her wellingtons; but she was humming under her
breath all the same as she pulled the door to behind her;

and the sun fell amiably on her cheek as she set off across the yard.

She was bent under the bonnet of her car when she heard the crunch of gravel as a vehicle turned into the drive. She straightened up carefully, still holding the dipstick and an oily rag, as a white Ford, flashy with spoilers and low-profile tyres, swept past and scrunched to a halt by the front door.

'Mind my gravel,' she murmured.

A man and a boy got out. The man was in his early forties, with lightly greying hair carefully cut. He was about Frances' own height (she was tall for a woman), and stocky. The boy was nine or ten and waiflike, with the large watchful eyes of a refugee in a charity poster. He looked vaguely familiar.

The man made for the front door; looked over and spotted Frances; and changed direction, coming towards her with a confident beam. She bent beneath the bonnet again and slipped the dipstick carefully back into its tube before meeting him with a vague smile.

'Frances! Miles Wetherby. We met at the school parents' evening, yes?'

'So we did,' she said, recollecting dimly.

Miles Wetherby was considered by many mothers to be one of The Pines' more delicious parents. He was a thoroughly modern man, democratic, bonhomous, committed to exercise and the saving of whales, of properly liberal outlook yet had contrived to rise nicely in monetarist, free-for-all Thatcherite Britain. He was almost an MP; everyone know that the Labour Party was only waiting for the occupant of a suitably safe seat to die before selecting Miles Wetherby. Meanwhile, he was active in local politics and community relations in a South London borough where his attacks on property speculators and his views on local policing regularly found their way into the national news. The Pines liked parents of his sort: famous in a thoroughly modern and acceptable way, iconoclastic without being threatening, pleasant to everyone, and destined to rise much higher. He was a single parent, which made him no less acceptable to that particular society—or as near as, since it was understood that there had been a long-term separation but no actual divorce from Thomas's mother, Judy Baker. Judy was in general well-liked; but in her absence, and in Miles's presence, it was agreed that she had clearly wronged him grievously.

They began to walk towards the house. 'I meant to call sooner, since you were so kind as to ask Thomas to play with your little girl, but I'm afraid business . . .'

They had reached the front door, and Frances pushed it open and led the way in. After the pale sunlight of the mild December morning the hall was dim and shadowed, though pleasantly warm. The low ceilings, the blackened oak and the russet brick soaked up such light as filtered through the eneven, bubbled glass of the ancient windows. Frances, used to the transition, habitually paused a moment when she brought others in, to let their eyes readjust. It gave her an opportunity now to get a better look at Wetherby while he peered interestedly into the shadows. She vaguely recalled now an invitation of a general sort, made without expecting it to be taken up, and was unsure whether to be pleased or otherwise that it had been.

'I expect Lucy's outside still. Come into the sitting-room while I find her. I'll have some coffee made; you'd like a cup?'

'That would be fine,' he replied with an expansive smile. 'You know, you've actually got some very nice pieces here, Frances.'

Yes, I did know, *actually*, she muttered under her breath; but aloud she simply said 'I like them,' and a moment later Frances' 'help', Bridget, came in, and Frances left Wetherby and his son in her care and went in search of Lucy.

Lucy looked Thomas over critically before taking him under her wing. The difference in maturity between a girl of almost eleven and a boy of only just ten was very marked; the more so as Thomas was so silent. Lucy endured

Wetherby's patronage stolidly ('She's got her mother's features, hasn't she? You're going to have the boys eating out
of your hand, Lucy, in a few years' time') and took the first
opportunity to whisk Thomas off to hold the tools and the
nails while she built her rabbit hutch.

Mr Wetherby ('Miles,' he reproved. 'Please!') did not
seem very anxious to leave, despite the Saturday morning
surgery which he claimed awaited him in his ward. Frances
easily resisted the temptation to invite him to stay to lunch;
whereupon he swallowed the last of his coffee and drove
away in the white Sierra, depositing a second helping of
gravel in the flowerbeds on the way. Frances wiped her
hands instinctively on the old pair of knickers which served
her as a rag, and which she now realized she had been
holding all the time, and went back to finish servicing the
car.

Wetherby reappeared as the winter dusk was thickening
into night, the headlights and spotlights of his car sweeping
brutally over the façade of the house like a searchlight.
Thomas, who had shown signs of enjoying his day as Lucy's
acolyte, returned to his place as his father's silent, diminutive shadow. Frances felt constrained to offer tea, which
Wetherby accepted with effusion, and it was six before
father and son climbed into the white car and drove away.
Before they left Frances found herself agreeing that Thomas
could come again; perhaps in the holiday, which was due
in a week or two. But Wetherby, it seemed, only had access
at weekends. The rest of the time Thomas was with his
mother. Frances was a little short with Wetherby after that;
but perhaps his work really was so demanding that he was
ready to leave Thomas even on those few days he was able
to see him.

'How did you and Thomas get on?' Frances asked Lucy
after the car had driven away. 'I know you! I hope you
didn't relegate him to a servant.'

'Did you know they were coming, Mum?'

'No, as a matter of fact. Why?'

Lucy frowned, and didn't reply directly. 'He didn't want to go.'

'Darling, I don't suppose it's easy for him if he only sees his father at weekends. There'll be another time to finish off the hutch, anyway.'

'I didn't mean Thomas,' Lucy replied witheringly. 'Besides, he doesn't see his dad for *months*.'

'I don't think that can be right,' said Frances absently, and they went to see what there was for dinner.

Four days later Miles Wetherby rang and asked if he could take Frances out to dinner.

'Well, Trooper?'

'Mum, you know Lucy Walker at school?'

'Don't think I do, do I?'

'You *must* do. Well, her mum lives in this super house, and she's got a rabbit which she keeps in a shed at the moment but we made a hutch for it.'

'Hold on, you've lost me. Start again!'

Trooper sighed exasperatedly. 'Dad took me to see them, right? Lucy Walker and her mum, right, in this big house. And Lucy and me, we built this hutch . . .'

'And Dad?'

'Oh, he went away, but he came back later. And she says I can go there again, but Dad said it'd have to be on one of his days. Mum, it wouldn't have to be, would it? *You* could take me.'

'What's she like, Lucy's mum?'

Trooper looked at her critically. 'Taller than you,' he said. 'But about as old.'

'Monkey! Was your dad nice to her?'

Trooper thought about it. 'Yes,' he decided. 'He was.'

'That explains it, then.'

'Explains what, Mum?'

'Why you dad is suddenly so concerned to be a good father and take up his right to see you at the weekend,' she replied tartly. 'If you want to know what you've been today, chum, you've been a prop for the latest performance of a terrible ham actor. Now come and have some tea, and then it's bath and bed.'

Judy's spirits had regained a sort of equanimity. Trooper's assessment visit to the children's unit had apparently convinced the people there that he was happy and well cared for and had no precocious knowledge of sexual matters which might be consistent with Judy abusing him. Mrs Kelso had revisited Judy and apologized—not for putting Judy through the ordeal, but apparently for the fact that it had not proved justified. Judy demanded to know where the initial allegation had come from, that Trooper was at risk. Mrs Kelso could not, or would not, say. Moreover, she gave Judy to understand that though the immediate sword was removed from over her head, a file once opened was never closed. Judy had no doubt her name now appeared on a register of parents to be watched. She was not innocent, she had just not been proved guilty.

She had told Heather Campbell about the incident. She had also, in an unguarded moment, spilled some of her anxiety to Kate Randall, one night when she was still waiting for the results of Trooper's assessment and they were driving back from the Mackenzies' house together. Now she half wished she had not; her instinct was to keep her private secrets very secret; but Kate had been calm and soothing, understanding her anguish.

The evening her mother and Miles Wetherby drove off to the restaurant in Westerham Lucy Walker sat on the piano stool in front of the baby grand, with her hands spread out stationary on the keys, and stared at the maker's name on the polished wood above the keyboard. The reserve which in Frances gave an impression of cool and poised competence was in Lucy precariously balanced on the edge of introversion. She was intelligent, and knew it; but she was also perceptive, unhappily so for a child, much more in fact than she would have chosen to be. She couldn't remember how old she had been when she first felt responsibility for her mother, but very early on she had perceived the anxious care she received from Frances; that care which led to Frances being quite prepared to be thought obsessive over her daughter. Lucy knew enough of her mother's work to realize that Frances was successful in business terms; what she feared above all, Lucy knew, was not being successful as a mother.

So their relationship had taken a curious turn. Although ostensibly Frances provided and Lucy received, in fact each planned ahead for the other, doing all within their power to remove hidden rocks from beneath the surface of daily life, so that their relationship was closer to that of orphaned sisters than mother and daughter.

Lucy was used to vetting men she met. Her mother was an attractive woman and Lucy was proud of the fact. Frances was sociable, single, relatively young and well-off. Lucy was not afraid of her mother's marrying; indeed sometimes she looked forward to having someone else to take her load of responsibility from her small shoulders. It was only the question of whether anybody could be found who was good enough. Lucy yearned for a Prince Charming, not for herself, but for her mother, even though she was fully aware that whoever married her mother would become her own stepfather. Lucy, who had never known her father and who watched her friends' fathers covertly at every opportunity, decided she must cross that bridge when she came to it.

Whenever Frances was asked out, Lucy took a watching brief, realistically not wasting her energies on anxiety until it happened a second, or a third time. Rarely had it gone further than that; but never before had there been someone who, like Miles Wetherby, had a pretext for calling at all sorts of times.

Lucy had never been so sure of anything in her life as that for her mother to get involved with Wetherby would be a terrible, irrevocable disaster.

CHAPTER 5

'For evil to triumph, it is only necessary that good men do nothing,' Ginnie Kemp quoted. 'And women, too, of course.'

Liz Pink hesitated, aware that she was at a disadvantage in arguing about an issue she was not one hundred per cent sure of .

'As soon as we started to think in terms of "rights" rather than *right*,' Ginnie pursued, 'we started down a slippery slope. *My* right to do what *I* want, and blow the cost to others. Why should we be so arrogant as to think our rights justify us in committing murder?'

Liz was on to the word like a hawk. 'That's just it! To you it's all murder, isn't it? Abortion. Well, I say women have been in subjection to their own fertility long enough. Why shouldn't we control it?'

Ginnie was amused. 'We can control it,' she pointed out. 'Would you like me to explain what contraceptives are for, Liz? Look, *that's* when you make the choice. If you were going to have a *dog* you'd make your mind up before you went to the kennels; you wouldn't bring the thing back and then say it was your right to drown it because you couldn't be bothered to look after it. It's too *late* when you find you're pregnant to talk of your "rights". Let's not wrap it up in a lot of pseudo-philosophical crap: what we're really talking about is not rights but convenience, and because we don't think it's convenient to be bothered with the child we've created we go to some nice sympathetic doctor and he kills it for us. Anyway, CAMEX isn't about abortion. Separate issue.'

'Oh, come on!' Liz protested. 'It's all part of the same thing, surely? Basically, you're trying to put the clock back.'

'My dear girl, your faith amazes me!'

Liz raised her eyebrows high at that. Whatever she felt

deep inside (and she was not sure whether she was ready to admit that even to herself) on the surface she had believed her agnosticism was seamless.

'Your faith,' Ginnie expanded, 'in the great god progress. Because we can, we should! Something we can do to-day must be good because we couldn't do it yesterday. Amazing!'

Liz grinned shamefacedly.

'Like a cup of coffee?'

'Love one.'

Ginnie went through to put the kettle on. After a minute or two Liz followed her and said, 'I don't know how we got on to that one. I'm sorry.'

Ginnie took down a couple of mugs from the rack. 'That's all right. We're as bad as each other. Only—I'm not trying to reopen the argument—CAMEX really isn't anything to do with being anti-abortion. Some of us are, some aren't.'

The kettle began to boil and she poured water into the mugs. Liz said, 'But you're against them using embryos for experiments.'

'Yes. But even that's not quite it. Do you know what really worries me?'

'Tell me.'

They took their mugs through into the other room. Ginnie resumed her seat. Liz leant against the window-sill, watching her, and blowing gently on her coffee.

'It's just this: who makes the decisions? You see, to most people, what a company like Medisearch does is not the remotest bit important. They don't think of it, because nobody's brought it to their attention. *I* know this legislation that's coming up won't even make a one-sentence item on the news, and even then the slant is that it will allow wonderful work which may lead to miracle cures for cancer and Down's Syndrome and help for infertile couples and all sorts of things like that. What we don't hear is that on the way companies like Medisearch are going to play God: decide which embryos to let live, which to let die. If a couple who've gone for in vitro fertilization die in a car accident, do you let that embryo die or use it for research? One day it's a potential child to a childless couple; the next, raw material for a doctoral thesis. Or why not try and see how long you can keep the thing alive? Ten days? Ten weeks? Have you *seen* what a baby's like at ten weeks, Liz? And *we* have to—*society* has to—decide whether we are prepared to let them do all this. Whether it is right that some of the biggest ethical questions we have been faced with in our lifetime should be decided by people who stand to make money out of the outcome.'

'Are politicians that much better qualified to do the deciding?'

'No; any more than you would be, or I would. But at the moment people aren't even aware that there is an issue. It's being bumbled through as if it was a piece of legislation about housing benefit or dog licences.'

'You just want to make people aware that something important is going on.'

'Oh, we want more than that; of course we do. We want Parliament to make sure that there are tough laws; that nothing goes through on the nod; that all proposed research involving embryos and foetuses is scrutinized ethically before it's allowed. We may not get any of that, but what we must do is stop people like Medisearch being able to make their own rules as they go along.'

'Um. I see.' Liz swilled the last of her coffee round in the mug and drank it. But seeing is not necessarily the same as agreeing, she thought doubtfully; and what your clever arguments don't do is reassure me that every CAMEX member is a similarly sober, rational, intellectual campaigner and not a rash idealist. And nor do they tell me what means CAMEX might see as justified by their ends. Even you, my friend from when we were tots: how do I know that you might not think yourself justified in breaking into Medisearch's lab, or setting fire to it?

'You want to join us,' Ginnie suggested.

'Oh God, I can't! We're supposed to keep our hands clean. Anyway, my boss wouldn't like it.'

'One of those? Old-time, narrow-minded copper?'

'No—he's good, in general. That's half the trouble. I mean, he's so good at not treating women as if being female was a distressing handicap that he sort of expects us not to have sexual characteristics at all. My joining CAMEX would be like leaving a tampon in his in-tray.'

'CAMEX isn't just for women.'

'Anyway, I couldn't join you if I'm not sure whether I agree with you even, could I?'

Ginnie replied drily, 'You wouldn't be the first person to allow your beliefs to be formed by your social life. You can be committed to anything, if once you decide you like the company you're travelling in.'

'What would worry me,' Liz said thoughtfully, 'is that you're not likely to achieve much anyway. I mean, be realistic: are you? A few letters; a few marches; it's unlikely to change the world, is it?'

'No,' agreed Ginnie. 'I'm afraid you may be right.'

Tina Blake was in the kitchen transferring packets of frozen food from a pile of plastic shopping-bags to the freezer. Sophy sidled in and began to forage for something for tea.

'I've got a pizza,' Tina said, putting the packet to one side. 'Your dad's coming home early for once in a blue moon. If you hang on half an hour, you can join us.'

'Umm . . .'

'Or is it too much to ask that we should all sit down to a meal together once in a while?' Tina asked meaningfully.

Sophy's eyes slid away. 'All right,' she said, opting for pacifism. 'I've got some things to do, then . . .' Exams were coming up in a few months' time, and Sophy had quickly learnt their value as a cast-iron all-purpose excuse. She wandered upstairs to her room and switched the television on, the sound turned low.

Ten minutes later she heard her father come in and his heavy tread on the stairs, and turned the volume right down, so that just the silent pictures jerked and danced on the screen. She waited for his footsteps to pass her door, willing him not to look in. Separateness had become the permanent state of each of them in the household, and Sophy felt as if she had an extra skin of hypersensitivity, like an anemone ready to shrink instantly from the threatening proximity of others.

When her father had gone downstairs again and she reckoned she had given her mother the right amount of time, Sophy switched off the set and wandered down. Sometimes she wondered what it would be like to have a brother or sister, and whether if she had, they would be close as some of the brothers and sisters at school were close, more like lovers sometimes than siblings. Somehow she couldn't imagine it. Her friends were mostly themselves only children: it was an unsought freemasonry. Sometimes she felt like little Trooper Baker: so lonely and pitifully stalwart.

In the kitchen the scene was treacherously domestic; her mother poking at the pizza with a spatula, her father leaning against the table holding a glass.

'Hello, Sophy,' he said.

'Hi.' She averted her eyes and crossed to play with the black cat in its basket by the back door.

'Anyway,' said Tina, obviously resuming a conversation which had been in progress before Sophy came in, 'it's worth it. Better than doing nothing.'

'They don't worry me,' John Blake replied, and drained the last of his drink.

'They worry *me*,' Tina said. 'And there's Tony. You always think Medisearch is yours to do with as you please. It isn't, John. I do wish you'd remember sometimes that it's not your personal property. We ought to have proper meetings, this sort of thing is precisely what we ought to talk about all together.' She set the pizza on the table, scraped cauliflower into a dish. 'Wash your hands, Sophy, if you've been playing with Dumbo. I'm sure that cat's got fleas.'

They sat at the table like strangers in a restaurant car. Sophy let her mind roam ahead to the weekend, calculating what she could afford to put off until Sunday night, whether she could get three essays done before next Tuesday without impinging on any of her evenings out, whether Judy Baker would want her to babysit for Trooper again.

'. . . Morris,' she heard her mother say suddenly. 'Isn't he, Sophy?'

'Sorry?'

'Mr Morris who teaches at your school.'

'He puts his hand up our skirts,' she remarked.

'Sophy!'

'He's always doing it. We don't mind. I don't think his wife gives him enough sex,' she said.

She intercepted her father's look, aimed at her mother, which plainly said, 'Don't take any notice; she's romancing again; teenagers will always say what they hope will shock.' Aloud, he said, 'He supports CAMEX, doesn't he? You know, the people who want to close us down.'

'Mm,' Sophy said, as non-committally as she could. She thought of Morris, and then of Judy Baker and Trooper. She wished she had told her parents who it was she babysat for.

'You see?' her mother was saying. 'If you just pretend they don't exist . . .' but then Sophy switched off again, concentrating on finishing her portion of the pizza, thinking of brothers and sisters again, and wondering whether Trooper minded growing up as an only child, like her.

Later, her mother came into her room. Sophy was sitting cross-legged on the bed, her books spread around her and on the floor, the television on but ignored and turned low.

'Darling,' Tina said, 'that wasn't true, was it? What you said about Mr Morris.'

'Yes,' Sophy said, bluffing it out, trying to get her mother to doubt whether it was not all an invention. 'He's always doing it.'

'He hasn't done it to you, has he?'

'He only likes girls with long hair,' Sophy improvised.

'Darling, this isn't a joke,' Tina said. 'You aren't having me on, are you? Are you making all this up?'

'Oh, *Mum*,' Sophy protested, 'don't go *on*.'

Tina looked at her dubiously. 'You're sure he hasn't . . .'

'I *told* you, Mum, he only likes girls with long hair,' Sophy said. 'Or fair hair. Or something. Nobody's been interfering with your little girl.'

Tina Blake wondered what she was supposed to believe. It seemed impossible this girl could be her own daughter, this almost-woman with her own existence and her own feelings and her own beliefs and her own activities of which Tina knew nothing. Depressed, she looked down at Sophy's streaked curls bent pointedly over her books. The bond between mother and daughter, she thought despondently: another of the dreams that hovered tantalizingly just out of sight for a few years before vanishing altogether. So many fictions. Romantic love. Career satisfaction. Motherhood. Fantasies to lure us on and blind us to the tedious realities.

Abruptly, Tina turned and left the room. Her daughter did not look up.

Only after the door had closed behind her mother did Sophy let out her breath in a long sigh. 'You stupid, stupid bitch, Sophy Blake,' she muttered, and reached out to turn up the volume of the television set.

CHAPTER 6

Detective Chief Inspector Alec Stainton walked into Inspector Glover's office with the report, which carried Glover's name at the foot, which he had plucked out of his in-tray five minutes earlier. It was a normal winter's day in the headquarters building, the strip-lights on against the poor light, condensation misting the windows, the air close and dry. The warm weather which had stimulated the unseasonable burgeoning of plants and trees had vanished in a night, exchanged for bitter winds and chill drizzles. Not that it had had any effect here; there was nothing to burgeon, if the tired collection of cacti on Glover's bookcase

was excepted, and they looked, as ever, unlikely to be affected by anything less than a second Deluge.

'This anonymous letter: anything in it, do you think?'

'Could be,' Glover replied cautiously. 'It's a bit vague
about what this Morris bloke's supposed to have done.
Anonymous: well, that's fair enough, if you're going to start
accusing schoolteachers of sticky fingers; but I'd like to see
some dates and places mentioned. Smells a bit second-hand
to me, and it crossed my mind that Bill Parkes at the *Post*
thought the same, which is why he's sent it on to us.'

'It's a nasty thing to accuse a man of,' Alec mused.
'Especially a schoolteacher. Know how it came?'

'Ordinary mail, addressed to "The Editor". Printed by
word-processor on plain unheaded paper. Parent; fellow-
teacher; jealous pupil; could have come from anywhere.
What do we do about it, that's the question.'

'Um . . . My instinct is the same as yours: someone casting mud, in the knowledge that it'll like as not stick. Better
have a word with the head teacher, though.'

'Done it. Chap named Crawford. Turns out a copy of the
letter was sent to him at the school, marked personal.'

'Hum. That rather puts a different complexion on things.
How does he propose to handle it?'

'Seems to have his head screwed on,' Glover replied.
'He'll have a quiet word with this Morris and keep his
eyes skinned. I wouldn't have thought he's the sort to start
wading in unnecessarily, and we've covered ourselves if
there does prove to be something in it.'

'All right. Give him a ring in a fortnight and see what
the score is.'

'Christmas holidays,' Glover reminded him smugly.

'Damn! In a week, then. Before the end of term, anyway.
If there is anything, he'll likely have got a sniff of it by then.
Working over Christmas?'

'Yes, thank God. Got the wife's family coming to stay.
Soon as I knew they were coming I rang Jack to put me on
the rota. Give me an excuse to escape when it all gets too
much.'

'With any luck there won't be too much going on. Let me have a photocopy of that, will you, Harry? Our anonymous accuser. We'll have another word about that when you've spoken to the headmaster again, OK?'

Clive Morris sat in the uncomfortable modern easy chair in the headmaster's office and felt prickles of panic nibbling at his spine and stomach. The headmaster, a diminutive, competent, leathery martinet, was eyeing him appraisingly, as if the truth of Morris's guilt or innocence was revealed in his face. Morris hoped desperately that the other man realized there was no difference between a guilty man and one who was just shit-scared.

'So there's nothing in it, Clive. You give me your word.'

'No! I mean, yes, I give you my word. I've told you, I can't imagine . . .'

'I'm giving you the chance to change your mind, Clive, because God knows it would be a difficult thing to admit to. So if you want to say anything different, now's the time to do it. Mind! Once you leave this room, it's too late. Now: you still say there's nothing in it?'

'For God's sake, you have to believe me . . .'

'I don't *have* to believe you, Clive.' There was a flash of steel in Crawford's voice, a warning. 'What I have to do is weigh what you've said against this.' He lifted the letter on the desk in front of him and let it fall.

'You can't believe a poison-pen letter! That isn't even signed! Please, Mr Crawford. Look: there's nothing in it. I'm happily married.'

Crawford swung round in his chair so that he was gazing out of the window, and not at Morris's glistening face. He was ashamed of his reaction against Morris, and hoped the other man couldn't see it. The teacher's small, paunchy body seemed vaguely obscene, with its neat small feet and tightly-stretched trousers and pleading, frightened, hairless features. It was easy to believe that this was the appearance of a man who interfered with the girls in his charge, frighteningly easy. Crawford had met Morris's wife Betty, and accepted unhappily that he disliked her too, a dull, dowdy woman, who might well make a man feel that life had passed him by.

'Look: ask them, Mr Crawford. Ask any of them. If any one of them says I have ever, ever, laid a finger . . . or so much as hinted . . .'

'How can I ask them? Don't be idiotic, Morris. Do you *want* this all round the school?'

'I don't have any option, do I?' Morris answered with sudden flat realism. 'You're not going to do nothing; not now. It's been brought to your attention, so you'll have to act as if it might be true. For me, the results are going to be much the same as if you had already decided I was guilty.'

'Nonsense, man!' Crawford retorted unconvincingly. 'All right,' he said a moment later. 'You can go. I'd better think about this. You're sure. . .?'

'Sure,' Morris said with some dignity, and left.

Crawford watched him go and then turned back to continue staring out of the window. Like head-teachers everywhere, he prided himself on knowing everything that went on in his school, and he was disturbed that he had had no inkling of this trouble until the arrival of the accusatory letter. He hated the situation, which was one where the accused was always guilty until proved innocent; and he hated Morris for thrusting it upon him. The best thing to do would be to get it thoroughly sifted at the earliest possibility and then to enlist outside help. It was no part of a headmaster's duty to shoulder unpleasant responsibilities alone.

He lifted the telephone receiver and dialled the number Inspector Glover had given him.

Of all the hours she spent at school, Sophy enjoyed swimming best. She was good at lessons, but she took that for granted and even felt slightly ashamed of it. It was at the swimming baths that she most keenly felt her own worth as she powered through her thirtieth length of the pool and climbed easily out afterwards, the water dripping off her regulation one-piece costume. She felt she was someone.

Her mood of complacency was not destined to last long this morning. 'You split on me,' Hannah hissed, as Sophy joined her in the changing-room and began to towel her hair.

'What do . . . ?'

'You promised not to tell! About . . . you know. Morris. You *swore*. I'm never going to believe a word you say again, Sophy Blake!'

The two girls were alone at their end of the changing-room, but Sophy instinctively looked round before replying forcefully, 'I haven't told. Not anyone!'

'So why did Mr Morris spend all morning in Mr Crawford's office? *And* look as if he'd seen a ghost when he came out? Tell me that! Because *I* haven't told anyone, except you, and that was a mistake, wasn't it? You did tell, Sophy, so don't try and pretend, you little liar!'

And Sophy suddenly remembered the other girl was right. For a moment she thought of continuing with her denial, but her habitual, painful honesty wouldn't let her. Nevertheless, she couldn't bring herself to speak at once, but absently peeled off her swimsuit and dropped it beside her bare feet on the damp tile floor.

'How do you know he was with Mr Crawford?' she temporized lamely. 'And even if he was, you don't know . . .'

'He was. Take my word for it. Julie Townsend was next door in the secretary's office and she saw him come out. And she heard Mr Crawford say . . .'

Sophy swallowed. 'Look, Hannah, I didn't tell, right? But . . .'

'Yes, but?' the other girl retorted scornfully.

'But Mum and Dad asked me about Mr Morris,' Sophy muttered, her face red, 'and I . . . I said he didn't always keep his . . . hands to himself.' She looked up. Hannah, clad in her bra and blouse, was watching her angrily with darkened face. 'I didn't think they'd even noticed, but they must have. But *they* wouldn't have got Morris into trouble, why should they?'

'God, Sophy, you're so dense. Because they're *parents*, that's why! I bet within five minutes they were on the phone to every other parent in the school. I bet you even said it was me he touched up! If you did, I'll never forgive you!'

'No.' Had she? Sophy thought back to that conversation a fortnight before. She was almost certain she hadn't said more than she'd told Hannah. 'Anyway,' she said defensively, 'he *ought* to be given a telling off. Mr Morris, I mean. You said yourself. He's a menace.'

But Hannah had turned away and was fishing her knickers out of the jumbled pile of her clothes. 'He ought to stop it, yes. But *I* don't want him to lose his job and never get another one.'

'Well, but it would be his own fault.' Sophy tried to imagine herself in Hannah's place, caught in the dusty lab with Mr Morris, and feeling his hand next to her skin. And suppose it had been some helpless thirteen-year-old, too scared to speak up, too scared to run away?

'Look,' Hannah said, turning back, buttoning her skirt, 'he's a dirty old man; but you have to *pity* him. Besides, I don't think he really is a dirty old man, not like that. He was just trying it on, and he stopped as soon as I told him. The poor sod probably doesn't get it from his wife and he has to spend his days cooped up with four hundred girls.'

'But it's wrong,' Sophy repeated.

Hannah sighed theatrically. 'I give up! Anyway, there's nothing we can do now, except for heaven's sake keep your mouth shut. That includes your mum and dad. Especially your mum and dad. Your trouble is, you're too trusting, Sophy Blake. You don't know you're alive. Now I should get a move on if I were you unless you intend to stand there with your mouth hanging open all day.'

Sophy closed her mouth and, glancing round, saw that she and Hannah were the only ones left in the changing-room. Hastily she reached for her clothes and scrambled them on. Hannah was right, she told herself miserably. All the same, swimming lesson hadn't been much fun today.

Clive Morris was suspended from work two days later, barely a week before the end of term, causing Inspector Glover to revise his opinion of Crawford's judgement. The following evening the local paper, keen to get into print before the case became *sub judice*, ran the story on page two under large headlines, adding that 'reports that students took part in sex parties have not been confirmed. Worried parents are today calling for a full inquiry into events at the school which has been dubbed "the School for Scandal".'

Glover passed the newspaper over to Alec Stainton and forked up a mouthful of steak and kidney pie. 'The only reports of orgies are in the pages of this paper,' he mumbled indistinctly. '"School for Scandal"' my arse! Nobody's called it that except the journalist who wrote this trash. And "dubbed". Why "dubbed", that's what I want to know? Bloody word's extinct except in the newspapers.'

'Journalese,' Alec observed absently, admiring the clever use of the passive verb. He passed the paper back. 'Looks like we were wrong about the headmaster.'

Glover swallowed too hastily, and it was a moment or two before he could reply. 'Silly sod,' he pronounced with scorn. 'Just running scared. Why the blazes didn't he just hang on a week and tell Morris not to come back at the start of next term? You'd think these blokes got some damage limitation training these days, but no, they still act first and think later. I suppose,' he reflected, 'it means he's got some definite proof.'

'Yes,' Alec replied. 'I'm afraid it probably does.'

Immersing herself even more deeply in CAMEX had been Kate Randall's way of coping when she lost her job. It was not the fact of being unemployed—in this part of the country that need not last long—so much as the manner of its happening, which had left her with a bruised ego and in need of a change. Previously, job moves had been made at her own choice. This time, she had been sacked.

Yet in a way it almost seemed meant that she should be freed from her job just at the time when the CAMEX campaign was approaching its crucial point, with the legislation shortly to be debated in Parliament which would lay down the principles on which future medical experimentation would be conducted. Ever since she joined CAMEX Kate had been depressed by the amateurism and inactivity of it. She did not consider her principles as deep and as carefully thought-out as those of, say, Ginnie Kemp, but that made it all the more incomprehensible that they should be prepared to let CAMEX stay vague, wishy-washy and ineffective.

CAMEX's structure gave regional committees, like the one which met at the Mackenzies', virtual autonomy—and the whole campaign was largely orientated towards the south-east of England anyway, because Westminster had to be the focus of its attention, and besides, most of the experimental laboratories were situated here. Kate was astounded to find herself on the Central South committee within six months, and to find that there was virtually no structure above the committee to direct it. Soon, simply by virtue of her strength of character and her intolerance of fudge and inefficiency, she found herself in the driving seat.

While daily work took so much of her time and energy, what Kate could achieve was limited; but even so, she had transformed CAMEX locally from a sort of social club which met to bewail the future into something approaching a respectable pressure group. The other committee members expressed wonder and admiration; Kate took stock of the gap between what had to be done, and what was being done, and forbore to disillusion them.

That being so, it was hardly surprising that even as she listened in disbelief as her boss accused her of dishonesty, even as she determinedly fought back tears at the injustice of it all, Kate's brain was calculating how she could live for six months until the crucial Parliamentary vote had come and gone, as full-time organizer of CAMEX.

From the dining table in her flat in Felbridge Kate had

since then organized the marches which had brought five town centres to a halt, uniting local churches, human rights groups, mother and toddler groups, two synagogues, sixth-formers and three local 'fringe religions' into a day of protest that headlined the local TV news and gained a mention on national television. She had computer-listed every Member of Parliament with a home or second home within fifty miles, prepared a brief profile of past declared views and voting patterns, and targeted the ten who in her judgement provided the best likelihood of being influenced by lobbying, and she had produced an information pack to be sent to each of these. She had written a leaflet for the general public outlining the issues and urging them to write to their MP, whose name and the House of Commons address and a suggested outline letter, were given, and she had worked hard to persuade supermarkets, schools and surgeries to let her leave copies in their reception areas, in addition to having them handed out on Saturday mornings in shopping centres by CAMEX supporters.

In short, she had done wonders, everybody agreed. Kate declared straightforwardly that she had only done the obvious; and that the obvious wouldn't be enough; and she kept quiet about the hate mail which had begun to arrive, and the apprehensive looks which Charlie Poole, who rented her spare bedroom and with whom she had come to think she had a future, had begun to direct at the piles of CAMEX papers overflowing into every corner of the flat; and she set herself to study the methods of those pressure groups who had *really* made a fuss—and achieved their aims.

Now Kate read the news of Clive Morris's suspension with disbelief which dissolved all too quickly.

'How *could* he?' she cried to Ginnie Kemp over the phone.

'Very easily, I'm afraid.'

'But we trusted him!'

'Kate,' Ginnie said, 'you're being irrational, which isn't at all like you. Clive's liking young girls and his belief in CAMEX aren't incompatible, for heaven's sake. Any more than if we had found out that he was a burglar, or a computer hacker.'

'But this is different. And those poor girls!'

'All right, I agree, but just bear in mind that Clive hasn't changed overnight. It's just that we've found out something rather nasty about the way he gets his sexual pleasures. If it's true. He hasn't been charged yet, don't forget, and you know what newspapers are. I should have thought you of all people wouldn't give someone up on the basis of a newspaper article.'

Kate found she could attend to nothing else that night. Like the thousands of people who read the newspaper story that evening, she knew in her heart that the allegations were well-founded. 'They wouldn't have suspended him if there was nothing in it, would they?' people said to one another; but Kate remembered instead her oppressive journeys home from CAMEX meetings. She wondered guiltily whether, if she had been more responsive to Clive, it might have prevented his offences against the schoolgirls in his charge. And then, abhorrence of what Morris had done was mingled with a sort of fascination—she couldn't help imagining all sorts of possibilities, and picturing him doing them—which disgusted her. It was all very well for Ginnie Kemp, telling her to 'see things in perspective'. All Kate could see was that Clive Morris was not the man she had believed him to be. He had deceived and betrayed her.

And CAMEX. When the initial disgust passed, that was what angered her most. All her careful, painstaking work in mobilizing and harnessing support for CAMEX, designed to peak as the time for the Parliamentary debate approached, had been jeopardized. As CAMEX's strength was a moral one, the suggestion of moral rottenness within its ranks would dissolve that support, that carefully-nurtured goodwill, like mist scattered by a storm. A bitter enemy driven to try and destroy all that CAMEX stood for could scarcely have dreamed up a more effective method of doing so.

*

After she had put the phone down on Kate Randall, Ginnie Kemp made herself a snack supper and set it beside her while she worked through some correspondence. Her husband was on call this weekend, and out on a home visit. She was on call herself, but in her case it was a matter of carrying a radiopager with her and not travelling too far from a telephone. She expected half a dozen calls over the weekend, most of them requiring a trip in to the gynæcology unit where she worked, half of them during the night. With luck she would still have the chance to sort through the arrears of paperwork which had built up over the week.

Swiftly she opened envelopes, snatching bites at her sandwich in between. Journals she put aside to join the pile to be read later. There were four bulletins from the Department of Health, and notices of meetings she would not be able to attend.

After the circulars, she started on the plain envelopes. A statement from her bank. A newsletter from a charity she supported.

The third envelope contained a letter from a firm of solicitors in Croydon advising her that they were suing her for negligence on behalf of a client, claiming damages in the sum of one million pounds.

CHAPTER 7

Frances Walker got up late and savoured her Saturday routine, putting the things together for her breakfast and leafing casually through the paper as she ate, while outside the wind whipped the naked branches of the trees and sent the high, wispy clouds scudding across the sky. Lucy dashed in in search of something to nibble, her cheeks pink from the chill, and disappeared as abruptly outside again, where she was adding extra refinements to the rabbit hutch.

It was gone eleven before Frances had cleared away her few dishes, checked her briefcase and got the car out.

Twenty minutes later, as she neared the Godstone turn-off from the motorway, the phone went.

'Hold on just a minute, will you?' she said.

Quickly she glanced in her mirror and pulled into the inside lane, indicating for the slip road.

There was a lay-by just off the roundabout almost beneath the motorway, and Frances turned in and switched the engine off. 'Sorry to keep you.'

'Frances, it's Kate. Kate Randall.'

'How nice to hear from you.'

'Listen, are you terribly busy? I want to come and see you.'

Until recently, Kate Randall had worked for Frances. She knew Kate as forceful, efficient, cheerful and polite, though reserved, and sacking her for dishonesty had been a painful business. The voice in the telephone was abrupt to the point of rudeness. Clearly something of more than ordinary importance was behind the call.

'I'm on my way to the office, Kate,' Frances said. 'I'll be there till lunch-time. This afternoon I have to take Lucy into Sevenoaks to dancing classes.' She paused. 'I'll be in this evening. Why don't you come for a meal?'

'I'd rather not,' the other girl's voice replied; and Frances was sure it sounded unnaturally constrained. 'I want a favour off you as it is; I'd rather not push my luck.'

'Nonsense. Come and eat. About eight. Lucy goes to bed at half past nine and then we can talk. Can you get over all right?'

'That's not a problem; I can probably borrow . . . I don't know . . . All right. I'll see you then.'

They rang off. Frances, as she turned on to the slip road again and rejoined the motorway, replayed the conversation in her mind and heard Kate's angry, bitten tones. They were the tones of someone who badly wanted help.

Frances turned back from the fireplace and met the straight look of the girl who sat tensely on the floral chintz of the old settee.

'Look, you're sure about this, are you?'

'Yes. You trust him, don't you?'

'Yes, I do; but he's a policeman like any other.'

Kate Randall smiled briefly. '*Just* like any other? I thought at one time you and he were rather fond of each other.'

Frances blushed. 'What I meant was, that he may agree to meet you because he's—' she searched for the word, and could find nothing more suitable than 'my friend—but if he decides to take what you say seriously he'll do so as a policeman. And anyway, he probably couldn't deal with it himself if he wanted to, he'd have to delegate it to some constable or sergeant, so the end result would be the same.'

'Never mind. Will you do it?'

Frances looked at the girl's gaunt face beneath the halo of coiled fair hair, and the dark smudges beneath her eyes, and nodded. 'Of course I will.'

DELTA COMMUNICATIONS, REDHILL, SURREY, UK
From the Managing Director's Office
Telex: Delcom.

Detective Chief Inspector Stainton
(Personal)

Dear Alec,

I am going to do what I usually deplore, namely presume upon an acquaintance. The truth is that I do not know what else I can do, so I hope you will forgive me if I am committing some terrible solecism in terms of police etiquette and be charitable enough to put it down to ignorance.

I wonder whether I could ask you to call round one evening. A friend of mine . . .

It was some time since Alec had had occasion to visit Frances Walker at the office in Redhill where she ran her business. They were sufficiently well acquainted for her to have suggested a meeting somewhere more comfortable if the purpose was simply social; but she was a woman who had her own strict mental etiquette about things. The meeting at the office meant business.

The fire-engine red Porsche was missing from the car park, but as Alec parked his own car and climbed out he saw that a magenta TVR was turning into the little industrial estate. He waited while it burbled between the units and nosed into the yard. It had a new registration. Frances Walker levered herself deftly out with only the merest glimpse of thigh and then dived back in, to reappear with a paper bag in her hands.

'Something to nibble while we talk,' she stated, holding it up, and led the way with her characteristic mixture of grace and diffidence to the entrance door, fumbling in her shoulder-bag for the keys.

When they were inside, upstairs in Frances' office, and the kettle had been switched on, she said, 'You're probably going to think I've wasted your time, I'm afraid. Only now I've got a tame policeman available the temptation is to use him.' She threw him a quick quizzical glance as she extracted eclairs from the paper bag and set them on a plate. The kettle steamed and bubbled and switched itself off. They both knew that she was giving him the opportunity to repay some of the favours he owed her; and they both knew too (or is it just me that thinks so, Alec wondered?) that it was in just such ways that they found excuses to keep in contact for the time being, without getting in deeper.

'What is it, then?' he asked, when they had both taken their first sip of tea and bite of eclair.

Frances pushed her chair back and he watched her as she crossed to a filing cabinet and unlocked it, a moderately tall, confident woman with shoulder-length brown hair and modest figure, who wore simple—almost severe—but expensive clothes. It was not often Alec could allow his eyes to linger on Frances' face, but now while she was absorbed leafing deftly through files he studied her profile, pondering on the possibility of Slavic ancestry in the high cheekbones and the smooth pale skin drawn over them like silk. That sculpted profile led people to judge her on first meeting haughty: that profile, and the green—in some lights—eyes which met yours so disconcertingly directly and then skittered away. Haughty, or pathologically private: even timid. A faint smile flitted across his own face. His eyes travelled over her unpronounced figure, and her long-fingered, mobile hands. She was a person one could watch for pleasure.

From the beginning Alec had acknowledged that Frances Walker possessed, in addition to this interesting body— and the adjective had something disparaging about it—an extremely acute mind. It was taking him a long time to decide how deeply he wanted to be involved with the woman to whom this mind and body belonged.

She slid the drawer shut and turned back to him. 'Look at these. This one first.'

Alec wiped a splash of cream off his fingers and picked up the sheet of paper she put in front of him. It was a letter, with a company letterhead which gave a London address but otherwise meant nothing to him. It was dated August of that year. The text was quite short, and underneath handwritten notes had been added in Frances Walker's handwriting. The letter, addressed to Dr Walker personally and marked 'Strictly Confidential' told her that the company's security consultants, who had been called in to investigate a security leak, had advised that the probable source was one of the company's outside contractors: one of whom was Delta Communications, of which Frances Walker was owner and managing director. Would she kindly contact the writer to arrange an appointment to discuss the matter? The writer was given as John P. Slater, Group Internal Security Manager.

Frances' notes recorded a telephone conversation in which Mr Slater had declined to elaborate on the content of his letter and a face-to-face meeting had been arranged.

'We do a lot of business for that company,' Frances said shortly.

'So in this case, when Mr Slater writes a peremptory letter, you bite back your anger and go and see him.'

'Yes; though I'd be a fool not to anyway. Any suggestion that Delta is a security risk and our business is on the skids. Almost everything we handle is sensitive from someone's point of view.'

'And I take it Mr Slater got you worried when you met?'

'Read this one. It's my notes of our meeting, made the same afternoon. I don't think I missed anything significant.'

She watched him seriously while he read the two pages of typed notes; and then reached absently for her tea as Alec sat back and considered what he had read.

Slater's company—Incorporated Allied Holdings—obviously had a number of divisions. More properly, perhaps, it was a series of companies under a corporate umbrella. Some of those divisions were concerned with matters where confidentiality was of the essence: it might be because of the defence angle; or to guard against product pirating; or because advance notice of company policy would play into the hands of 'raiders'.

For all these reasons, IAH maintained in-house security staff and also hired external experts. The internal people had discovered the leak: the outsiders had been engaged to track it down.

They had tracked it down to Delta Communications. More precisely, they had tracked it down to one employee. IAH had issued a simple ultimatum: either Dr Walker sack this employee forthwith, or no part of IAH would deal with Delta again—and they would write that prohibition into every contract put out by every division of the company. IAH, in short, would blacklist Delta throughout the business world.

Alec looked up. 'So you sacked him,' he said.

'Her.' Frances turned in a burst of energy which sent her cashmere skirt flaring and revealed the tension within her, and crossed to the window. He watched the shadows the streetlights cast on her cheek. From time to time car headlights lit her features harshly as they swept past on the road.

'Yes, I sacked her. You see, the evidence is irrefutable, isn't it? Slater named the document, where it was found. His spies had "retrieved" it from the offices of a merchant bank who advise one of their rivals. He showed me a photocopy. There were only two options: either Kate had leaked it, or I had myself.'

Alec watched a muscle in her cheek working and wondered what there was in this sorry little tale to evoke such a response. She turned again, and crossed to the side table and poured them each more tea. She passed him his cup with a humourless, apologetic smile.

'And now you're hating yourself,' he said gently.

She shook her head. 'I haven't finished. I had Kate in, of course—this was a couple of months ago. Confronted her with the evidence as Slater had given it to me. The thing is, I'd have sworn that girl was honest! Asked her why the hell she'd done such a stupid thing. Was it money? What was it?'

'And what *was* it?'

'She wouldn't tell me. Because she just said she'd never done it. So how could she give me a motive, if she'd never done it? We went round in circles like that for a long time.'

Alec looked down at the notes on the desk in front of him. There didn't seem much room for denial. And what possible motive could Slater have for concocting a story in order to get some insignificant typist in a very minor service company fired from her job? But something held him back from uttering the simple conclusion—the girl was lying to save her job—because if it *was* that simple Frances Walker would accept it, however distasteful, and wouldn't be suffering qualms of conscience. And wouldn't have called on him for help, either.

'Do I know her?' he asked instead. 'This girl Kate, I mean.'

'I expect you've seen her. She used to be my personal assistant. Slim, fair hair worn long.'

'Wears a miniskirt? I followed her up the stairs the first time I came.'

Frances' face flickered and relaxed a fraction. 'That was last year. Fashions have changed.'

Alec said simply, 'And you believed her.'

'I couldn't,' Frances said. 'How could I? Can you see any way that evidence can be made to mean anything else?'

'So you sacked her.'

'Yes. She took it well, poor kid. That made me feel she must be guilty, or she'd have kicked up more of a fuss. But she could see as well as I could that I'd no option.'

'In fact, you'd have had to sack her whether you believed her or not. Wouldn't you?'

Frances hesitated. 'I don't know,' she said. 'Yes, I expect you're right. I'd have had to, wouldn't I?'

Now it was Alec's turn to stand up and cross to the window. This side of the building faced on to a back street and he gazed down on the slick, damp pavement. Cars skimmed silently past from time to time, the hiss of their wheels blanketed by the double-glazing, but the damp dark night seemed to have washed all forms of life from the face of the world. He wanted to tell her that he respected her scruples—which he did, but it wasn't easy to say without sounding unbearably smug himself. And he still wanted badly to know why she was so upset by the incident. Was it simply that she was nervy anyway for some reason (he found himself wondering about her time of the month), or that she hadn't the stamina for the seamier side of her work—or was there something else?

As if reading his thoughts, Frances said, 'Kate rang me the other night. She came over for a meal.'

'Ah!'

'Well, it turns out she's a member of this pressure group, CAMEX, which has been in the papers recently. I didn't know. She's got it into her head that the group is being persecuted, Alec. Systematically. And looking back, she thinks this was all part of the plot.' She shrugged. 'That's all.'

Alec's heart sank. CAMEX was beginning to take on the shape of an albatross ready to drape itself round his neck.

To his mind, people who joined groups like CAMEX were just the sort who *would* steal confidential documents and pass them on—and would concoct some high-principled reason for doing so.

Frances was waiting for his reaction. She seemed more like her normal cool self again, so maybe what she had really wanted was just to talk it through with someone, yet he had the feeling that she was looking for something more personal than she would have admitted to, and needed comforting and reassurance. It was a new light on her.

'Well,' he began, 'whether or not the girl was right about that, you couldn't have taken any other action than you did. And frankly, I think what she said about it all being a fiendish plot is just balderdash. Wishful thinking—or paranoia. As a matter of fact we *are* investigating another member of CAMEX, but it's just coincidence. And it's a grubby little case which does nothing to make me respect the sort of people something like CAMEX appeals to. No; don't worry; there was nothing else you could have done.'

'Thank you,' she said absently, 'I just wanted to hear someone else tell me I was right.' And maybe it was the hint of disappointment in her posture, or some fractional inflection in her voice, but Alec knew at once that he had failed to provide what she had hoped for. In the next instant he realized the significance of the different words they had chosen: Frances Walker didn't want to be told that what she had done was unavoidable. What was nagging at her, nagging enough for her to appeal for someone else's opinion, was whether what she had done was right. As simple as that.

They left soon after that. Dr Walker seemed to have recovered her customary maddening self-possession, which revealed just enough for you to suspect there was an interesting and maybe lovely woman underneath, without ever letting you get close enough to find out for sure. Alec told her—which she already knew—that there was nothing, from a professional point of view, which he could do to pursue the matter.

He asked after her daughter Lucy as they went down-stairs, and learnt that Thursday was her piano-lesson night. Dr Walker, who was a single parent, sometimes invited Alec to tease her about her obsessionality where Lucy was concerned; but not tonight. Had she time for a meal together in town, Alec asked, or at least a drink? Not tonight, said Dr Walker, thanks all the same.

When they were both unlocking their cars, and Alec was already preparing to spend the evening feeling resentful, he changed his mind and went over instead to the sports car. Frances Walker was already half-in the driving seat and she paused, her hand on the open door, and looked up. The internal light showed splashes of mud on her nylon-clad legs from the wet car park and her cashmere skirt fell back from her knees in the intricacies of getting into a low-slung sports car; but it hid her expression and her eyes were in shadow. She made no move to pull her skirt down.

'I'm sorry,' Alec said. 'I forgot that you knew Kate and I didn't. I should have given that more weight. Having said all that, I still think that letting her go was the right thing to do. The fact that a lot of valuable business hung on it doesn't affect that. And thank you for telling me about it. I appreciated that.'

He turned away feeling a bit of a fool but otherwise marginally better. As he started the engine of his car the TVR's lights came on and it passed him. The horn tooted cheerfully and he saw Frances' hand come up in a wave. Then it was turning into the road and squatted down on its springs as she accelerated away.

By the time Alec had turned out of the car park all that was to be seen of it was two broad dull tyre-tracks on the sleek wet surface of the deserted road through the estate. Dr Walker, he recalled, only drove fast when she was happy.

CHAPTER 8

Detective Chief Inspector Alec Stainton and Miles Wetherby Esquire met two days later at a cocktail party given by a firm of Reigate estate agents to celebrate the approach of Christmas and—coincidentally—the opening of a new branch. As both men recognized, it was a case of hate at first sight.

Perhaps hate was too extreme; but Alec, as a gap in the crush revealed Wetherby across the room bending solicitously over Frances—who, unbelievably, looked flushed and was laughing, her hair dancing as she lifted her head to reply—found it difficult to think of any other term which was strong enough and sufficiently all-embracing to cover his antipathy; and besides, hate suggested something irrational, and that described his reaction to Wetherby perfectly.

It certainly had no one origin. The way Wetherby made up to Frances, whom Alec was escorting tonight at her invitation, was a factor certainly, and the first thing Alec noticed, even before he registered Wetherby's carefully elegant greying hair and leather brogues and too-smiling face. The man might have been an American television evangelist, or a small-time film star; he had the same suspect sincerity. Throughout the evening Wetherby cultivated Frances with an easy charm which to Alec was blatantly rapacious, though it was only later that Alec realized that Wetherby had contrived the meeting, and that it was not their first.

Alec, of course, was not jealous, since he had no *locus standi* where Frances was concerned. He was entitled, however, he told himself, to raise his hackles when he had to watch her subjected to such cheap and practised voraciousness. Altogether then, Alec decided as the throng intervened and the antipathy sparking between them like a perverse current subsided for a while, Wetherby was a loud-mouthed, immodest, vain, plausible, too-smooth-by-half middle-aged poseur.

Which made it all the more remarkable that Frances with her common sense and acute intelligence could be taken in by him.

It was a question he asked himself a hundred times in the course of the next two hours.

The journey back to Frances' house on the edge of the Kent weald was strained. Alec had never before known a time when he was unhappy in Frances' presence, and the knowledge that his dislike of Wetherby had made him ungracious was depressing. It seemed Frances too felt they had arrived at the end of their relationship, for she was silent for most of the journey.

It was not an occasion for lingering when he dropped her off. Nevertheless, to Alec's surprise as Frances put her hand on the door handle to climb out she said, 'Alec, can I ask you something?'

He looked at her, startled, where she sat shadowed against the faintly lighter window. 'Of course you can.'

'A favour. Would you meet—'

'Wetherby?'

'*No!* Kate Randall.'

He was aware of her watching him in the darkness and said quickly, before he could think better of it, 'Of course I will.'

Frances nodded. 'Good. I don't think you'll regret it. She's a nice girl.' She rested a hand briefly on his arm. A valediction? A stay of execution? Then she was gone.

Only as he drove away did Alec wonder whether Frances had deliberately thrown them a lifeline.

'It's going to be nice to be rich,' Tina said to the ceiling.

Darby rolled over on the bed until he was able to look at her. She was vainly proud of her flat stomach and the firm-ness of her breasts, which were indeed remarkable for a woman of almost forty who was also a mother; but he gazed instead at the very fine, intricate web of wrinkles in her face which hinted at vulnerability, in contrast to her outward toughness.

'I hadn't thought of it,' he said.

'No; I honestly believe you hadn't. Do you know, I believe you work for the pleasure of it,' she said, her voice light with surprise. 'You'll probably give it all away.'

He laughed. 'Counting your chickens.'

Still staring up at the ceiling of his bedroom, Tina shook her head fractionally. 'I believe in you. I even believe in John. It'll work, and we'll be rich. You probably will give it all away, though.'

Darby laughed again, and began to trace with his finger the faint brown line that led down the skin of her stomach. 'I'll buy myself a house,' he suggested. The flat was only rented; he never had had a house of his own.

'Good.' Tina was tired of meeting in Darby's depressing flat, making love in this dreary bedroom. 'And then?'

'I'll buy myself some furniture to put in it.'

'And then?'

His finger had reached the dark wiry curls of her hair, and he teased them carelessly. 'A holiday? I don't know. A car?'

'I think you're the most unworldly person I know,' Tina reflected. 'Ow!'

He rolled over again on to his back, so that they lay side by side, not touching. 'It can't buy you happiness,' he remarked. 'Or love; or skill at your job; or friends; or health, in the long term; or contentment.'

'It can buy you everything else, though,' Tina said feelingly. 'And it's going to. And no group of cranks is going to stand in my way.'

Frances Walker moved fast and arranged the meeting three days later. Nobody's home ground would do, so a restaurant was chosen as the meeting-place. Sharing a meal together would place them all on an equal footing; and it is difficult to browbeat someone with whom you are breaking bread. Who she thought might do the browbeating was not clear.

She guessed Alec would have mixed feelings at the prospect of meeting Kate Randall. CAMEX was a run-of-the-mill pressure group to which bank managers and farmers' wives and dentists and carpet fitters and nuns and rabbis belonged throughout the country, but Frances was well aware that in this little patch of southern England CAMEX had a specific antagonist in the shape of Medisearch, and a serving policeman would not be keen to find himself dining with a woman whose weekend hobby might prove to be posting letter-bombs or burning down research laboratories.

The restaurant was at Brasted, near Sevenoaks. In spring, summer or autumn the drive through the Sussex countryside and over the Chart into Kent could be as near to blissful as it is possible to be on the roads of south-east England, but on the December night arranged for the meeting Alec was only conscious of the slithery wetness of the lanes, of warnings of frost; of dazzling headlights and muddy spray and drivers hurrying home from office parties.

Both women were already in the small bar-cum-lounge when Alec arrived, drinks on the low table beside them, and he watched them unobserved as he made his way across. Cheery men in business suits all but filled the room, joking like schoolboys playing truant. Male laughter overflowed as anecdotes were recounted. Alec wondered how Frances had secured a table for their own little party so close to Christmas.

Eighteen months before, Alec had met Kate Randall briefly when he first visited Delta Communications and she showed him upstairs into Frances' room. Little had registered beyond the shortness of her skirt and a general impression of small, pleasant features and conventional long fair hair.

He saw now that she was older than he had imagined; or maybe it was the purpose of their meeting which gave her a serious, rather withdrawn look. The blonde hair had been pinned up into a snood 1940s-style revealing pale features and a high forehead, and she frowned as she studied the menu, as if shortsighted She wore an Icelandic-patterned jersey and corduroy skirt, and a single loop of very small artificial pearls at her neck, and they were the clothes of a woman who had thought long and hard about the way she wanted to appear that night.

Frances Walker was rather similarly dressed, though her lambswool jersey was plainer and her suede skirt fell to soft leather boots. She glanced up and spotted Alec drawing near, and welcomed him with a small smile and a steady look which he thought had something of warning in it. The girl, following Frances' glance, stared seriously and then smiled.

'Sorry to keep you. How are you?'

'Hello, Alec. You remember Kate. I'll get you a drink while you think what you want to order.'

Over the meal, with much prompting from Frances, Kate outlined her reason for wanting to see Alec and ask his advice. It was simply that she had arrived at the conviction that CAMEX was being subjected to deliberate attacks designed to destroy it. She had identified five incidents, she said, ranging from tyre-slashing to the unaccountable interest the Social Services had suddenly taken in Judy Baker. Once launched on the subject, she was lucid and forceful, and Alec listened with growing respect.

'The weak point,' Alec said ruminatively when she had concluded, 'is that each of the incidents seems to stand on its own basis of fact. It's only the coincidence of them all occurring so close together which enables you to put a sinister interpretation on them, isn't it?'

'But,' she insisted, '*do* they have a basis of fact?' Her fair hair swung forward as she leaned towards him to urge her point. 'They're all allegations—that's all. Take the one against Judy: it's the classic guilty-until-proved-innocent, and even after that people will say there was no smoke without fire!'

'Mm, but you could have said as much about the case against Clive Morris, and now it looks as if that *is* well-founded.'

'Pity he wasn't charged straightaway,' Frances remarked. 'Then at least his name would have been kept out of the papers, surely.'

'Precisely!' Kate seized on the point. 'As soon as that happened, guilty or innocent, the damage was done, wasn't it?'

'Is he known to be linked to CAMEX?' Alec asked. 'I haven't seen any reference to that in the papers.'

'That's probably being held back until it can do the maximum damage. But even if it isn't, Clive's lost to us as an activist. He won't have the stomach for it—and we wouldn't be able to take the risk if he had. The same with Ginnie: she's already said she'll have to pull out until this court case is sorted out. Two of our committee taken away just as things are getting crucial! And Judy—she's not on the committee, but she's a useful worker. How much of her energies will CAMEX get in the face of the threat of losing her son?'

'But when you lost your own job,' Alec pointed out, 'which you claim is part of the same series of persecutions, it had the opposite effect: it freed you to work full-time for CAMEX.'

Kate nodded. 'Yes; that's one in the eye for them, who-ever they are. They must have thought it would mean I lost heart; but instead it's meant I can work flat out.'

'Can I ask . . .'

'What I'm living on? The dole; plus contributions from sympathizers. I can't do it for long, but I shan't have to. By the spring it will all have been decided, and either we'll have won our campaign, or the bill will have been passed.'

They ordered desserts from the trolley. Frances pressed Kate to indulge; she herself chose only cheese and biscuits.

Alec said, 'I'm doubtful whether all the things you've mentioned could have been orchestrated. OK, tyre-slashing is child's play and an anonymous letter to a newspaper or to Social Services is very easy to write; but a malpractice suit against a doctor . . . and Allied International's part in your losing your job. What do you think, Frances? It's your ground rather than mine.'

Frances said, 'I'd like to do a little more research on that. I've put one or two inquiries in motion. It's not inconceivable.'

'There's nothing I can do,' Alec said finally, as they sat over coffee, 'except bear it in mind. I'm afraid it doesn't amount to any sort of coherent case.'

Kate Randall's shoulders sagged fractionally, but she nodded firmly. 'If you can bear it in mind, that's all I wanted.'

Though less than she had hoped for, of course. But in all truth, what *could* he do? The most serious incidents were the allegations against Morris and Dr Kemp; and one of those had been pretty well substantiated, while the other was out of his jurisdiction completely. What did the rest of Kate Randall's 'conspiracy' amount to? Allied International's pressure on Frances to sack Kate was not criminal, even if cruel and possibly unfounded (and could he assume that?) Tyre-slashing . . .

'It does sound rather a lot of coincidences,' Frances suggested gently.

'Of course it is,' Alec said. 'But I can't allocate police resources on that basis. I'm sure Kate appreciates that. But look: if anything else happens which seems to fit into the same pattern, I'd be very interested to hear.'

'Well,' Kate said matter-of-factly, 'I suppose I'd better hope for something to happen which is serious enough to convince you.'

'Hark at that wind,' Frances said as they emerged into the darkness. It was shaping up for a winter of storms, and beyond the car park lighting they could hear soughing and creaking. 'It's getting worse.'

'Will you be all right?' Alec asked, thinking of the trees which surrounded her house.

'We survived the hurricane,' she observed. 'There can't be much more to come down.' But touched by his concern, she laid a hand lightly on his arm. 'Drive carefully,' she said. She turned to Kate, who was unlocking the door of a small Renault. 'You too,' she said. 'We don't want any more coincidences.'

The girl nodded as she folded herself into the driving seat, and before he turned away to his own car Alec saw her bend to fasten her seat-belt with deft, decisive movements.

He no longer thought of her as diffident or lightweight. He had seen and heard enough this evening to lead him to believe that she was a very formidable young woman.

CHAPTER 9

Christmas was upon them with a vengeance now. There was a permanent queue of cars for the multi-storey car park, trailing back round the corner into the High Street to jam the junction. Harassed shoppers stepped off the congested pavement in front of harassed motorists. Alec, going out one lunchtime expecting to do his shopping in one crisp, efficient trip round five shops, found himself back in the office forty minutes late, short tempered, and with half his list of presents still unbought.

Crossing briskly from Boots to Marks and Spencer on his way back to the office, Alec had found his path temporarily barred by a cheerful girl with hair in bunches, thrusting a leaflet into his hand. Other shoppers had seen the trap in advance and were neatly side-stepping with averted gaze as if suddenly intent on making some vital purchase before the shops closed, but it was too late for him to do so, and rather than be needlessly graceless he took the proffered leaflet. It was a CAMEX broadsheet. He climbed the steps to the police building thoughtfully.

As it happened, his in-tray was even fuller than usual, for the messenger had been round in his absence with a fresh set of files, papers and memoranda. As he shuffled the reports together Alec reflected that here in his hands he held all the evidence any policeman needed to persuade him that the festive season was upon them: credit-card fraud, shoplifting, domestic violence, theft and suicide all moved into higher gear as the celebration approached.

There was laughter from the next-door office, followed by a crash and the sound of raised voices. On an impulse, Alec dropped the reports back in his in-tray and wandered out into the corridor to see what all the fuss was about.

Liz Pink and Nelson had been hanging decorations. Liz, alternately sucking and shaking her hand, changed in mid-sentence from tigress to lamb as Alec appeared in the doorway.

Alec looked from the end of the red paperchain in Liz's other hand to the overturned chair in the corner of the room.

'Just pick the chair up and hold it still, Nelson,' he suggested, and as the sergeant sprang forward to do so he took the paperchain from Liz's hand, picked a drawing-pin from the tin on the filing cabinet and, standing on the chair, reached easily up into the corner, pushed the pin into the plaster and climbed down once more.

'Spare me a minute, Liz, will you?'

Back in his own room Liz stood cheerfully before him. He was tempted to dampen her high spirits by some harsh remark but realized in time that he had no wish to make her the whipping-boy for his own troubles. Wryly he reflected that old age was making him soft.

'Have you read those briefings I gave you?'

'Yes, sir. And the law reports. Sorry if we were disturbing you, sir. Nelson was reading out the circular about the office party. We were laying odds on the likelihood of Mr Fletcher bringing his Dubonnet rosé again.'

'I shouldn't put any money against it: he always does. God knows why. He's the only one who can stand the stuff. Look, if you've read the law reports, I've something else I'd like you to do. Just some research, really. This group CAMEX: the one who organized that march a few weeks back. I came across one of their members the other day, indirectly.' Liz nodded warily. 'We're not inquiring into them formally, but see what you can find out. Press reports, any contacts. You can give me a verbal report at the end of a week, and I'll tell you then whether to go any further.'

'I can do that, sir. I've got to be in court on Thursday, but . . .'

'Well, fit this in when you can. After Christmas will do. I've just got a feeling about it. Call it a bee in my bonnet.'

Liz opened her mouth to mention her friendship with Ginnie Kemp, then decided against it. Instead she simply nodded and returned to her room. This time she closed the door firmly behind her.

'Well!' Nelson greeted her wonderingly. 'Chief Inspector Stainton hanging paper chains? Now I've seen everything.'

'Wonders will never cease,' agreed Liz. 'Come on, then, if you want these things up. What comes next? What about one of these streamers?'

Alec attended the office party and reluctantly drank warm Dubonnet rosé out of a plastic cup, and the next day, Christmas Eve, drove to his sister's house near West Wittering.

When it rained, Alec thought, the book forgotten in his lap, the sea and the sky became barely different shades of grey; like the test card he used to watch on the television as a child, waiting for *Watch With Mother* to begin. The rain hung smokily in the air, a universal wetness.

'What are you looking so glum about? Here: have a nut.'

Alec took the shelled brazil nut his sister was holding out to him. In her lap, wool rampaged in a riot of colour as she finished a winter jumper for one of the children.

'Come on: tell,' she demanded, wielding the nutcrackers again. 'I know you like being enigmatic, but you can't expect to get away with it here. Damn! Now I've made a mess. Anyway, Eddie wants his uncle to play with him, and you did promise.'

Alec stretched lazily and put his book to one side. 'It's nice to be needed.' And he got up and went to kneel by his

six-year-old nephew who was puzzling over the instruction
leaflet for his new construction set.

Tessa Livingstone watched the two of them fondly for a
moment, and then bundled her knitting together and
crossed to draw the curtains and shut out the grey
December sea and the gathering dusk. The small earnest
boy who was her son and the spare, withdrawn man who
was her brother absorbed themselves together in the possibilities of the new toy, and Tessa wondered whether it was
an illusion that Alec seemed more withdrawn even than
usual, and whether asking him down to share the family
Christmas really had been the good idea it had seemed.

By the time Tessa had been sixteen and capable of being
an adult companion for her brothers they had left home.
Jeremy was in the Navy and Alec was about to start his
first term at Sandhurst. That was fifteen years ago: and
now the two men were almost middle-aged, Jeremy captain
of a frigate, Alec a detective chief inspector; and she, their
gawky, despised sister—she sometimes looked in the mirror
in bewilderment at the contented married woman with a
young family which she had become. Eddie's birth, and
more especially Alec's being godfather to him, had brought
Tessa and Alec together in a way they had never known
before, and when their father died their newly-discovered
tie of affection became permanent.

Pity it hadn't had the same effect on her and Christopher,
she thought with a stab of self-pity. She left godparent and
godson, heads bent over their work, to themselves and went
through to the kitchen to check the pans; and to stop herself
going any further down the road to misery she began to
speculate what it was which had happened in this last year
to unsettle Alec.

Because that had always been the problem, she told herself. Since he had come out of the army, a tightlipped and
noticeably cynical twenty-seven-year-old, and joined the
police force, she felt he had never really relaxed with himself; and consequently his relationships with others had
been tense too, and unencouraging of sympathy. Only with

her, through Eddie's mediation, and now with Eddie himself (now that he was no longer a small child but a definite
person) had there been some willingness to lower the bar-
riers; and even then only to a certain point.

She wished she could believe him capable of lowering
them altogether. For she felt that she was going to need her
brother's support before very long.

Later, when the children were being tucked into their beds
by Christopher, Tessa, idly dangling an empty glass at
arm's length as she lay back in her chair, said: 'What did
you mean about being needed, Alec?'

He raised his eyes reluctantly from the *Telegraph's* Christmas crossword. 'Did I say that?'

'Yes, you did, and you know it. And you didn't just mean
Eddie and his Lego set, so don't try and pull the wool over
my eyes, brother mine.'

He smiled. 'Oh, it just seemed rather pleasant to be able
to meet a simple need. Someone asked me for something
rather more complex a few weeks ago. It was nice to be
someone she felt she could turn to, but in the event I rather
made a muck of it.'

Tessa opened an interrogative eye. 'She?'

'She. There: that's given you something to speculate
about, hasn't it? But you know, Tess, I do have friends of
both sexes. So don't let your eager little mind get carried
away. Incidentally, I think there's a piece missing from
Eddie's Lego set.'

'Don't change the subject.' Tessa considered how she
might draw more information out of her brother, but her
mind refused to work. She wondered whether she was tipsy,
and decided she was just pleasantly tired; but the thought
depressed her none the less.

Christopher came back in. 'All tucked up,' he said; but
Alec did not fail to notice that he addressed a point in the
air somewhere between his wife and his brother-in-law.

He wished he had the first idea about how to begin to
help.

CHAPTER 10

Christmas came and went. Alec heard nothing more directly about CAMEX for nearly a month; though, in the way that happens once one's mind is alerted to something, he began to notice references in the newspapers to the debates which were to take place on the parliamentary bill in the spring, and to the activities of CAMEX groups and other lobbyists up and down the country.

Three weeks into the new year, the question of CAMEX re-entered Alec's consideration with a bang. Alec was intent on the details of a new training schedule when Inspector Harry Glover put his head round the door of Alec's office, walked across to the desk and flourished a sheet of paper in Alec's direction.

'Have a look at that,' Glover said shortly. Alec took it and glanced down it with a sinking heart.

'*One: Members will hold themselves ready to carry out whatever acts the committee may consider appropriate for forwarding the aims of CAMEX,*' Chief Superintendent Blackett read out half an hour later in a voice pregnant with sarcasm. '*Two: Members must be made to acknowledge that their allegiance to CAMEX outweighs any so-called responsibility to act within conventional definitions of legality. Since in the real world it must be accepted that some members will continue to have outmoded ideas of what constitutes "acceptable" campaigning, a register should be kept, for the eyes of the committee only, of members fully committed to our aims and fully prepared to implement them by all available means.*' He looked up. 'Does that load of garbage mean what I think it means?'

'It gets worse,' Glover observed.

'*Three: Should the means recommended by the committee involve a significant risk of injury or loss of life, whether to members or non-members, the committee should not for that reason only abandon any otherwise fruitful course of action. Four: Those directly in-volved in the activities against which CAMEX is fighting should be regarded as legitimate targets and CAMEX will not hold itself responsible for injuries or death which such people bring upon themselves by their involvement in those activities. Five . . .'*

He threw the photocopied sheet down on the desk top in front of him. 'Where did we get this pile of shit?'

'John Clavell had it through the post this morning,' Glover informed him. 'No covering note. The original's being done over for prints.'

Clavell was the constituency's Conservative MP.

Glover continued, 'The original was printed, using a daisywheel, the way it's laid out suggests a low-budget home-computer set-up; but what Clavell was sent was a photocopy too, suggesting maybe whoever sent it had access to the document second-hand.'

'What do you make of it?'

'Well,' Glover replied cautiously, 'it did just strike me that there've been rather a lot of anonymous tip-offs lately to do with CAMEX. Makes you wonder whether they haven't got a mole in their midst.'

'Maybe,' Blackett grunted sceptically. 'Personally, I wouldn't have thought an organization like that is worth betraying. You either join because you support it, or you leave it alone.'

'Yes, but it'll be like any group,' Glover suggested. 'No sooner is it running than you get splinter groups: those who think it's too radical, not radical enough. Like old-time Trotskyites and Stalinists. Maybe there is a revisionist CAMEX at the throat of a neo-CAMEX.'

'They can chew each other into pieces for all I care,' Blackett said, flicking the sheet of paper with a yellowed fingernail. 'But this looks like trouble.' He sank into heavy thought for a moment or two, hunched over his desk. 'Alec?' he said at last.

'I suppose,' Alec ventured, 'we have to assume it's genuine?'

Blackett looked up from beneath his shaggy eyebrows. 'Go on.'

'This "memorandum": it's all jargon. Any of us could run it off in half an hour. It isn't signed or initialled, there's no reference, no heading to the paper. In the last six months,' Alec said, 'one of CAMEX's members has lost her job; one, a doctor, has had her car tyres slashed and then been informed she's to be sued and reported to the GMC disciplinary committee; that schoolmaster, Morris, is a CAMEX member, too, don't forget. It's the sort of issue over which tempers run high.'

Blackett sat back in his chair, which bore the strain in silence. 'Are you going to be the one to decide that we can just file this and forget it?' he asked with a sour smile.

That was exactly the problem. Whoever had written that memorandum, whether it was genuine or a fake, they couldn't afford to dismiss it.

'I suppose we don't have any lead into CAMEX, do we?' Glover asked without much hope. 'I mean, who might be pressed into telling us whether this is genuine or not?'

'I'm rather afraid,' Alec admitted slowly, 'that we do.'

'I thought we might,' Blackett said enigmatically, with a hard stare in Alec's direction. 'Better get on with it, then.'

'This is fake,' Kate Randall said, and her large round eyes looked up at Glover in horror. 'You've got to believe me!'

Glover scrutinized the girl's tense, anxious face impassively. Of course the Randall girl was worried—desperately worried. You would be, wouldn't you, if your organization produced a document as explosive as this and it got into the hands of the police. Or equally, of course, if you found yourself helpless at the centre of a smear campaign.

'Don't tell me what I have to believe,' he said. 'I can't *afford* to believe you. On the other hand . . .'

'Yes?'

'On the other hand, Chief Inspector Stainton has told

me about your meeting with him, and he's told me that
that meeting was at your instigation.'

The girl let out her breath with an audible sigh. 'It's all
part of the same thing,' she protested. 'Like I told Mr
Stainton. It's obvious. It's a campaign to discredit
CAMEX. First simple things like tyre-slashing. Then it's
personal smears. Now this. What's so bloody is, it's going
to work.'

The girl was remarkably self-possessed, all the same.
Many men and women, after they had been in this room a
while, were on the verge of tears (sometimes simulated;
Glover often compared the acting he saw on television
adversely with that which he encountered professionally).
Not this girl: she was plainly a tough cookie.

'Are you telling me your committee never drew up this
document?'

'Never. We've never even discussed anything like this.
There's nobody who would *suggest* it. We're not terrorists,
for heaven's sake!'

'*How do you know?*'

'What do you mean?'

'Come on! You're a bright girl. Work it out for yourself.
If,' Glover pointed out deliberately, 'there *were* people in
CAMEX—maybe not even in your local chapter—who *did*
plan along these lines . . . well, you'd never know, would
you? Because, knowing your views, they'd never include
you in any of their deliberations. Proving a negative. Can
you *prove* to me that there is no militant wing, or action
group, or whatever, anywhere in CAMEX? Can you? Come
on, love!'

'If it was one of our committee's resolutions,' she said
dully, 'it would have our reference and the date, and anyway, our minutes are written in a book.'

'Not on computer, so's they can be copied and sent out
to committee members before the next meeting?'

She shook her head sorrowfully. 'You don't realize.
CAMEX has no money. We can't afford luxuries like that.'

*

Eight miles away John Clavell added bitters to the gin he
had poured Alec, and swirled the mixture around in the
glass while the pink tinge suffused the alcohol.

'Personally I don't believe the thing's genuine,' he said.
'On the other hand, I didn't show it to Christine because
I didn't want to upset her, so to that extent you could say
I took it seriously. There you are, that should be about
right.'

'Thanks. Why not? Believe it, I mean.'

Clavell took his seat, put his own drink down on the table
beside him, and scratched his ear. 'Doesn't seem their style,
I suppose. It's not what I've come to expect of CAMEX.
Not the way they've played things up till now.'

'How have they played things?'

'Too damned softly, to be honest. They're a good bunch
of people who sincerely believe that we're making a big
mistake over this issue, but they've never really taken the
gloves off in the way you have to these days if you want to
be an effective pressure group. Having said that,' he added
thoughtfully, 'they have rather pepped their ideas up in the
last month or two.'

'Perhaps they sense that time is running out. Perhaps
they realize they've been too nice about things so far and
have swung the other way.'

Clavell shook his head dubiously. 'Time *is* running out,
of course; but still . . .'

Alec sipped his pink gin. 'You seem to have a lot of
sympathy for them, John.'

'I have.'

'But you don't intend to vote against the bill?'

'I don't.' He hesitated. 'I don't mind admitting I have
my doubts about whether I'm right, but at the end of the
day, I tell myself that it's going to happen, nobody's going
to hold back anything which can be passed off as progress,
so it's better to vote for the Bill and ensure that as many
safeguards as possible are built into it.'

'There speaks a politician,' Alec observed cynically.

'But an honest one. Mind you, I don't like the idea of

putting money into the pockets of people like Blake; that does stick in my craw.'

'Blake?'

'John Blake, who runs our own contribution to progress. You must have read about the Medisearch laboratory out on the Technology Park. There was a lot of fuss last year because it was claimed the council had paid them sweeteners to locate within the area. There are strong rumours that Blake's backed by Dutch money, and he'll be a millionaire in a year or two. I don't *like* putting my vote where it pleases the big commercial interests. I'm inclined to go along with CAMEX and say that in an issue like this, there shouldn't *be* commercial interests.'

'Leave all the research to government laboratories?'

'Then you've got to fund them.'

'But you can use the profits for the public good.'

The MP laughed. 'That's taking a long view. You'll never make a politician, Alec, if you persist with olde-worlde ideas like *that*.'

'Thank God for that,' Alec said drily. 'Who do you think sent the thing, by the way?'

'No idea; and why to me? The aim presumably is to discredit CAMEX and persuade me to take no notice of their lobbying; but whoever sent it could have had much wider effect by copying it to the national papers—or the rest of the House, come to that.'

Alec shook his head. 'We've checked.' He looked at Clavell assessingly. 'What about Blake?'

'Blake?' Clavell froze in the act of reaching Alec a plate of crisps. 'Yes,' he said slowly. 'I see what you're getting at.'

'If you're right about CAMEX being ineffective, Blake has nothing to worry about,' Alec pointed out. 'But does he know that? And does he share your view of their effectiveness?'

It was close to five in the afternoon when Kate Randall finally left the police station. The incessant wind had brought rain, blowing it slantwise across the road, glistening in the headlights of the traffic streaming out of the town. Oncoming cars formed an unbroken stream, swish-swish-swishing past, their lights on, white and spiteful. It was the time of year when reason said the days were drawing out, but the body was worn down with cold and darkness and could not believe that there would ever be a spring.

The lights were off in the flat. Turning the car into the parking area, Kate saw the windows glistening darkly, uncurtained. She climbed the stairs, and her key in the lock seemed to turn noisily, as on to empty rooms.

At first it was difficult to see what made the living-room seem empty. Then she realized: half the records were gone, and the tape-player. In the kitchen the teapot was gone; and the rack of knives. In the bathroom beyond, no razor, no aftershave, no brown sponge-bag.

Wearily Kate pushed at the half-open door of the spare room. There was no need to look in the wardrobe; it was enough that Charlie's suitcase was gone from the top of it. Emptily, Kate sat on the stripped bed, while the rain pattered carelessly against the window and the streetlight outside cast its orange glow on to the ceiling. She swung her feet on to the bed, lay back, stared at the ceiling for a while, then closed her eyes and willed herself into sleep.

Clive Morris was finally charged two days later. Delicate investigation revealed that he had interfered with up to a dozen girls to one degree or another over the last couple of years, some at school, some at a youth club with which he had helped. Of these, three cases could be treated as representative, with victims who were ready to attest to what had happened, and old enough to be reasonably reliable witnesses. That was more than enough for Inspector Glover, at least for the time being. Morris was invited to the police station again, where he cried and, to Glover's relief, at last made a statement admitting to offences stretching back to the time of his mother's death three years before. It might not, after all, be necessary to subject any

of his victims to the trauma of giving evidence against him.
Glover sent off his file to the Crown Prosecution Service
and congratulated himself on a job well done.

CHAPTER 11

At first it was just one more blustery day; but as the hours
passed there came a ferocity to the wind, and as the long
winter shadows melted into dusk it became apparent that
this latest storm was different from the others. The wind
screamed and moaned round the buildings, interspersed
with gusts which thundered as if a giant was beating a
carpet above the rooftops. Flurries of rain beat against the
windows like exuberant children, and then were gone, hurried away by the wind. It wasn't particularly cold, but those
who went out at lunch-time returned with ruddy faces,
gasping and grinning after battling with the elements.
    In the car park in Redhill someone opened a car door
only to have it snatched out of his hand and slammed
against the paintwork of the vehicle alongside. A van driver
delivering catering packs of coffee and tea to replenish the
vending machines was knocked back against his vehicle; he
lost his grip on the boxes and before they could reach the
ground the wind whirled them ten yards away. One burst,
and coffee drove like spindrift down the car park; the other
was driven against a van wheel, where it waited submissively to be retrieved. Two hundred yards away, a wooden
pallet leant carelessly against a wall shifted, turned, and
began to bowl end-over-end across the concrete.
    By six there was little sign of the wind abating. As
Frances struggled to lock the door of the office it tugged at
her clothing and snatched spitefully at her scarf. The car
rocked, as she settled herself into it, with the gusts which
raced across the now almost empty tarmac of the little
trading estate. On the main road traffic moved cautiously,
speeding up outside town. Frances fiddled for the radio for

a traffic report, and then caught quickly at the wheel as the road emerged from a cutting and the car moved bodily sideways in the force of the wind.

Out on the M25 things were no better, though it was a relief to be out of reach of falling trees. Frances was appalled at the viciousness of the wind as the motorway emerged from the shelter of Titsey Hill and ran along parallel with the North Downs towards Riverhead, and steeled herself for the five-minute run from the exit through the tight, sunken lanes to her house.

And then she was home, and the solid old house hunched its shoulders to the blasts and seemed merely to sink a little more deeply into its sheltering hollow.

Frances had lost sixteen trees in the storms of October 1987 and the woodlands outside her boundary had been ravaged as in a great game of spillikins. But it had taught her respect for the Kentish clothier who had built the old house, tucking it cannily into the folds of the wooded weald. Long ago it had weathered the storm which scattered the Armada, and now its timbers, brick, and tiles were all set by the passing of the years. Like an old, twisted countryman who casually shoulders a hundredweight sack which a young townsman can barely lift, so Frances' house had looked out over the new vistas opened up by the storm, untroubled while newer structures shivered and succumbed; and this time, Frances had little fear that things would be worse.

'I'll be with you in a moment, Miles. Come in and say hello to Lucy. Lucy, it's Mr Wetherby.'

Miles Wetherby, smart and affable in his charcoal grey suit, put out his hand to the girl. 'Hello, Lucy.'

Lucy ignored the hand, stared aloofly at a point just short of Wetherby's chin, and made no reply. Wetherby's mouth hardened. Frances was still turned away, hunting in her bag for keys and credit cards, but she sensed the animosity in the room as Lucy turned away and walked through into the sitting-room.

'Lucy? Mr Wetherby was speaking to you.' Frances' voice expressed puzzlement rather than anger; Lucy was a quiet but invariably a polite girl and it did not at first occur to Frances what was happening. Lucy turned her head a fraction so that her mother could see her closed face, but didn't pause. A moment later they heard *Für Elise* issue from the baby grand in the other room.

'What's got into her?' Frances wondered aloud. 'OK, Miles, sorry to keep you waiting. I can't find my cheque-book—must be in my other bag, but I've got an Amex with me.'

Miles held the door for Frances, his face revealing neither anger at Lucy's response nor pique that Frances insisted on taking the means to pay for herself. A moment later Lucy, on the second reprise of the theme, heard the bark of the exhaust of Wetherby's car above the roar of the storm, and the faint crunch of gravel as he let the clutch in too fiercely.

'She won't like that,' Lucy said out loud, with satisfaction. Her fingers continued to run unfalteringly over the keyboard. She played the piece to the end, and then went in search of companionship in the shape of Bridget, her mother's live-in help.

Judy Baker listened to the wind as she dressed to go out. It howled and wailed in the chimney, beat itself against the walls, shifted tiles with tiny chinks, and would not be ignored.

She wanted to ignore it. It was one of the hateful things about living in the country—there weren't many, and she tried to forget them, but from time to time they pressed themselves insistently on her consciousness. They were all natural, and therefore could not be fought: the elements and events for which earlier centuries had reserved gods' names. Thunder was one (how much more crushing it was, here, than ever it had been in Cheam or Brixton). Fog was another, unrelieved by streetlights and signposts and passing red buses. Strong winds were a third. Never, in town, had she felt the force of the wind untrammelled. Even in the great storm of 1987 when Cheam's parks and avenues lost their limes, their sycamores and their beeches, and tiles, greenhouses and carports whirled away into the night sky, Judy had felt safe, surrounded as she was in every direction by ten miles of man's construction. Let the storm rage as it would, it could not easily erase five centuries of building in brick and stone.

But here, man's achievement felt a frailer and an altogether more precarious thing: in particular, the two cottages, joined siamese-like at the waist, stood up uncertainly and might at any moment decide to kneel, sit or lie down to escape the brunt of the vicious blows of the wind.

Judy herself, however, was in better shape now to cope with country demons and ancient gods. Earlier in the evening she had caught Trooper glancing at her sidelong to gauge her reaction, and Judy had grinned at him unashamed. For once she was able to give him the security parents owe children: it was her responsibility to sustain their modest home, and the rising wind was not about to deflect her from that task.

All the same, Judy wished the noise would simply *stop*. To distract herself she spent more than usual care on her choice of clothes for the evening, finally selecting a short dark skirt which depended for decency on wearing legwarmers beneath it; and a white blouse with a cheeky tie. Judy's small face, always suggestive of youth, and skinny legs turned the ensemble into a fair pastiche of schoolgirl adolescence, and after a moment's thought she fetched a ponytail hairpiece from a drawer and pinned it into her dark short hair before bending to the mirror on the dressing-table to concentrate on making her make-up invisible.

Twenty minutes later she cuffed Trooper affectionately on the shoulder and they fought their way out to the car to fetch Sophy Blake to babysit; and it was arguable, had there been any observer to notice, whether the driver or the passenger of the car looked the older.

*

Kate Randall shivered as she waited in the downstairs lobby for her lift to turn up. The storm chimed with her feelings, which were turbulent and unpredictable and frequently violent. As the minutes passed and the car did not arrive, she tapped her foot, and beat a tattoo against the wall with her gloved hand. As if drawn by magnetism her hand moved to the pocket of her jacket, and she half-drew out the envelope she had received that morning, before resolutely pushing it back in and zipping the pocket shut. The contents were after all well enough known to her now; and they didn't improve on rereading. She shivered again; and at that moment one pair of the series of headlights passing on the main road swung round and shone straight into her eyes. Blinking, she pushed the glass door open and walked out into the violent night.

Alec Stainton drew the curtain across the broad bay window and turned his back on the wild night.

'You'd better stay the night, Tess.'

His sister Tessa shook her head and began to gather together coat, gloves and bag. 'A good night for a murder,' she offered.

He smiled. 'For burglary, more like. Wind like this is a godsend to the breaking-and-entering brigade. Who's going to hear a window smash or a lock tear out of a doorframe?'

'Alec . . .'

But he was out in the hall, drawing the curtains there too, and Tessa sighed and tugged on her jacket. Things between her and Christopher were bad—bad enough to send her sixty miles on a wild night to seek her brother's reassurance and advice. But she had been chasing a will-o'-the-wisp. Alec, of all people, to give advice in an affair of the heart? Nobody better to consult in any practical matter—but life, or at least her life, had never been about practicalities.

'Sure you won't stay? You could ring Christopher.'

'No, thanks; I wouldn't be easy in my mind; and it's main roads most of the way—I'll be all right.'

'Make sure you are.' He smiled affectionately at her, and she smiled ruefully back. He saw her downstairs and into her car, and waited under the little porte-cochère until her tail-lights had receded down the drive.

Then he slammed the door and stumped back upstairs to relieve his foul mood and his anger with himself in a bitter flood of invective which echoed tauntingly round the empty flat.

It was late. Sophy sat watching the television distractedly. Every few minutes her eyes strayed to the clock on the mantelpiece. Each time the hands had moved only a fraction; yet move they did, relentlessly, and it was already far later than she was used to staying. On the screen a smiling woman in a pastel woollen dress encouraged two couples as they revealed the secrets of their marriages. The picture flickered suddenly and the ceiling light blinked, and Sophy shivered. She willed the storm to subside, but every time she managed to persuade herself that the gusts were less fierce, a specially violent blow seemed to rock the tiny cottage.

All movement had long ceased from the cottage next door. Sophy had heard the signature tune of the radio news at nine, and shortly afterwards the muffled sound of a door banging as old Mr Weeding made his way to bed. Trooper was in bed too, and sleeping with a peace and ease which Sophy could only envy.

'And how do you and Belinda deal with this little problem of yours, Alan?' asked the woman on the screen with excessive interest.

'At first we thought we would just have to live with it,' Belinda answered, leaning forward, 'but then we discovered that if Alan, you know, took his time over the sort of foreplay . . .'

'Tom and Wendy,' the interviewer turned to the other couple, 'have you ever had problems with premature ejaculation? Tom?'

'Well, funny you should . . .'

The frank and fearless programme ended. Sophy jumped up, and hunted for the remote control. The clock drew her eyes like a magnet: half past midnight, and she had never before been later than half past eleven when she had been baby-sitting for Judy. Her parents would explode. How was she to get home if Judy didn't come back soon? Desperately she calculated how long it would take her to walk the distance that in the car they covered so quickly; but she knew that she could never venture out into the dark while the wind beat like this. Had Mr Weeding a car? She was almost sure he had not.

It was a long while before it occurred to her that she could ring her parents to come and collect her. But then she thought of Trooper. What would happen to him? The wind was still pressing round the cottage like a python preparing to squeeze, and Sophy was frightened.

'Where's Mum?'

'Trooper!' She couldn't keep the relief out of her voice. 'You should be in bed!'

The boy came forward, his face tense and adult above his red dressing-gown and Superman pyjamas.

'Mum not back?'

'No; she's ever so late, and I don't know what I should do. D'you think I should ring the police? It's an awful night.' Sophy realized as soon as the words were spoken that they were not the most prudent in the circumstances; but Trooper seemed not to have registered their implication. Nor did he seem to think much of the idea of looking to the police for help and even in her anxiety Sophy found that response disturbing in a ten-year-old.

'Wish that wind'd stop,' Trooper remarked bravely after a while. Sophy nodded.

'What do we do, then?' he asked.

'I don't know, Trooper; I wish I did. D'you think we could wake Mr Weeding?'

Trooper stood indecisively for a minute and Sophy watched him hopefully. It seemed all wrong, but it was Trooper who knew how to cope.

'I'll ring Aunty Hev,' he said finally, and crossed to the telephone where it hung on the wall by the door, beside a message board.

'It's awfully late,' Sophy said doubtfully, but Trooper had already taken the phone off the hook and was tapping out a number on the keypad. It seemed to ring for an awfully long time, but Trooper just stood there, as if in no doubt of its being answered in the end.

'It's me, Aunty Hev,' he said in the end. 'Please can you come round? I'm afraid something's happened to Mum.' He listened for a moment, then put the phone back and turned calmly to Sophy.

'She'll be round in ten minutes,' he said. 'We could make her a cup of tea.'

A gust of wind clapped derisively against the side of the house and the light flickered for a moment. When it came on again at its normal brightness it revealed to Trooper his babysitter crouched in a chair, her head in her hands, sobbing her heart out. He stared at her, and then padded out into the kitchen to fill the kettle.

In her tile-hung yeoman's house crouched on the Kentish scarp Frances Walker slept deeply, dreaming of sailing at sea in strong weather, on a boat crewed by Miles Wetherby and Alec Stainton. They kept disputing the captaincy, until she cried out that if that was the way they behaved, she'd jump overboard and swim ashore; whereupon she found herself running alone and unaccountably naked through the endless galleries of the British Museum, while the sightless eyes of mummies and sea-creatures and shrunken heads gazed lasciviously at her. She woke to a cackle of derisive laughter; but it was only the wind. Of course.

Others were not so lucky. A man died, staggering home from a night-club along a suburban high street, when a tile blown from a roof fractured his skull. A sales rep, hurrying home from a continental trip, drove round a corner into a van that had been blown on to its side, and was killed. An old woman had a miraculous escape when a chimney fell across her bed.

The storm raged all night, and by morning had blown itself out. Country lanes and main roads were strewn with debris, from twigs to broken branches. Great trees lay up-ended in the fields, discs of soil and snowdrops clinging to their roots. Interestedly, people drew back their curtains and peered out into the still-dark morning; tried electric light switches; lifted the telephone.

By half past seven many of those who commuted had already departed for work, nosing carefully along the lanes, the daily routine pleasurably upset by this fit of temper on the part of nature. Those who were left donned wellingtons and jackets and ventured out to see how the landscape had changed overnight.

Arthur Stead and his setter set out for their customary morning run expectantly. Arthur looked at the waving tree-tops and decided they had not the same frenzy they had had the evening before; he and Patch would be safe enough, especially if they kept out in the open. The dog, full of beans, tugged eagerly at the leash. Once over the road and on to the common Arthur slipped the leash and the dog bounded on ahead. Arthur followed more sedately, breathing in the heady fresh air and noting what had been brought down.

Near the car park was one of the characteristic copses of birch which were scattered over the common where it had been undergrazed over the years. The rough car park was much used in the summer by ramblers and picnickers, and at most times of the year by courting couples. The copse, Arthur realized as he drew nearer, looked thinner than it had when he had been here a day or two before, and its chief feature, a well-grown pine which had been here long before the scrub birch grew up, no longer towered above its neighbours. Patch had vanished into the undergrowth. Stead, assuring himself that the wind really was far less strong, followed the side path the dog had taken among the trees.

There lay the great pine, brought low now after its lordly life. Patch was nuzzling round it, pattering to and fro, lifting his leg. And beyond . . .

That was the point at which Mr Stead's heart skipped a beat as he saw the dull gleam of painted metal among the tangled debris. Calling to Patch, he slipped his leash on and scrambled down the low bank. He had to go quite a long way round to avoid the tangled limbs, for the mighty pine had brought lesser trees down with it as it fell, before he could begin to approach the car across which the trunk of the pine lay so firmly. It was a small blue hatchback, well out of his reach, deeply enmeshed in the tangle of branches. It was badly crushed, half lifted off its wheels on one side, almost pressed to the ground on the other by the heavy, gnarled limb which lay across the roof and bonnet. Stead had braced himself for the expected sight, the crushed body in the driver's seat, and felt almost let down that nothing was visible. Or was it, he thought, with a sinking heart, as he pushed his way through the brash of branches.

The body was there all right. It lay almost on the ground, head down, hunched by the side of the vehicle. Bare, pale flesh was clearly visible. There was nothing wrong with Arthur Stead's eyes and he saw quite clearly, without the need to thrust himself any further in among the clinging, whipping debris, that it was a woman; a young woman, her hair tumbled forward over her congested, discoloured face, and there was no doubt at all (he shuddered, turning away from the ruin of the back of her head) that she was quite, quite dead.

CHAPTER 12

Apart from those deaths which are plainly murder from the start—the wife standing tearfully over her husband's body; the man who walks into the police station and confesses to having beaten his mother to death—and those which are never recognized as murder at all (and who knows how many of those there are?): apart from these, murder investigations often begin with a vague unease, on the part of a doctor hesitant to sign a death certificate or a policeman reluctant to close his notebook—a feeling that something about the death is not quite right.

Thus when, the morning after the storm, Detective-Sergeant Nelson radioed through a message for Detective Chief Inspector Stainton at twenty-five minutes past eleven to the effect that there was something about the death up on the common that he was unhappy about, Alec glanced instinctively at his diary to see what could be cancelled, left the coffee steaming in the mug on his desk and the stack of reports and files in his in-tray, and within four minutes was turning out of the car park, buckling himself into his seat-belt as he went. The wind was subsiding every minute like a mortally wounded foe, though from time to time a spurt of hailstones rattled against the windscreen.

Up on the common the air was fresh and invigorating, driving the rain squalls away into Kent leaving a wide chromium-coloured sky against which the leafless trees stood sharply delineated. The scattering of parked cars came into sight as Alec crested a brow. A uniformed constable stood at the entrance to the car park in front of a fluttering orange tape, and Alec drove past and pulled off the road a hundred yards further on, in front of the pathologist's Volvo.

Alec climbed out and tugged on his Barbour as he walked back down the road. Nelson was already walking up to meet him.

'I think we've got a murder on our hands,' he said simply as they came up to each other. He gestured to the right, and the two men crossed the verge and jumped over a drainage ditch. A sheep path wound through the undergrowth, and shortly they came out on to the rim of the car park. Their slight elevation on the surrounding bank turned the car park into a miniature amphitheatre. Twenty yards away the mangled remains of a blue car lay pressed beneath the fallen pine, and beside it, almost hidden by the smashed branches, the pathologist, Ransome, bent over a huddled bundle.

'Tell me,' Alec said.

Nelson took a couple of Polaroid photographs from his clipboard. 'Have a look at these. This one—you see the general setup. Nasty accident, isn't it? And it looks as if the tree's right on top of the body. But now . . . see . . . this one, which shows the body from a different angle.'

Alec took the second photo Nelson handed him, and his pulse quickened. The huddle of clothes, which seemed to bear no relation to anything human, was in reality a good six feet from the nearest limb of the fallen tree. He looked across at Ransome again, who was now standing up and holding something to the light.

Alec studied the two photographs once more. 'I'll warn Blackett,' he said. 'SOCO?'

'Waiting for your say-so. I'm afraid he may find the car park's been a bit churned up,' Nelson said. 'When I got here the local plod had driven his car right up to the body, and two apes were standing around with chain-saws all set to clear the tree. Sorry, sir. Nothing's been touched since.'

'Keep your apologies for Mr Fletcher,' Alec grunted, rising. 'Right: let's get weaving. Run a trace on the car?'

'Registered to a Judy Baker, age thirty-four, which fits.'

Alec nodded and turned away, heading for Nelson's blue police Rover to use the radio. 'Don't let Dr Ransome disappear,' he instructed over his shoulder. 'Let's see what we can salvage from the wreckage.'

The van towing the murder caravan stalled on the steep, greasy hill, and nothing they could do would get it to pull away again. In the end a Land-Rover had to be brought out, and the caravan was unhitched and towed up to the car park. Three uniformed constables spent most of the afternoon trying to get it to sit level.

Alec looked round critically at the usual organized bedlam. Orange tape fluttered among the trees, encircling the whole car park and a ten-yard-deep strip of the surrounding heathland. It was still raining, driven by a blustery wind, the dampness coming in flurries which sought out the chinks in clothing and spattered noisily against waterproofs. Arc lamps turned the winter evening into cruel white in which scientific and Scene of Crime teams still ferreted and probed like ghoulish spirits in the endless mud into which any clues had probably long ago been crushed, while outside the circle of light the blackness was total. And still it rained.

Down in the caravan they had got their priorities sorted out and the kettle was boiling five minutes after the power supply had been connected. Telephone lines were being run to a junction box on one of the poles by the roadside. Alec took the mug of coffee he was handed gratefully, and promptly burnt his tongue on it.

'It's a bit hot, sir,' Simms warned him belatedly.

David Fletcher, the greying Scene of Crime Officer, stamped in and shook the moisture from his cap. Simms winced as spots of damp appeared on a virgin pad of foolscap on the desk. Already the caravan was beginning to seem distinctly crowded.

Fletcher nodded to Alec, and took the mug Simms passed him.

'Damn!'

'Bit hot, sir. Sorry.'

Alec waited patiently. Fletcher blew on his coffee. 'Bloody hopeless!' he complained.

Alec smiled homourlessly. Of all the places one would choose to come across a dead body, from the point of view of gathering clues open commonland on the morning after a hurricane and in continuous rain had to come pretty low on the list. Moreover, the officer first on the scene had rightly attended first to the dead woman to make sure there was no chance of reviving her. After that, and the doctor's more expert but equally fruitless ministrations, the corpse was hardly in its pristine innocence; and the ground of the car park resembled a relief model of the battle of the

Somme, rendered more noxious by the little piles of shit left behind by Arthur Stead's dog Patch. After all that, Fletcher and the civilian experts were supposed to collect scientific evidence for analysis?

Alec became aware that Fletcher was watching him shrewdly, and raised his eyebrows interrogatively as he took a cautious sip from the plastic cup.

'Well, now! The car. Usual abundance of fingerprints, including at least two different sets on the steering-wheel. Plenty of hairs, dog and human, black, blonde, you name it; usual rubbish in the glovebox and door-pockets. Quarter-bottle of Gordon's, two-thirds empty; receipt for same, pushed into a door-pocket. Dated yesterday. Blood, of course, and not all of it from this incident, by the looks of it, because there's seepage as well as splatter and it's older too.'

Alec raised his eyebrows.

Fletcher made a face. 'You don't need me to suggest a dozen explanations.'

'Innocent ones?'

'Depends what you mean by innocent, doesn't it?' He drained his mug and the two of them walked back up the slope. Outside the glare of the lights it was properly dark now. The road was quiet. An hour ago homegoing commuters had used it as a short cut to Uckfield and Crowborough from Crawley and Gatwick; now it had reverted to anonymity, an ancient, windswept trackway over the bracken-clad, deer-bitten common. Tomorrow morning it would slip back into the twentieth century for the morning commuter and school runs. By then Alec would be making his report to Chief Superintendent Blackett. He had better think what he was going to say.

Fletcher said: 'Shoulder-bag on the passenger seat. Thank God for women's handbags, I always say. The day they go out of fashion is the day I take up growing dahlias instead. Credit cards, membership cards, letters. There's a rather nasty letter you'll want to look at later, Alec.'

'Yes? What about the murder weapon?'

Fletcher shook his head. 'No dice. Ransome reckons something round and jagged, doesn't he, a stone, a—'

A shout from the far side of the car park interrupted him. The two men raised their heads like pointers catching the scent.

'Sounds like somebody's found something,' Fletcher said with satisfaction, and altered course in the direction of the sound. A figure emerged from the scrub of birch and brambles and held up something in a plastic bag.

'By the way,' Fletcher said, 'I mentioned there was a can of petrol in the boot?'

'No,' Alec said. 'You didn't.'

'Full.'

'So?'

'I did just wonder, seeing as she had a CAMEX membership card in her bag . . .'

'You didn't mention that, either,' Alec observed drily. 'It looks as if there could be more to Miss Judy Baker than meets the eye.'

'Judy Baker my foot,' Fletcher said, saving his best card until last. 'I don't know whose car she was driving, but if the contents of the bag are anything to go by, the name of the dead woman was Randall. Kate Randall.'

'Oh no!' muttered Alec. 'Oh God!'

'Found it, sir!' One of Fletcher's team bounded up like a puppy that's retrieved a stick, and held up the plastic bag. It was indeed a stick inside, of sorts; or, more accurately, a length of broken branch, a foot or so long, three or four inches in diameter. It was cruelly jagged where twigs and subsidiary branches had been snapped off, and in the white glare of the arc lights Alec could clearly see a dark thick encrustation at one end; and embedded in it, shining, three or four long pale hairs.

Alec left Nelson and Liz Pink to cope with the welter of things still to be done next morning to set up the spare office as a murder room. As he strode down the corridor to the stairs he passed the open door. Box files and piles of papers were stacked on the desks and the floor; Sally Field sat at the PBX taking calls. The clatter and bustle lifted Alec's spirits a little, reminding him of the sense of shared purpose which sometimes accompanied murder investigations, an antidote to the depressing catalogue of evil such investigations disclosed.

Two hours later Ransome, the pathologist, leant back against the sink and peeled off his gloves. The body which had sheltered Kate Randall lay violated and disregarded on the ceramic slab behind them, awaiting the cosmetic attentions of the mortuary assistant. Alec, who had had to sit in on quite enough post-mortems in his time, had found it harder than usual to dissociate his mind from the bloody rituals. For a brief while after the shock of Fletcher's information, he had tried to persuade himself that the handbag on the passenger seat did not automatically mean that Kate Randall was the murder victim. But now here was the body under the fluorescent lights on the slab: he could not deceive himself any longer.

From Alec's point of view it was the earlier stages of the post-mortem, the examination of the clothing and the outside of the body, which were most likely to yield information of immediate relevance, and he could not afford to escape into anger and exasperation. All the same, he felt Kate should be crying out in protest as her body was humped about and peered at, her hair which had pulled free of its pins remarked upon, her trousers and woolly tights (but her legs were cold enough now) stripped off, her body kneaded and probed; but she just lay there inert and unresponsive and her eyes stared up at the ceiling.

Fortunately there was no necessity to watch when Ransome got down to the serious business of cutting up. When he started to excise the features Alec permitted himself to turn away and, as he listened to the pathologist's running commentary into the dictation machine, the body mercifully became a mere lifeless source of clues to a crime.

'The tree didn't kill her?' Nelson said with satisfaction.

Ransome laughed. 'Do yourself a favour! You saw for

yourself! No, this poor bitch died from a deliberate blow to the skull, crushing the side of the head. It killed her all right; and unless there were two people battered to death in that spot that night, that—' he gestured at the log, the presumed murder weapon, which lay on a side table—'is the weapon that was used. Wait till we get the tissue matched, but it's ten pounds to a brass farthing the brains on that hunk of wood came from this poor darling's skull.'

Alec shifted his weight, and Ransome suddenly busied himself with scrubbing his hands. Most policemen relished pathologists' gallows humour; Ransome, Alec knew, had momentarily forgotten that he had one of the few exceptions in the room with him.

'When will you know about the alcohol?' Alec asked. They had all remarked on the smell of alcohol when the body was opened, and Alec remembered the quarter-bottle of gin that had been in the car. Kate Randall's drinking habits were just one of the intimate secrets Alec would have to make his business.

Ransome nodded. 'I'll let you know what we find when the samples have been tested. But either way I don't see that it alters the picture much. She was certainly alive when the blow was inflicted. Unconsciousness supervened at once, and death came probably within a few minutes.'

He glanced at Alec, who nodded gloomily. Ransome had estimated death at between eleven at night and two in the morning. They could get closer than that if they could find out at what time the tree had fallen. When had the storm started to die down? That would provide a latest possible time for the killing. The tree had to have fallen after Kate Randall was battered to death . . .

The dead girl's clothing had not been intact. As befitted the winter weather, she had been wearing a woolly hat, jeans, a thick jacket with a jersey beneath, and a blouse and bra beneath that. The first photographs showed the jacket and jersey up under her armpits as she lay head down crouched on hands and knees, and her jeans, tights and knickers round her thighs. Beneath her jersey, the blouse had been torn open, and the bra, still done up, wrenched above her breasts. Ransome had shown Alec how there was blood in the creases of the jacket and jersey, proving that they had been interfered with after the blow had been struck. There was no corresponding blood in the creases of the jeans, but the inside of the waistband was bloodily splashed. Poor girl, she had been struck from behind as she crouched in the dark with her trousers round her thighs, relieving herself. She had been, for the record, a virgin.

Kate Randall had been hit from slightly above. The blow had smashed her skull despite the cushioning effect of her pinned-up long hair and woolly hat, and had knocked her forward on to her hands and forehead. A right-handed attacker must have been behind his victim to have inflicted such a blow on the rear right side of the dead girl's head.

The stump of wood lay neutrally in its protective bag. In his imagination Alec hefted it in his hand.

'The murderer would have been unable to avoid getting blood on himself,' Ransome observed, following the direction of Alec's gaze. Alec nodded again. 'Not necessarily a great deal: look for small streaks, like exclamation marks. If you find anything that looks promising, we'll run a serological test.' He smiled sympathetically. 'I'll give you all the help I can. Once you've found the culprit, I should think we ought to be able to nail him.'

CHAPTER 13

'We don't know what Kate Randall was doing up on the common,' Alec remarked that afternoon to Liz as he glanced down the press briefing which the PRO had prepared for issue in time for the evening news bulletins. 'We don't know where she had been, nor where she was going. We don't know who, if anyone, was with her. There's nothing like starting a new case with a clean sheet!'

'She must have believed she was alone,' Liz pondered. 'Or been with someone she knew very well indeed.'

'Who says there weren't two vehicles?' Alec remarked absently, adding his initials to the distribution list.

'There can't have been,' Liz said, with the readiness to jump to conclusions which she had not yet learned always to curb. 'Because otherwise she'd never have been so stupid as to get out of the car. I mean, this was late at night, in a lonely spot. If she turned into the car park, and another car's headlights followed her in, she'd have noticed and driven straight out again.'

'What about a car already there before Kate Randall arrived?' he prompted. 'Would she have noticed it? If she had caught it in her headlights, yes; but if it was tucked away in a corner, with its own lights off? Or someone on foot, come to that. Walking the dog, like the chap who found her. Unlikely, maybe, at midnight in a storm, but people do daft things.'

'Crime of opportunity, you mean, sir? Some bloke sitting parked there to get away from the wife, sees a car turn in and a girl get out?'

'I don't know. I suspect she may have been parked there some time. Long enough to polish off the best part of a quarter-bottle of gin, possibly.'

'The advantage of that theory is, it rules out anything to do with CAMEX as a motive,' Liz pointed out.

The CAMEX connection: the fly in the ointment. That was what had given Alec the conviction that this would be no simple murder case where someone had wielded a broken branch in the heat of the moment and now just waited to be arrested for the catharsis of confession. That was why Alec's reaction to Kate Randall's death had resentment uglily mixed in with the shock and anger. That was why he had been skirting round the issue with unlikely hypotheses all last night and this morning.

Would he be approaching the case differently if Kate Randall had never come to see him with her tale of persecutions? How many coincidences did you need before 'jumping to conclusions' became acknowledging the obvious?

'Yet she could have had an appointment and not realized that the other party was there before her,' Liz pursued remorselessly. 'Certainly a sexual motive just doesn't ring true to me.'

'Go on,' he said, wanting to hear why Liz was uneasy, and add it to his own sense of doubt.

'Well,' she began. 'All right, the clothing suggests the presence of a man, but we know nothing had actually happened. And if there was a man and they had gone to the car park to have a cuddle, what happened to him afterwards? Did he walk home? And then there's this, isn't there?' She nudged the sheet of paper on the desk between them. 'Where does this letter fit in?'

The letter thrust into Kate's handbag had been nasty and full of hate; proposing brutish things, mostly sexual, which the writer would enjoy doing to her, and suggesting sexual inadequacies as the reason women joined an organization like CAMEX. The original, handwritten, was now in the hands of a graphologist. So far the only tentative conclusion was that it had probably been written by a woman.

Suddenly Liz frowned. 'And . . . did you ever know of a man who would cuddle a woman while *she* was in the driving seat and *he* only in the passenger seat?'

Alec laughed, and nodded.

'It offends every male instinct there is,' she went on. 'No: if that was why they'd gone there, then either they'd have transferred to the back seat, or the bloke would have been behind the wheel. It just doesn't ring true, does it? When did he kill her? She hadn't had sex, and there was no bruising of the genitals.'

'And,' Alec reminded her, 'her shoulder-bag was on the passenger seat.'

'So,' Liz mused, voicing the inevitable conclusion, 'the stuff with the clothing was done afterwards. By a man who couldn't resist it with a girl helpless there before him, even though he had just clubbed her to death? Sounds more like a blind to me! To suggest a sexual motive where in fact none exists. Possibly the killer didn't know her well enough to realize that she might well be sexually inexperienced. Of course,' she added more doubtfully, 'as a blind it isn't terribly subtle. Not if we've got it all worked out in five minutes flat.'

That depended, Alec thought as Liz moved to answer the telephone, on what it was a blind for. Still the same questions arose and would not be answered. Was Kate Randall alone in the blue Renault? Had there been a second car? Where had she been, that kept her out so late on such a foul night?

Above all, was the charade with the dead girl's clothing just to cover up the *motive* for the killing: or was it, maybe, a way of diverting attention in a different way?

Had Kate Randall been killed by a woman?

Reluctantly Alec faced up to the fact that CAMEX must be the first avenue for exploration. It was the one thing they knew for sure about Kate; the one known source of friends, and the one undoubted means by which an attractive, competent young woman might have made enemies. Yet logic was against it in so far as no enemy could have known Kate would have been on the common in just such a place at just such a time—and on such a night—unless there had been a prior appointment. And why should Kate agree to such a spot, such a time, for a meeting which could as well have been effected in her flat?

'It's Nelson,' Liz announced, breaking into his deliberations, her hand over the mouthpiece of the telephone. 'The owner of the Renault: he's brought her in. Says do you want to come down, or shall he go ahead?'

Alec shook his head. 'I dare say he can manage on his own.' At least they might establish why Kate Randall's body had been lying beside another woman's car. With a jigsaw puzzle it didn't much matter where you started.

'OK,' Liz said into the telephone. She put it down, and glanced at her wristwatch. 'Time I was getting along to meet Mrs Randall.' She turned to Alec. 'Nothing you want me to get from her in particular?'

Alec looked up, and shook his head. Liz nodded, and made for the door. When her hand was out to open it, Alec said, 'Be nice to her, Liz.'

'Yes, sir; of course.' And Liz let herself swiftly out. Poor old soul, she thought, meaning her boss, not the dead girl's mother. Going soft in the head. But she didn't think any the worse of him for that.

Nelson gestured to Sally Field and she slipped out of the interview room and stood with him in the corridor. 'Any reaction?' he murmured.

'Hard to say, sir.' Sally replied eagerly. 'She's very much on edge, but then she seems rather the nervy type anyway.'

'Has she said anything?'

' "I didn't do it." '

'Aye, aye!' Nelson raised his eyebrows appreciatively. 'She said that?'

Sally nodded. The tea-trolley appeared out of the room ahead, and they stood back to let it pass. 'And she asked about Thomas: that's her son.'

Nelson reached for the door handle and smiled grimly. 'Right!' he said, and turned the handle and led the way in.

The interview room had that stale atmosphere insepar-able from waiting-rooms in government offices. Nobody actually works in them—they are just set aside for the pass-ing of time. The windows stay tight shut, and for long periods the door is shut too and the room empty, maturing its flat, acid smell of old cigarette smoke and sweat and despondency. Re-entering, Sally realized just how frowsty the interview room was. Nelson had long ago ceased to notice.

Sally slipped into her chair in the corner, and Nelson sat down heavily opposite Judy Baker, who looked back at him from the far side of the scarred table.

On first impression she seemed small: small and young. Her features were childlike in their proportions, and though her dark hair was curled, it clung close to her small skull like a fairy's cap. She looked straight at Nelson from large blue eyes, and he noticed the fine webs traced in her skin and realized scornfully that she was not so young after all. There was something in her poise which was catlike, and he sensed a catlike readiness for evasion, a willingness to do anything for a quiet life. Her fingers picked at each other in a way that belied her forthright gaze. She'd lie as soon as look at you; but Nelson would have the truth out of her if it took him all day, and after what she had said to Sally Field he was sure there was more to be unearthed than merely the ins and outs of her lending her car to Kate Randall.

'How long am I going to be here?' she asked; but her voice was hesitant, as if she had no conviction of an answer.

'That depends on you, love,' Nelson said. 'We're not keeping you here against your will, are we? You came here voluntarily, didn't you?'

'Did I?' she replied bitterly. 'First I've heard of it.'

'So you see it's all up to you. Tell me the truth and you might be out of here in no time. It's not as if you're under arrest, love. I assure you, it's very different altogether.'

'The truth about what?'

'The truth,' Nelson said deliberately, 'about the murder—' he paused deliberately after the word, watching for its effect—'of Kate Randall.'

But Judy Baker must be a very cool character indeed, for her large eyes remained disconcertingly blank and she said nothing. Her fingers continued to pick at each other, and then suddenly she stopped herself abruptly, and folded her hands together. Nelson decided that her stare was too steady altogether; she was on a very short tether indeed! A nutter, no doubt.

Picking his approach carefully, he began to question her about her friendship with Kate Randall.

'Unsatisfactory,' Alec said aloud, stabbing the stop button of the tape recorder, and swivelled in his chair so that he could gaze out over the car park and the rooftops to the distant downs looming out of the smoke-like rain.

Two hours with Judy Baker had confirmed Nelson in his impression that she was living on her nerves, but he had not got as far as he intended in getting the truth out of her. Half way through she had asked for cigarettes, and thereafter smoked one after the other until there were only three or four left in the packet. After a while Nelson had stopped enjoying questioning her and lost the assurance of an early breakthrough. Every time he pressed her there was a tightening of her inner tension, and Nelson had tried twice to provoke a release of that tension, an outburst directed against himself or his questions, but it had not come. Only her features seemed to grow older and tighter, and the lines round her eyes were etched a little more deeply, and all the pressure which he hoped would explode outward, in anger and admission, was inwardly absorbed, to build up somewhere inside. As the interview stretched into the second hour he began to get angry with her, and he was uncomfortable now, aware that his anger was clearly audible on the tape. Mr Stainton's 'Unsatisfactory' related to more than just Judy Baker's failure to confess to a crime for which, Nelson was beginning to realize, there had been precious little basis for thinking her a suspect.

The framework of fact according to Judy's version had been simple to establish; thereafter, all Nelson's efforts had been directed towards penetrating that shell, and cracking the story which, he still felt reasonably sure, was far short of the truth.

According to Judy, the fact that Kate was found in her car was simply accounted for. Kate had used the Renault three or four times in the last couple of months. Two weeks ago Judy had let Kate have the car on semi-permanent loan. It sounded a tissue of falsehoods to Nelson. It was not the way people behaved.

'Where was she going, the times you lent her the car?'

'I don't know.'

'And you mean you didn't ask?'

'No.'

'I suppose you didn't check she was insured to drive it, either?'

'No.'

'It's more than likely that she wasn't. If she'd had an accident you'd have been stuck, wouldn't you?'

'I'm stuck now,' Judy had replied, but though the words bore a trace of humour, even Nelson picked up the desperation underlying them, and seized on it gratefully.

'I'm glad you realize that. Randall paid you for the use of your car?'

'No. And her name is Kate.'

'*Was.* You were with her, weren't you. This rigmarole about giving her the car on long-term loan!'

'You must be a very mean man,' she had replied levelly. 'I pity the friend who asks you for a help. You'd ration it and weigh it; if you gave it at all.'

That shouldn't have riled him; things were said in the interview room which were often designed to hurt; it was a part of the game of mutual provocation and usually Nelson put it behind him at once; but he prided himself on being open-handed and generous, and he was uncomfortably aware now that he had let that barbed remark get under his hide.

'So you gave your car to Randall, and you walk everywhere now, do you? Fitness freak, are you?'

'I bought myself another car. I was going to do that anyway. I just brought it forward. When Kate didn't need the Renault any more, I'd have sold it.'

'Jesus! What is this? A Hovis commercial?'

Judy Baker stood up. 'I'm not staying. I . . . You can't behave like this . . . I . . .'

'Sit down! You'll go when I tell you you can, and not before.'

'You can't keep me without charging me . . .'

'Been in the nick before, have you? Know all your rights?'

Judy looked as if she wanted to protest; but she sat down, reaching for another cigarette. Sally noticed the way her hands trembled, and the flame of the lighter wavered around the end of the cigarette. She looked down at her notepad and felt embarrassed. The tape whirred steadily round in its metal box.

'What did you keep in the boot of your car?'

She looked up. 'I've no idea. Spare tyre. The tools, jack, I don't know.'

'Can of petrol?'

'Was there?'

'You tell me.'

'And I tell you, I don't know. It was . . . it was Kate's, to do with what she liked.'

And so it had gone on, Nelson bent on extracting some detail which would suggest that Judy Baker and Kate Randall had been together in the blue Renault on the night of the storm. Judy answered all his questions, with no more than the bare minimum of detail, and all the time Sally Field sensed the fire building up inside her, waiting to explode.

Once she thought Nelson had released it.

'Where were you that night?'

'Out.'

'Where?'

'None of your business.'

'Out late, were you?'

That seemed to get to her. She fiddled with her lighter, then nodded.

'With Randall,' he asserted.

'*No.*'

'You went off with Randall,' he repeated. 'And you left young—what's his name?—Thomas alone. Rough on the kid, that. Thing like that can scar a kid for life! Might have burnt the house down . . . Not the action of a loving mother, is it? Done that before, had you? Often?'

'You bastard!' Judy Baker was on her feet; and Sally saw she was not so small after all. Her cigarette had fallen to the table and rolled almost to the edge, smoking. Then in an instant she had sunk back into her seat, her face deader, washed more clean, the lines a little deeper. With an effort she reached for the cigarette, examined it, stubbed it out among the other butts in the tin ashtray. 'No,' she said flatly. And after that she answered the rest of Nelson's questions monosyllabically, with no pretence that she was any more interested in trying to help.

Judy Baker's reaction to the charge of neglecting her son was probably the most interesting thing that came out of the interview, Alec pondered. That, and the knowledge that something was eating away inside her. Maybe they were one and the same.

And the knowledge that within Nelson there was this well of professional brutality only too ready to spill over.

'You've let her go?'

Nelson nodded. 'We can always pull her in again, sir. If you want, I can—'

'How was she getting home?'

'What?'

'Never mind,' Alec said wearily. 'All right, you can go.'

Sophy Blake was at school when she heard the news of the body on the common. Indeed, Alec Stainton would have been intrigued to learn just how quickly after the discovery of the body, a roughly accurate version of the finding was circulating in office canteens, Sainsbury's, and the local schools.

'Your dad'll be pleased,' Hannah remarked at lunch-time, by which stage the identity of the dead woman as a leading, but unnamed, member of CAMEX was being added to the gossip.

'He probably did it,' Damon Roberts leered. One or two of the group of boys and girls sauntering along the corridor looked uncomfortable.

'That's sick,' Hannah pronounced, and Roberts reddened, not having meant to be offensive, only witty.

'Now my mum'll stop me going up on the common,' one of the girls prophesied. 'You know when that foreign woman was found, right? In the lay-by, the one with no hands—' this was a notorious, sensational and ghoulish murder which had made national news four years earlier— 'well, I wasn't allowed to ride Trixie on the common for almost a year, until she forgot about it.'

The group walked on thoughtfully, for some of the boys were old enough to borrow parental cars, and the common was a useful stopping-off point when taking a girl out. For the girls, practising the arts of pleasing and resisting in its brackeny dells, shadowed car parks and sunny swards was an accepted rite of passage.

Sophy's thoughts were different. 'A woman who belonged to CAMEX' was just a detail to the others; but that cursory description was enough to awaken terrible fears in Sophy Blake. She had told her mother about Mr Morris, embroidering the tale a little for effect, and within weeks Mr Morris had been suspended, and everyone knew (even without the article in the paper) that he was being investigated with a view to prosecution for indecent assault. Mr Morris was himself a leading supporter of CAMEX. Now a woman had died: and she too was high in the CAMEX hierarchy. Sophy Blake had never come across the phrase *Cui Bono?* but she was quite well aware of the concept. Who had the incentive to set about destroying CAMEX? The fragile basis of her trust in her family and home and parents seemed to shiver and crack, and beneath was only a black void.

She began to feel her head ache, dully, and told herself that her period was coming on. When the rest of the group reached the entrance lobby and turned towards the doors, en route to the shops, Sophy walked on along the corridor, alone and lonely, towards her locker, wrestling with her fears. Including the awful, heart-stopping fear that the dead woman might prove to be the one member of CAMEX she knew personally; whose child she had babysat; whom she had finally spoken of to her mother over Christmas: Judy Baker.

CHAPTER 14

The mortuary assistant whisked the curtain across the little window and Mrs Randall turned away reluctantly. It was the last opportunity she would ever have to look upon the face of her daughter, even though Liz didn't suppose the sagging re-sewn face seen through the window was very like Kate's face in life.

'Why don't we see if we can find somewhere nice for a cup of tea,' Liz suggested.

They wound through the echoing corridors and pushed open a door, and crossed the car park towards the gate. The day was calm and mild. A scum of debris—twigs, plastic bags, larger branches—showing like a tidemark against walls and hedges testified to the storm of a day or two earlier. The sun appeared through a tear in the clouds and Liz unzipped her jacket and turned her face up to it gratefully. Mrs Randall kept her coat buttoned up, and her head down.

There was a café close to the hospital gates, a chintzy, olde-worlde place where you sat upstairs and looked down on the scurrying heads below while the proprietress was dilatory about bringing the 'home-made' cakes. Liz had used it once or twice for a similar purpose; it was a place of low whispers, and never crowded, and the slow service made questions natural.

'You'll miss her very much,' Liz said gently. She had long ago learned that clichés were merciful sometimes.

'She was twenty-nine,' Mrs Randall said obliquely. It was a way of telling Liz they had not been close but that it was no one's fault. 'Harry died fifteen years ago.'

'Kate was your only child.'

'It would have been selfish of me to keep her. I could have. She didn't want to go to college. She said, Mum, I oughtn't to leave you, all on your own. Well, it wouldn't have done. I made her take up her place at college. When you've worked hard for something it seems criminal to throw it away, I wasn't having that. Of course, after that she never lived at home again.'

Liz nodded understandingly. It was easy to be understanding; she herself had left home at nineteen and never lived with her parents again. It was the pattern of modern life. At least her own parents still had each other. There was a lot to be said for the old way, leaving school only to start at the factory down the road, living with your parents until you married.

'Did she tell you a lot about her life down here? I'm thinking about the usual things: boyfriends, work. And there was CAMEX, too.' Why am I asking about boyfriends? Liz wondered, remembering the post-mortem findings; and then: Why not? What a grubby little mind I've got!

The tea came; mock-Georgian pots, hand-thrown crockery. Liz had ordered two substantial slabs of gooey cake, and she pushed one encouragingly towards Mrs Randall. The stunned look was beginning to pass from the older woman's face. Liz recognized the family similarity: the heavy-lidded eyes, in Mrs Randall's case behind glasses; the thick fair hair, which the mother had scorned to retouch as it became streaked with grey; the spare frame.

'There *was* a boy, I think,' Mrs Randall said, gazing at the slab of cake but making no move to eat it. 'Katie mentioned him, I remember. She frightened them off. Oh dear!'

Liz nudged the plate a little closer to the other woman, and said helpfully, 'Because she was too clever, you mean?'

'Men don't mind you being clever,' Mrs Randall pronounced, 'but they prefer you to *hide* it. *We* all knew that. But girls of Katie's generation, they wouldn't be told, and then they were upset when all the boys steered clear.'

'This boyfriend Kate mentioned, though,' Liz probed. 'She didn't give a name?'

'Colin? Keith?' Mrs Randall frowned and shook her head. 'You learn not to ask, you see,' she said bitterly. As if she had at last received permission, she picked up the piece of cake and took a bite. For a few minutes the two women chewed in silence.

Liz took a sip of tea. 'Kate never . . . had a tendency to drown her sorrows in drink?'

Mrs Randall looked scandalized. 'Never! Not,' she added more reasonably, 'that she was much of a one for letting on when she did have . . . sorrows.'

'What did you think of CAMEX? Are you a member?' Liz hurried to change the subject, not wanting to seem to attack the dead girl lest Mrs Randall take offence and clam up.

'No!' Glad to have an external subject to vent her emotion on, Mrs Randall expanded at length on the organization which had seduced her daughter's commitment and talents. 'An unpaid office-girl, that's what she was,' Mrs Randall declared. 'I don't hold with all these pressure groups and whatever they call themselves.'

'Perhaps your daughter felt it was an issue she had to make a stand on.'

'Why couldn't she choose something peaceful, if she wanted to take up with a cause?' Mrs Randall complained. 'Heaven knows, there are enough organizations which need someone with her skills! And if she was at a loose end she could have helped out with Meals on Wheels.'

'You regard CAMEX as . . . not peaceful?'

'You never know,' Mrs Randall pronounced, 'what these groups are going to do next, do you? One minute it's a pressure group, the next it could be setting light to people's houses and putting bombs under politicians' cars.'

'Did Kate . . . *say* anything to give you the impression that that was the way CAMEX might go in the future?'

'No,' Mrs Randall replied. She seemed to feel suddenly that she had been too forthcoming, for her manner became very proper and polite; and she made great play with finishing her cake and pouring more tea. But she couldn't resist adding, as if she had to empty her memory of complaints before she could start to grieve, 'The trouble with

Katie was, she never knew when to stop. Always the same. Right from a baby. Anything she did, it had to be her whole life. I always said, one day she would go too far. More tea?—and then I must be going.'

'Thank you,' Liz said. 'Thank you very much.'

Alec's decision that the CAMEX connection would prove the speediest way of building up the background to Kate Randall's life was quickly put into effect. Local police officers within a circle of fifty miles' radius found themselves requested to call on CAMEX members in their patch and ask about Kate Randall, and Sally Field, under Nelson's guidance, began the task of collating the information which was garnered. Alec found both of them in the incident room next morning, bent over the computer keyboard. Liz Pink was there too, on the telephone.

'I'd like you to find this Charlie Poole,' Alec said to Nelson. 'I'd be interested to know just where he fits in— especially as he seems to have done a runner.'

After her chat over the teacups with Mrs Randall, Liz had devoted what was left of the afternoon to uncovering the identity of Kate Randall's boyfriend, and she had struck lucky. Against the odds, she found that a Charlie Poole was entered against Kate's address on the poll tax register. There had been no sign of him when the flat had been examined—and no sign that he had ever been there; but 'Charlie' was close enough to 'Colin' and 'Keith' for her to be morally certain of the identification. Whether he had ever actually lived in the flat was problematical; but there was no doubt in Alec's mind that he would have to be found, and quickly. Putting Nelson on the task left him free to use Liz for a second, and more sympathetic, approach to Judy Baker.

That left one big question-mark, and Liz, turning from the telephone, put into words the problem he had been mentally stalling. 'What do we do about Medisearch?'

Alec nodded, making his mind up. 'I'd better go and see them,' he agreed.

*

Alec met John Blake in the latter's spartan office at
Medisearch that afternoon. Getting that far had been
something of an achievement, since the gate guard seemed
to be under the impression that he was in sole charge of
something on the scale of Aldermaston or Porton Down.
There was much to-ing and fro-ing of telephone messages
before Alec and Sally Field were handed blue plastic tags
and allowed through the barrier.

Medisearch occupied a new building on what the town
hopefully called its Technology Park. The smoked-glass,
outside-frame buildings mostly housed businesses which
would have coped equally well on an old-fashioned industrial estate, but money had been spent on landscaping and
the density was low. Alec and Sally walked to meet their
own reflections in the glass walls, past saplings and peren-
nials and the company's name on a stainless-steel plate set
in rough-hewn granite.

The main entrance gave on to an open office area where
a middle-aged woman typed industriously on a word-
processor and a shaggy-headed young man stood bent
over a desk filling in a form. A coffee-machine stood in a
corner; the only decoration was a tired-looking rubber-
plant.

Both the young man and the woman looked up as if
surprised to see something so remarkable as a pair of visitors. Alec said he had come to see Dr Blake: Detective Chief
Inspector Stainton. He proffered his warrant card and the
blue plastic tag; neither seemed of much interest.

'Is he in?' the young man asked the woman.

'No idea,' she replied; and, to Alec, 'He does know you're
coming?'

'We fixed it up on the phone.'

The young man looked puzzled, then turned back to his
form, as if visitors were not his department. The woman
went out to see if Blake was in the building. They waited,
and Alec thought that it didn't seem much like a place that
was at the burning edge of medical breakthrough; he'd seen
mortuaries with more life in them.

'That's all right; Dr Blake's in, and he'll see you, Mr Stainton,' the woman said, returning, treating him to a pleasant smile now everything was satisfactorily resolved. 'Like to come this way?'

Blake's office was a few paces down a corridor. The whole place was remarkably quiet. Sally wondered how you set about research, anyway? Lots of people tucked away out of sight, thinking, she told herself with a smile.

Blake to some extent compensated for the underwhelming impression made by Medisearch so far. Alec found himself shaking the cold hand of a man of medium height who was probably in his fifties, with nondescript greying hair above a greying face saved from being equally nondescript by forcefulness of expression and a pair of sharp blue eyes. He wore the sort of spectacles which are designed to suggest business acumen and a jet-set social life though the lenses, Alec noticed, were of a thickness more appropriate to the round pebble glasses of the comic-strip professor. The room was bare and stark—by design, clearly, as all the furniture was minimalist and the paintings on the wall were pale pastel abstracts. The inevitable computer, printer, fax and photocopier were all carefully blended to the overall design.

Though the hand which shook Alec's was cold, Blake's greeting was otherwise friendly, and as they sat down and Alec said he thought they ought to have a word about CAMEX a wry smile hovered round his features.

'I wondered, when I heard the news, how long it would be before you were knocking on our door. Two and two sometimes make five, you know. CAMEX are a thorn in our flesh I don't mind admitting; but fortunately the public doesn't take them too seriously. In some kinds of business the free advertising they are giving us would be worth thousands: in ours, it's just a minor irritation. A fact of life.'

'A bunch of harmless cranks?'

'Cranks, certainly. I suppose they're entitled to their views, free country and all that. Harmless? I hope so. If only they are content with their present level of activities.'

'What sort of thing do you think they might go on to, then?'

'Who knows? You've seen we're very careful about letting people in here. Though that's partly because it's so vital that the sterile areas aren't infringed. But I'm sure, Chief Inspector, we've both seen instances of so-called peaceful protest spilling over into something nastier. Personal attacks . . .'

'Physical ones, you mean?'

'I was thinking more of libellous rumours, nasty smear stories.'

'Has there been anything of that sort?' Alec asked, wondering just why that line of thought had been in the forefront of Blake's mind.

Blake shook his head. 'Not yet, that I know of. But it will come, I've no doubt.'

Alec asked, 'How many people do you have, working here?'

'Oh, only a dozen or so, all told. Four other scientists, apart from myself, and the rest are support staff.'

'And what are these medical products you are making, then?'

Blake laughed. 'Nothing. This is purely a research establishment. We're doing the work which will enable doctors in five or ten years' time to prescribe a drug which will cure cancer; which will save parents the terrible trauma of giving birth to a handicapped child; which will enable childless couples to have a baby; or help a woman plan her family without sacrificing her career. It's people like us beavering away in our little laboratories which will make that possible. If CAMEX and their ilk don't prevent us, that is.'

'If you don't make anything,' Alec wondered aloud, not caring terribly much for the commercial, 'who pays for it?'

Blake's expression sharpened a fraction; then he remembered, perhaps, that Alec was a simple policeman asking an innocent question, and smiled, 'There is funding involved, of course. We are eligible for a certain amount in government grants; pharmaceutical companies allocate

sums for research like ours; some of our people have
a certain amount of university funding, and so forth.
It's rather a headache keeping track of it all, actually; dribs
and drabs, but it adds up to just about enough to keep us
going. Now, is there anything more I can help you
with?'

'Only to keep us informed if you do hear that any of your
staff *are* made the object of any sort of personal attack. We
might be able to take some action . . .' Alec could be as
disingenuous as the next man; unless perhaps the next man
happened to be John Blake.

Blake stood up. 'I appreciate that, Chief Inspector, I
appreciate that very much. As I say, you can't really take
people like CAMEX seriously; but even dinosaurs can be
clumsy with their feet, can't they? And—' he met Alec's
eye and added firmly, 'we really don't need to indulge in
crude deterrence.' He ran his hand lightly over the surface
of the computer. 'If you want to know where I was on
the night of the storm,' he volunteered carefully, 'I was in
Amsterdam. The Hotel Van Der Hoel. I expect you will be
able to check the register, if you wish.'

'I expect we shall.' Alec crossed to the door; Blake held
it open for him, and then just remembered to do so for Sally
too.

'Anyway,' Alec felt bound to remark as they walked down
the corridor together towards the entrance, 'you don't seem
much bothered about the death of Kate Randall.'

Blake stopped in his tracks. 'My dear chap! Have I given
that impression?' He resumed walking. 'It's tragic—of
course it is! A young girl, even an impetuous and misguided
one—there must be parents . . . friends . . . And murdered,
too! What a terrible thing!'

'Oh, well,' Alec couldn't help returning acidly, 'at least
she had the chance to be born first.' And they took their
leave, leaving Dr John Blake standing at the glass door,
shaking his head sorrowfully at the tragedies and misunder-
standings of the poor ignorant world.

*

'Always resist the temptation to have the last word,' Alec said wryly as they walked away.

'He talked like a press release,' Sally complained. 'Why do doctors always treat everybody else like children!'

'Mm. He's not a medical doctor, of course,' Alec said thoughtfully. 'His PhD was in biochemistry, wasn't it? Nor are the other directors, Darby, is it, and Sachs.'

Sachs was a biologist who had spent much of his career with ICI, until resigning eighteen months before to join Darby and Blake in setting up Medisearch. There was a fourth member of the team, Lawrence, a non-scientist, who had been sponsorship-hunter for one of the minor universities and now fulfilled the same role for Medisearch. It annoyed Alec that he should be fobbed off with all this talk of disinterested research when even an ignorant policeman could be expected to see with half an eye that any company which discovered and developed the sort of drugs Blake had been talking of would very quickly become extremely rich indeed. No doubt they were all genuinely anxious to play their part in relieving suffering and preventing unnecessary and painful deaths; but it was vaguely insulting not to acknowledge that they would also do very well out of it, if successful.

And because they would do very well out of it, someone was prepared to subsidize Medisearch in its present, unproductive phase. He remembered what Clavell had said of rumours of Dutch money, and wondered if that was what Blake had been doing in Amsterdam. Anyway, what Blake had fed him about shoestring budgets, footling research grants and university hand-outs must be so much bullshit, and he said as much to Sally Field.

'Why don't we find out who's really backing them, sir?' she offered, meaning: *I* could do that.

Alec looked up from his thoughts. 'Because we can't justify it, that's why. What reason have we got? All we've got to link Blake and Co to Kate Randall's murder is the fact that CAMEX don't like Medisearch, and Medisearch don't like CAMEX. Doesn't add up to anything. Certainly not enough to justify spending time on digging deeper.'

Then why are we digging at all? Sally wondered, and what have we been doing this morning?

'Don't worry,' Alec said, reading her despondent face, 'I'll make sure you get to see some of the action.' He made a dismissive gesture, as if sweeping Medisearch and CAMEX alike to one side.

'One moment, sir, if you please! Your security tags, if you don't mind.' The gate guard was out of his little sentry-box pretty smartly to block their way. They handed over the blue pieces of plastic.

It wasn't real, Sally thought, as she stood on the pavement while Mr Stainton unlocked the car. She gave a little shiver; the February afternoon was well advanced; the illusion of spring had vanished abruptly. She looked back at the single-storey complex of glass buildings. She had thought when they arrived that it looked more like a new primary school than a research laboratory; now it put her in mind of the reflecting sunglasses movie stars wear when they want to appear enigmatic. What would they have found if they had been able to penetrate into one of the sterile areas where the real work went on? What *did* go on? Somehow, when you thought about it like that, the antics of a group like CAMEX didn't seem so senseless after all.

She climbed into the car, and Mr Stainton started the engine and pulled away from the kerb. As they passed the gatehouse, the guard came out and stood watching them go. He didn't wave.

The pair of cottages seemed equally deserted when Liz Pink drew up outside. The gardens were both meticulously tidy, as much as any garden can be in winter, but there was no other sign of habitation: no smoke from Judy Baker's chimney, and none from her neighbour's, no light though the afternoon was overcast and dusk would soon be falling, no sound of television or radio. And no answer to the door when Liz knocked.

She tried the left-hand cottage first, Mrs Baker's, ringing the bell and then, because perhaps it was broken, knocking as well. Her knuckles made a feeble sound on the solid, blank, grey-painted door. The bay window was uncurtained and dark (the next-door bay, she saw, was also dark; but in there the curtains were drawn), the whole house silent and dead.

There was a letterbox, and Liz bent down to peer through. The bottom half of a staircase was visible, rising directly before her. A door led off the little entrance hall into the sitting-room. So far as she could see, there was no post or newspapers lying on the floor beneath the letterbox. She thought she sensed a faint mustiness in the air.

The afternoon was chilly and drizzly; a rapid shower of drips chased each other off the tile-hanging as Liz stood back to look at the upstairs windows, and smacked her in the eye before trickling clammily down her neck.

'Shit,' she said aloud, daring someone to be there to hear her. Reluctantly she stepped on to the sopping grass and leant over the little flower border to peer into the darkened living-room.

Chairs; a few built-in shelves; a coffee mug loomed palely on an occasional table. Dried flowers in the grate. No body on the patterned floral carpet.

A pathway led round the side of the house. The down-pipes gurgled into a drain but the rain itself fell almost noiselessly. Liz peered into an empty kitchen—washing-up piled on the draining board, she noticed—and pushed open a promising-looking door, which proved to lead into a coal-hole, with no connection with the inside of the house.

She glanced again at the other cottage. Was there a hint of light seeping round the drawn curtains? Was that the pale shadow of a wisp of smoke against the darkening sky? Marching round in her now soggy boots, Liz knocked loudly on the door.

'I'm a police officer,' she shouted, feeling foolish. 'Is there anybody in? Will you open the door, please!'

But other than the drip, drip, drip of moisture off the tiles there was no reply. Liz squelched back to her car and got in, slamming the door. Serve her right for not speaking out and making Mr Stainton send Nelson to clean up his own mess! It was Nelson who had fucked up the interview of a potential key source of information, going in as if he was having a heart-to-heart with Al Capone about the St Valentine's Day Massacre; and now that same key source had predictably done a runner. She turned the key, her foot down on the accelerator, made the engine roar and pulled away from the kerb, the wheels slipping on the mess of wet leaves in the gutter; and consequently never noticed the curtains of the house next to Judy Baker's twitch as if caught by the breeze of her passage, and settle back into place.

Unlike Sophy Blake, Alec Stainton was familiar with the term *Cui bono* and as he mixed himself a modest gin and tonic by way of dutch courage in his flat that evening, he found the words forming themselves unbidden on his lips. He wished Kate Randall's claim of a vendetta against CAMEX didn't now seem only too frighteningly plausible. He thought with a shudder of the can of petrol in the back of her car. The stakes were clearly higher than Alec had considered, and who was to say they were not high enough for murder?

He swirled the clear liquid around in the glass, took a sip, and moved reluctantly to the telephone. Tomorrow the name of the dead girl would be released to the press. Before that happened, he knew he must tell Frances. With an unwonted lack of enthusiasm he picked up the receiver and tapped out Frances Walker's number.

CHAPTER 15

While all the usual routine of searching for clues to a casual killer ground into action—stopping cars on the road over the common to question drivers who might have passed that way on the fateful night; priming the newspapers with stories and appeals for help; and the behind-the-scenes analysis of the Renault, the broken branch, and the detritus of cigarette packets and crisp packets and condoms garnered by the Scene of Crime personnel—while all that was going on, the search for Judy Baker slipped into a higher gear. Her suggestive absence from her cottage, her friendship with Kate Randall, her ownership of the blue Renault beside which Kate had died—all made it a matter of urgency to find her. Liz, reporting her fruitless trip, had immediately been put in charge of finding her. Already she had unearthed one interesting item: namely, that the cottage did not belong to Judy Baker at all. It, and its neighbour, were farm cottages, belonging to a farm a quarter of a mile away; both were rented.

That might be significant in itself, Alec pondered, listening to Liz's preliminary report. Rented cottages were not so very common, even in rural areas, in the south-east these days. Those that survived were relics of an earlier generation, almost all occupied by the elderly. As these died, and the cottages fell vacant, they were invariably modernized and sold, the vacant possession value far exceeding the value as a continuing, let investment. So what was Judy Baker, born in 1955 (according to the details of her driving licence on the Police National Computer; there was no entry under her name in the Criminal Records Office), doing renting a desirable residence in gin-and-Jaguar Surrey? Or more particularly, what was the owner doing letting her stay there? Interesting!

Other than that, those few neighbours who had been interviewed in a limited house-to-house in the immediate area had had little to say about Judy Baker. 'Reserved' was a word used of her more than once; 'timid', someone suggested; 'haunted', said someone with a more active imagination.

She had a son, Thomas, who was mentioned occasionally in the context of babysitters and schooling: he was eight or nine, it seemed. Nobody knew anything about a wider family—or about a husband. She had never mentioned one to her CAMEX acquaintances either, and some surprise was occasioned when it was pointed out that she referred to herself as 'Mrs Baker'; the group operated on Christian name terms, and some of them hadn't even known Judy's surname, let alone that she was (or had been) married.

Nobody, unfortunately, admitted to being a good friend of Judy Baker. It was beginning to look as if her only close friend was Kate Randall, which lent credence to the idea of Judy lending Kate her car, but robbed the police at one go of their best sources of information about both the missing woman and the dead one. One other usual source of information was also a non-starter: it appeared that Judy Baker, like Kate Randall, did not have a job.

That, to Alec, was a second fact worth noting about a single woman with a child to support, and in an area where demand for employees exceeded supply; well worth pursuing further. Possibly when they delved deeper they would find that even if she did not have the conventional office job which was the norm for this part of the country, she would have *some* form of work: delivering leaflets, or acting as agent for a mail-order firm, or 'helping out' in the area's better-off households. Meanwhile, his hands were largely tied, since her cottage could not be searched in her absence when there were so few substantial grounds for the suspicions he was, nevertheless, increasingly feeling against her.

Nelson meanwhile was busy trying to locate the other missing person, Charlie Poole. At first, that poll tax registration was the only proof of his very existence, and a second interview with local CAMEX supporters was largely in vain. Ginnie Kemp knew Kate had shared her flat; but she didn't know more about Charlie than his Christian name, and could not speculate on what the relationship might have been. Other CAMEX members seemed surprised by the idea that Kate Randall had been living with someone in either sense of the words, and found the idea of her having a lover difficult to adapt to, giving the impression that they had always felt Kate wasn't that sort of girl. She wasn't, Nelson did not scruple to reassure them; she was a virgin. Indeed? responded those he interviewed, with various degrees of interest. Fancy that! However, as they knew nothing of Charlie, clearly they could not know what had now happened to him.

But there was one CAMEX member whom Nelson expected to be able to tell him about Kate Randall's private life; and Nelson found him at home, in his small Victorian semi in Blindley Heath, watching children's television.

To Nelson, men like Clive Morris were a pretty low form of life. Morris was of a physical type—rotund, tight in his clothes, shiny-skinned, like a grown-up version of Dickens' Fat Boy—that the fit, rugger-playing Nelson found instinctively antipathetic. He had seen Morris before, when the latter had been invited by Inspector Glover to come into the police station 'for a chat'. Nelson had seen the two men together, known what it was Morris was 'helping' with, and felt a physical repugnance to the man who was suspected of indecency and looked so likely to commit it.

By his own obscure logic Nelson had great hopes that Morris would know a good deal about Kate Randall and her private life. Nelson pictured Morris following her with his button eyes, angling for a good view of cleavage or leg; always on the spot when the unintentional revelation occurred, the undone button, the rucked-up skirt. Nelson wasn't interested in speculating as to why a society eager, even desperate, to tolerate any and every practice resulting in consummated heterosexual intercourse nevertheless dealt increasingly harshly with men of Morris's type; it was enough for him that that attitude chimed in with his own sense that Morris, a man who lusted after women and was reduced to putting his hands up schoolgirls' skirts, was detestable.

Morris was at first reluctant to talk of Kate Randall's private life. Nelson put his reticence down at once to hypocrisy; but whether the scruples were genuine or not, loneliness and despair easily overcame them. Though he was not aware of it, Nelson was Morris's first human contact in three days; a fact which would not much have worried him if he had known it.

In fact Morris had both liked Kate, and been unable to stop himself lusting after her. Her death seemed to him a great shame; one of those matters which show the rottenness of chance, when a good person like her could be snuffed out while many more worthless ones (and he included himself) lived on. He didn't gain pleasure from talking about the dead girl's private life, but it seemed to him that it was one of the few contributions he could make towards the finding of her killer, and the pursuing of justice.

'I can't believe this,' Nelson reported back to Alec. 'Are you sure Ransome's got it right?'

'Why shouldn't he have done?'

'Why, this Charlie Poole's a health service administrator,' Nelson explained, 'which means we should be able to track him down fairly easily. He and the Randall girl met about six months ago. They got on OK, so Poole moves into the flat, doesn't he; there's vague talk of getting married. And then Ransome tells us she was a *virgin?*'

'They still exist, you know,' Alec pointed out restrainedly. Sometimes he doubted Nelson's basic intelligence; which wasn't going to help when the explosion between Nelson and Liz Pink came, he thought unhappily, because he would almost certainly find himself siding with Liz; and in a situation like that, siding with either party would be a mistake he could not afford.

'Anyway,' Nelson went on hastily, 'Morris says Poole took off after Glover started questioning Randall about CAMEX; after the CAMEX memorandum; that would be getting on for a month ago.'

'How does he know?' Alec had wondered.

Nelson shrugged dismissively. 'Nosing around. 'S how he gets his thrills. There's no doubt he fancied Randall himself.'

'Did you ask where Morris was the other night?' Alec asked.

'No; I never thought to.' Nelson looked up speculatively. Alec shook his head. 'Doesn't matter for now.'

'I should have done; bloke like that . . .'

'It doesn't matter,' Alec had repeated irritably. Bloke like what, indeed? A pathetic man with a ruined career, that was all.

Later, alone in his office, recalling his irritation, he wondered whether he had been right to quench Nelson's enthusiasm for Morris as a suspect. He stared out of the window meditatively, acknowledging that while Nelson was ready to consider Morris as a suspect simply because the man was so cut out for one, he himself was perversely tempted to refuse to do so for the very same reason.

Suddenly it occurred to him that for the last couple of months there had been not two but *three* CAMEX members with time on their hands. 'The devil finds work . . . ?' he wondered aloud in the empty silence of his office. Coincidence? Glover, he remembered, had speculated at the existence of some sort of CAMEX caucus. Was it beyond the bounds of probability to imagine that just such a caucus might have formed almost accidentally when Clive Morris, Judy Baker and Kate Randall all found themselves at leisure during the day—and might have met the night Kate Randall died to plan or even to execute . . . what? Might a full can of petrol mean more than the prudence of a woman who doesn't want to run out of fuel in a lonely spot?

He considered practicalities. Kate and Judy Baker had the use of a car, but one of the cruellest results of Morris's follies had been that, as Nelson had reported and Glover confirmed, his wife had left him, taking their two daughters with her, and incidentally taking the car. If they had met, where and how had they managed it? Might this be support for the theory that there were other people in the car when Kate Randall drove into the car park where she met her death? On the other hand, that car park was well south of any route she ought logically to have taken, whether she was travelling to or from her flat, Morris's house, or Judy Baker's cottage.

Then again: two lonely people. Might Kate have suggested, or agreed to, going up on the common with Morris? Might Charlie's defection have left her in need of comfort, any comfort, from any source?

But then of course they'd have gone to her flat; or Morris's empty house. And on such a night, too, he reminded himself. Sensible people did not park their cars beneath trees in weather such as there had been the night Kate Randall died.

Every hypothesis failed to ring true. Each depended on a fantastic rickety structure of supposition balanced like an upside-down pyramid on one simple coincidence; and each ran counter to the sort of people Kate Randall and Clive Morris were. Kate was, must have been, a woman of strong principle and perhaps of religious conviction; and Morris would presumably not now be in trouble for behaving indecently with underage girls if he were capable of establishing easy relations with women of his own generation. Alec would have to see him himself, there was no doubt, to try and arrive at some more rational sort of assessment— and to put the questions Nelson had omitted to ask.

Liz Pink wanted to find Judy Baker before Nelson found Charlie Poole. It was a petty ambition and even an unwise one: more tactful to let Nelson edge ahead of her in such a trivial respect, easing the resentment when she outran him in all the ways that mattered—as she was determined to do.

She was realizing now that she and Nelson didn't really like each other. Nelson, she noticed, had not yet woken up to this fact, for after all they had worked together well enough when Liz was a detective-constable. Now, however, that they were equals in rank, and with the needle of Liz's ambition (and potential) it would not be long before superficial amicability soured into active hostility. They had few interests in common, for Liz, she was quite certain, had the better mind—Nelson's interests were not cerebral. That meant, too, that their approach to their work was different, hers speculative and intuitive, his plodding and sometimes abrasive; and it meant that Liz was instinctively (she felt) on Chief Inspector Stainton's wavelength. True, Chief Superintendent Blackett distrusted her, as he distrusted all 'clever' policemen until they proved there was substance to their cleverness; but Mr Stainton's was the opinion that immediately mattered.

Moreover, Liz found herself increasingly out of sorts with Nelson's treatment of her as a woman. Women police officers were plainly to him on a par with women drivers— inherently less capable, to be tolerated but patronized.

Now Liz was faced with the problem of finding a woman who had disappeared—a woman with money, and a car. There were obvious avenues to be explored: friends and relatives to whom she might have run. But the avenues quickly turned into cul-de-sacs. There were no close friends, with the possible exceptions of Kate Randall, who was beyond providing assistance, and Heather Campbell, who rented Judy the cottage. Liz pulled the dog-eared telephone directory out of her desk drawer; but the Campbells' number, when she dialled it, rang and rang to no reply. Of relatives there seemed to be only a sister, Isobel, married, and living near Guildford. On the telephone Isobel was unforthcoming, but Liz confirmed that Judy was not there, and arranged that Isobel would stay in the following afternoon, to be visited by herself or Nelson.

Re-emerging from these mental cul-de-sacs Liz gave her mind to the possibility of approaching her goal cross-country, as it were. She could not locate Judy? Very well, she would locate Thomas, on the assumption that where the son was, there the mother would be also. Turning to the directory once again, Liz looked up the telephone numbers of the three primary schools closest to Judy Baker's cottage. If Thomas had vanished with his mother he must be absent from school; and she ought at least to be able to find out whether it was by prior arrangement. A premeditated trip was a very different thing from a sudden, guilty flight.

In the event she rang only one of the numbers.

'Thomas . . . ?' the headmistress queried, after having satisfied herself of Liz's *bona fides*.

'Baker,' Liz repeated. 'The mother is a Mrs Judy Baker, from the cottages just outside the village.'

'No, he's not one of ours,' came the discouraging reply—for this was the closest, and most likely, of the primary schools. Liz opened her mouth to make her polite and brisk thanks, when the helpful middle-aged female voice went on, 'A lot of them *are* privately educated, you know, around here.'

'Yes, well,' Liz said, 'though I don't think this Mrs Baker probably has very much money. Thank—'

'Do you want to know or not?' the voice interrupted tartly, removing any lingering doubts Liz may have had as to whether she was talking to a schoolmistress. Liz sat up straight.

'Well, yes.'

'Thomas goes to a preparatory school. The Pines; over beyond Dormansland. It's one of the better ones, actually. Almost worth the fees it charges, which are not peanuts, so I shouldn't assume Mrs Baker is on the breadline, if I were you. Does that satisfy you?'

'It certainly does,' Liz said gratefully. 'You've been a great help.'

The Pines did not see fit to advertise in *Yellow Pages*; Liz found the number hidden discreetly in the ordinary phone book, and rang it with some curiosity. She spoke to a secretary and waited a long time to be connected to the headmaster Mr Stracey who, having been forewarned that she was not a potential parent, was brisk and businesslike.

'Thomas? Yes; yes, I can confirm he is a pupil here,' the headmaster said, in a tone which suggested that more detailed information would be regarded as classified.

'I'd be grateful if you can tell me,' Liz said, 'whether he is in school today; and if not, whether you knew in advance that he was going to have time off?'

'Time off when? Thomas Baker isn't absent. I'm afraid

someone has misled you, young lady.' He sounded as if the prospect gave him satisfaction. 'I have seen him myself this morning.'

'But . . . who brought him in? Do you know? We have reason to believe that Mrs Baker has gone away. So who is looking after Thomas?'

'If Mrs Baker has gone away, I'm afraid I regard that as her private business. You will appreciate, I'm sure, that I don't feel able to discuss parents' arrangements and private lives on the telephone.'

'This is a police inquiry, Mr Stracey.'

'And I'm sure you realize the need to approach every-thing in the proper form. I can only suggest you, ah, your superior writes to me here, officially, and I shall be only too pleased to assist any genuine police inquiry in any way I am at liberty to do so without disclosing, ah, privileged information.'

'Cocky bastard,' Liz said, but only after she had put the phone down. 'Privileged information my arse. Who does he think he is?'

She sat for a moment staring at the telephone receiver, and then got to her feet and went out into the corridor and knocked on Mr Stainton's door. There was no reply, and opening it she saw the room was deserted. Thoughtfully she made her way back to her own room and jotted down a record of her telephone conversations.

So Thomas was attending school as usual. Ten to one Judy was holed up with her sister, or some crony nearby; but the memory of the woman Nelson had described, and the paradoxical picture of Judy Baker which was beginning to emerge, made her pause and wonder if it was going to prove quite so simple. What sort of woman was she? And what sort of woman goes away on the spur of the moment and leaves her eight-year-old child behind?

Alec, reading Liz's note an hour and a half later, won-dered about that too, then dismissed the idea. Thomas was still attending school: therefore he had not been abandoned; arrangements must have been made for him, he was staying with friends or relatives, or with Judy herself close by. Alec scribbled a few words on the note and moved it to his out-tray, and picked another sheet off the pile of papers awaiting his attention.

'We've got a possible sighting, sir.'

'We have?' The surprise Alec felt at this news mirrored that which he saw in Johnson's expression. Given the wildness of the weather on the night of Kate Randall's death, he had fully resigned himself to the unlikelihood of anyone coming forward with stories of what they had seen on the common that night.

'It's a lad, sir,' Johnson confirmed. 'Aged nineteen; trainee baker; name of Russell. He was up there with his girlfriend.'

Paul Russell hadn't been very enthusiastic about the idea of talking to the police. It seemed a bad idea in principle, just as he always thought it important to be as unspecific as possible when his parents asked where he had been or what he had been doing. If you did not defend yourself in this way, your life became increasingly invaded. Further, he shrunk from exposing to the gaze of other people the way he and Fliss felt for each other. In love, he was more than ever inclined to be reticent. When they were with their other friends they didn't walk together; the shared secrecy was part of the wonder of their intimacy.

On the other hand, Paul perfectly recognized that Fliss was able to get him to do most things that she wanted, and when she insisted that he should approach the police about what they had seen he knew he would end up doing it. What they had seen didn't amount in fact to very much: just a car parked by the side of the road; but on that wild night they had noticed it, because it was the only thing which spoilt the feeling that they had the entire common to themselves. As Paul Russell told Johnson about it, he experienced again that almost painful happiness he had known, driving across the deserted roads, the car buffeted by the wind, with Fliss curled up on the seat beside him in the dark, her hand stroking the back of his neck as he drove. He could have driven forever.

'A Ford Sierra?' Alec repeated.

'Yes, sir.'

'Hmm.' If a boy of nineteen said so, then that was probably what it had been. The car had been tucked into one of the tracks which abounded on the common; maybe the one which came out by the car park where Kate's body had been found, but on that Paul Russell wisely refused to commit himself. A light colour; could have been white; couldn't tell exactly which model of Sierra because not all the car had been visible, and it had only been caught in Paul Russell's headlights for an instant as he and Fliss drifted past in their dark cocoon of love.

It wasn't much, Alec thought; but it was all they were likely to get.

CHAPTER 16

Heather Campbell ran a breeding kennels. Her few neighbours could hardly complain of the dogs barking, for the farm lay only half a mile from the end of the runway at Gatwick. Liz parked her car as an Air Canada 747 staggered into the air in a thunder of engines; looking up she could see every detail of its undersides revealed in indecent clarity.

The house was an attractive one in the Sussex farmhouse style, with an agreeable air of wear and tear about it which suggested wellingtons and battered chairs and dogs.

Dogs there certainly were; though not as overwhelmingly evident as in boarding kennels where animals pine and moan day in and day out for owners in Malaga and Bali. There was no doubt, she told herself, her nose wrinkling, as she rang the front door bell, that principally it was the smell you were aware of; though the occasional deep-throated bark issued from the low wooden buildings she could see round the side of the house.

'Hello; you're the policewoman, I take it?'

Another plane was building up for take-off as Liz turned to meet the woman she had come to see, and she just had time to say hastily, 'Yes; Liz Pink; I rang you,' before its thunder enveloped them in an almost palpable cloud.

Heather Campbell, in her mid-thirties, was a handsome, rangy, strong-looking woman in jeans and dun-coloured jersey with a green body-warmer buttoned up and bespattered green wellingtons. She looked Liz over quite frankly as they waited for the noise to fade, from rather prominent brown eyes which were sharp but not unhumorous, and brushed a stray wisp of dark hair back from her cheek with the back of her wrist.

'Let's go round,' she suggested as soon as words were possible, and nodded towards the rear of the house. Liz followed her past wooden buildings and chain-link compounds, in one of which a startlingly large shaggy dog watched them impassively, before wagging its tail cautiously three times.

The back porch where Mrs Campbell kicked off her boots smelt heavily of dog, but the kitchen beyond was better, and double-glazed against the noise. It was comfortably unfitted, with unmatching chairs and a deal table and a red Aga on top of which a black cat snoozed lazily.

Heather Campbell padded round in her stockinged feet filling the kettle and fetching a half-consumed packet of chocolate biscuits. 'I keep the dogs out of here; you can have too much of a good thing and they're gigantic sods anyway. I love 'em but my husband doesn't, though as he never shows his face in the kitchen anyway I suppose it doesn't matter. Milk? Sugar? Help yourself to a biscuit. Oh, plates . . .' Her voice had the unmistakable porcelain ring which signals attendance at one of the country's top girls' schools.

'I can manage without.'

'Good. Not very civilized. We can go through if you like,

though frankly I'd rather not, you never know what you might have on your jeans; me, I mean, not you. During the day I live like this; Tim doesn't get home till half past seven, bless his cotton socks, tired out after making lots of money in the City, by which time I'm bathed and changed and sweet-smelling and wearing a skirt and stockings and all the ingredients of a happy marriage.' She handed Liz a mug of coffee. 'That all right? You don't look like a policewoman.'

'Fortunately they let us in in all shapes and sizes,' Liz responded.

The other woman grinned. 'It's having only the dogs to talk to all day; they don't answer back, which is very bad for one.'

Another jet passed over; but here inside it was no more intrusive than a vacuum cleaner in a nearby room. Liz felt comfortably at home, and decided she would have a house like this before too long—homely and welcoming to strangers, untidy because it was more enjoyable that way, without being messy or inefficient. She wondered what the other rooms were like, where well-groomed Heather played the dutiful wife for something-in-the-city Tim, and gave up the effort as impossible.

'Now,' said Mrs Campbell, and there was a hint of formidability in her voice which drew Liz's mind back to the task in hand with a jolt, 'what are you here for?'

'To ask you about Judy Baker,' Liz replied directly. 'We think she might be able to help us about a death which took place on the common on the night of the storm. But she's proving . . . elusive.'

'Why should you think she can help you?'

'I'd rather talk to her about that.'

'Indeed! Well, then, why should you think *I* can help you find Judy Baker?'

'She lives in your cottage.'

'That doesn't make me her keeper.'

'No . . .' There was a pregnant pause. Liz looked round

the kitchen carefully. 'But you are her friend as well as her landlord, aren't you?' she suggested finally.

Mrs Campbell was suddenly very still, and Liz knew her instinctive awareness of the atmosphere in the kitchen had been correct; Heather Campbell was wary. 'Yes, I suppose you could say so,' she agreed. She took another biscuit, crumbling it absently in her fingers. 'I don't know anything that will help you, though' she said. 'I'm sorry.'

'When did you last see her?'

The sharp brown eyes fixed themselves unwinkingly on Liz while Heather Campbell's brow furrowed. 'About a week ago, I think. Might have been the day after the storm or the day after that. There's a shop in the village. I wanted some butter, we were out; Judy was in there with Troo . . . with Thomas, buying vegetables. I stopped for a chat on my way to the till.'

'How did she seem?'

'She didn't seem anything,' the other woman replied. 'Not that I noticed. Can't even remember what we talked about. The weather, I expect; the winds.'

'She didn't mention any plans to go away?'

'I believe she did say something of the sort; I'm afraid I didn't pay much attention. We were only passing the time of day, and I was rushing, as usual.

'Did she say how long she planned to be away from home? You must have gained some idea! Just the evening? Overnight? A week?'

'I . . . got the impression it might be for a few days.'

'You're sure she didn't mention where she was going?' Liz repeated.

'Sure.'

'Nor who she was going to see?'

'Quite sure. I'm sorry I can't help you.'

She didn't seem very sorry, and her story sounded like so much crap. It was a pity, because Liz felt that Heather Campbell was a likeable sort of person in other circumstances. When you met people as a police officer, their hostility could sometimes get a little depressing.

'You've a key to Judy Baker's cottage, of course?' she said.

'Yes, I have. But if you think you're going to go barging in there while Judy's away, you've another think coming,' Mrs Campbell told her. 'Tenants have a right to peaceful enjoyment; I'd have thought you people would know that!'

Liz sighed, and got up. As if she repented her acerbity, Heather Campbell said in a more conciliatory tone, 'Come and have a look at my girls before you go.'

Liz pushed her notebook into her bag and followed Heather Campbell, who was already in the porch tugging wellingtons over her thick socks. The aeroplanes were still clawing into the air, or for all Liz knew maybe the same bored pilot was simply going round and round. But noise apart, the afternoon was bright and mild, and under the trees crocuses lifted gaping mouths sunwards.

Heather's 'girls' were Irish Wolfhound bitches, penned in ones and twos and threes in various stages of pregnancy, motherhood or merely anticipation. Liz ambled round on the outside of the wire, while Heather Campbell did things with buckets and feed scoops and shovels.

'You knew Judy was married?' Heather called out.

'Married?' Liz echoed.

'Didn't last. Heaven knows why she married him in the first place. He was a lecturer at Keele, where Judy went to university. I think she soon decided he was lured by the idea of the Baker millions, but of course Judy was used to that; and anyway, it was all tied up in trusts and what-not.'

'Were there . . .' But at that moment another jet unstuck from the Gatwick runway eight hundred yards away. Heather merely shook her head, and Liz waited and tried again. 'Were there really millions?'

Heather slipped the catch on a gate and came out. 'Judy's father was the Baker of Baker's Biscuits; didn't you know? She went back to her maiden name when the marriage went wonky. Millions? I doubt it. Could have been a couple of hundred thousand. Might have been more, because Baker's was snapped up by—who was it? Rowntree, or General Foods, or some such. As I say, I believe there was some sort of trust. This was ten years ago.'

'So Judy decided her husband was only fortune-seeking?'

The two women walked along to another set of pens. 'So she dumped him back where she had found him. For all I know he's there still, if Mrs Thatcher didn't have him cut as an economy. Come and meet Max.'

Liz was a big girl, almost as tall as Heather Campbell and more substantially built (she had cried when she first put on her WPC's uniform and looked in the mirror; since then the move to CID and then sergeant's pay had enabled her to dress so as to play down her curves); and she was quite used to large dogs, even ostensibly fierce ones, since they usually came accompanied by an equally large dog-handler, generally bearded, and dog and handler were invariably both softies with people they liked.

Max was something else. He could have picked up one of the police Alsatians and tossed it in the air as a terrier does a rat. On all four shaggy paws—where Liz devoutly hoped he would stay—he was able to nuzzle her breasts while barely raising his head—and he did.

'Max likes women,' Heather said, apologetically, burying her hand happily in the dog's grey fleece. 'Only he's not terribly discriminating. Are you, my boy! You can't blame him,' she added to Liz, 'seeing as the whole of his existence is devoted to sex. So far as Max is concerned, I feed him and keep him warm and exercise him, and I run a splendid harem for him. Every time he sees a bitch she's dying for him and all he has to do is go in and do it. It's a dog's paradise, isn't it, old boy?'

'Or a man's,' Liz suggested.

'Ah!' Heather raised her head from the dog's mooning eyes. 'I always think it's vaguely insulting to the dogs to start anthropomorphizing.'

'Sorry! But it did rather strike me that way. I mean . . .'

The older woman shrugged, so that Liz suddenly felt

rather stupid. 'He really is a very splendid dog,' she offered, to make amends.

'Going to make friends, then?' Heather said to the dog, and to her dismay Liz watched it raise itself on to its hind legs with a little push of its forefeet. It kept its balance well enough but she knew there was only one way it could stay like that, and braced itself as a couple of uncertain steps brought it up to her. Max draped his shaggy forelegs gratefully over Liz's shoulders and subsided. Liz found herself helplessly supporting half the weight of six and a half feet of Irish Wolfhound, a great shaggy satyr embracing her as if for some grotesque and intimate dance. 'The damn brute,' she recounted later to her boyfriend, 'was actually licking the top of my head!'

She stayed like that for several minutes while Heather filled Max's water bucket and forked a nauseating mixture of meal and meat into his feed trough, whereupon the gigantic dog casually abandoned Liz, flopped down on to all fours again and padded off to sustain his bulk and potency. 'You bitch!' Liz muttered at Heather's back. 'You knew he'd do that!'

'Les was a bit like that,' Heather said abruptly turning towards her. 'In a dog it's endearing. In a man it's vile. I sometimes think Les is the vilest man I've ever known.'

When Isobel Syme, née Baker, received Nelson graciously, he knew he was in for a hard time.

She was a small woman, punctiliously dressed in a tweed skirt and angora jumper, the correct degree of formality, apparently, for entertaining policemen on official business; or perhaps it was her everyday wear, he told himself gloomily. There was a recognizable kinship between her features and those of Judy Baker, though careful make-up, in Isobel's case, spoilt them. What had impressed Nelson in spite of himself about Judy was the nervous energy she radiated. Sexual energy, to a large extent; and her small, neat, heart-shaped face demanded to be called puckish. Isobel was empty of sexual life, and though she seemed to have decided that puckishness—or any other trait suggestive of a sense of humour—was in bad taste, he recognized its tedious cousin, archness, in the way she introduced him to her husband.

Donald Syme drifted forward vaguely to shake, or at least touch, Nelson's hand; but then Isobel steered Nelson to a deep uncomfortable seat, and herself took the one opposite, on the other side of the dancing sanitized flames of the clever 'real' gasfire, and Donald Syme seemed to fade into the wallpaper again.

'So you want to ask us about Judy,' Isobel began. 'We guessed this would happen, didn't we, Donald? It was only a question of time.'

'Do you know where she is?' Nelson inquired, trying the blunt approach.

Isobel looked sad. 'Alas, no. We don't see as much of Judy as we ought to, do we, Donald?—but then, I'm afraid she's a strange girl, Sergeant, as you've no doubt already heard.'

'When did you last see your sister?' Nelson side-stepped.

'Oh, we were trying to remember, before you came, Sergeant. You know, I think it must be eighteen months ago. It sounds terrible, doesn't it?' she said, looking if anything rather pleased with herself.

'So you aren't close?'

'It's better to be honest, don't you think? You certainly don't want me to try and mislead you; that wouldn't help anyone, would it? I suppose the truth is, Judy has always gone her own way. My husband would tell you, she isn't always easy to get on with, is she, Donald? Even as girls, we weren't close.'

'In what ways,' Nelson asked, 'is she difficult?'

'There! Now I've given you the impression there's something *disturbed* about her! Of course, she and I are such different kinds of people. She was always the impulsive one, even as a child, getting into scrapes, rowing with Dad. Then she left home to go to university, and the next thing we knew, she was married. To one of these left-wing people,' she amplified, as if they might be a peculiar race Nelson was unacquainted with.

'I gather he was a lecturer at Keele University?'

'Ye-es. Though,' Isobel went on more enthusiastically, 'he seems to be doing quite well for himself now. Politically, you know. Miles Wetherby—he's quite often on the television news, isn't he, Donald?'

Nelson made a note.

'Incidentally,' Isobel inquired, 'you didn't say *why* all this interest in my poor sister all of a sudden. I take it she's done something awful.'

Nelson picked up the note of resignation in her voice. He remembered she had said, it was only a matter of time. 'It wouldn't come as any surprise?'

'Not . . . Oh, dear! Let's say I would be disappointed to hear she'd . . . again . . . Is it that poor child? I'm sure he'd be far better off in care of some sort. Isn't that an awful thing to say about one's own sister? So she's . . .' She waited hopefully.

'She's disappeared,' Nelson said simply.

'And you . . . particularly want to find her? I mean,' Isobel expanded, 'I rather thought you people didn't take much notice these days if people went off . . . unless you had a more, let's say a more *pressing* reason?'

'A woman's body was found in a car park on a common south of East Grinstead on the night of the storm, ten days ago,' Nelson said. 'There was a car near the body. We've established that that car is registered in the name of your sister, Judy Baker. We'd rather like to be able to ask her some more questions about that, but unfortunately she's missing from her home, and nobody yet has been able to tell us where she might be.'

'Oh!' said Isobel, and Nelson felt a passing satisfaction that something he had said had been able to faze her.

Donald Syme, on the other side of the room, unexpectedly cleared his throat. 'I think we might offer the sergeant a cup of tea, don't you, darling? Why don't you put the kettle on.'

'Yes; yes, of course, I should have . . . excuse me.'

When the two men were left alone, silence descended on the room. Nelson could hear cups clattering, a kettle being filled, muffled by the intervening wall.

'She's an alcoholic,' Donald Syme said suddenly, his voice falling heavily among the chintzy chairs and fussy occasional tables.

'She . . . ?' Nelson stuttered, startled.

'Judy is an alcoholic. She and Isobel have hated each other's guts since they were children. Isobel believes they aren't true sisters, you know; lot of rubbish, of course. Just as she always believes Judy's brat Thomas isn't Miles's. That could be true enough, given the sort of woman Judy is.'

Nelson scrabbled his way out of this avalanche of information. 'And is she left-wing too?' he asked, but the irony which was intended to express his scepticism disappeared somewhere between his mind and his lips, and he was not surprised when Donald Syme answered perfectly reasonably, 'I shouldn't be at all surprised.'

The door swung open. 'Here we are,' Isobel's recovered social voice said. 'How do you like it? Milk? Sugar?' And Nelson with a sinking heart took a cup of tea which, even by the standards of women entertaining policemen, was pretty nearly the weakest it had ever been his misfortune to have to drink.

CHAPTER 17

'I'm sure she knows where Baker is!' Liz said.

She and Mr Stainton were driving to The Pines. The Chief Inspector had been dismissive of Stracey's pussy-footing. Letters to and fro would be slow, and give the headmaster too much scope for hiding behind fine phrases. Instead, an appointment had been made to see him immediately school ended, and Mr Stainton had judged it more economical in the long run to see Stracey himself. Liz, looking forward to witnessing an interview which promised to be short and sweet, and enjoying the fact that someone else was behind the wheel as they wound their way in the failing light through the damp lanes which in winter never seemed to dry out, let her mind roam over her conversation with Heather Campbell, and had now come up against a conclusion so obvious she wondered how she had over-looked it from the start. 'God, I'm thick!' she exclaimed in disgust. 'Why the hell didn't I push harder?'

The mildness of Mr Stainton's reply only confirmed that he had seen the true picture straight away.

'It's arguable whether you'd have been justified at this stage,' he said; 'unless you felt she was telling you down-right lies. Seems to me she was more concerned just to lead you up the garden path. All this stuff about the husband—when she was being so reticent about Judy herself.'

'Might be worth checking him, all the same, sir? I mean, maybe that's where she is. Any port in a storm sort of thing,' Liz replied gloomily.

'You got the name?'

'Les somebody,' Liz said, leafing through her notebook. 'Yes: here we are, but it's not Les any more. That was in his lefty university lecturer days.'

'Sorry, Liz, I'm not with you.'

'He's changed his name. Or rather, it was his name all along, but it didn't sound democratic enough. Miles Leslie Wetherby. Les. Or, now, Miles. Miles Wetherby.'

'Wetherby?' he echoed, aghast.

The old man's going senile, Liz told herself despairingly. 'That's right,' she said aloud. 'Want me to fix for one of us to go and see him?'

'Looks as if we shall have to,' Alec agreed reluctantly. He drove on in silence, coming to terms with this ironic twist in the investigation. After a while, to get his mind out of the Wetherby groove, Alec began to speculate on the extent to which the Campbell woman had misled Liz. What was at the root of her evasiveness? Simple protectiveness of her friend—or did she know there was a definite link between Kate Randall's death and the missing Judy Baker?

One possibility which had not escaped him, and which worried him a good deal, was that Judy Baker had not disappeared by choice. It was perfectly possible that she was lying dead herself somewhere. On the common itself, perhaps: bodies sometimes stayed hidden for years, often within a few yards of busy roads or paths. He knew that too well: he had had to look at some of them. But in that case too, where was her car? There was a general call out for it, but to no avail. Most likely it was where Judy was; tucked away out of sight in a driveway or garage.

'So you want me to fix something up, sir?'

'Sorry, Liz?'

'Wetherby. Will you see him yourself?'

'No,' Alec said. 'No, I don't think that would be a good idea at all.'

'Lionel Stracey, Chief Inspector. Come on in.'

The man who strode with practised confidence forward to shake Alec's hand was attractive; and by God, didn't he know it! Fortyish, thick wavy brown hair, craggy features, hands manicured, charcoal suit tailored to flatter an athlete's body: if ever there was an ideal form for the proprietor of a private school, Stracey had it. No doubt the prospectus sent out to parents was flattering to the school, but if any doting mothers were in doubt as to whether The Pines was worthy of receiving a child of young Ben or young Amy's sensitivity and forwardness, an interview with Lionel Stracey would have felled them like ninepins. Alec let the other man out-grip him and followed him into his office—or, as Stracey referred to it, 'my study'.

Liz, following dutifully a step behind, readily acknowledged Stracey's charms, though she did not wholly trust them. They were of the sort encountered in men who overwhelmed you with their attentions prior to suggesting a weekend trip to a country house hotel, where they would have your knickers off you before you had unpacked your toothbrush. Come Monday, it was 'I-thought-we-both-realized-it-was-just-a-pleasant-interlude', and come Tuesday, all you got was the message on the answerphone. Moreover, in the present situation she was galled by Stracey's response to Mr Stainton's bearing, and his tie, and the cut of his suit, and his accent: all unspoken recognition symbols, disposing Stracey to answer Mr Stainton's questions as he would never have answered Liz's.

Glancing round the study as she took a seat, Liz noticed the discreetly framed degree certificate hanging behind the desk. Jason Lionel Stracey, she could just make out, and thought with satisfaction of the ragging Stracey must have received about that 'Lionel' when he was a schoolboy himself. Now, though, what a godsend such a name must be to the proprietor of The Pines!

Stracey's handsome features registered tragedy when Alec spoke of the death of Kate Randall; concern when he mentioned Judy Baker and her absence from home; pride when Alec touched on Miles Wetherby; proprietorial concern when Thomas's name came up.

'Poor Mrs Baker.' Stracey nodded understandingly. 'Hers hasn't been an easy life, of course. Young Thomas is a remarkable lad. I often think adversity brings out the best in children, Chief Inspector. I wish I could say it did in adults! We have a good deal to learn from our children, in some ways.'

Less of the 'our' thought Liz; unless Mr Stainton had secrets he wasn't telling.

Liz listened with mixed admiration and resentment while her boss efficiently extracted what little Lionel Stracey knew of the whereabouts of Judy Baker, and smiled glumly to herself as the information Stracey had tagged as 'privileged' on the telephone came tumbling out in the headmaster's smooth plummy accents.

Two days earlier Thomas's form teacher had mentioned that the boy was staying with his aunt—there was some difficulty because he didn't have all his school things with him, and had turned up for gym in trainers instead of regulation shoes. 'We try and maintain very high standards here at The Pines, of course, and so normally we come down heavily on infringements of school regulations. After all, if we don't prepare our pupils they will find their public schools when they get to them a rude awakening.'

Oh, neat! Liz thought, and hoped Mr Stainton was savouring Stracey's promotional dexterity. Liz's own school had been one where a girl who stuck to the dress regulations would have been laughed out of court by her peers.

'His aunt?' Alec queried. He glanced at Liz, one eyebrow raised, but she shrugged her ignorance. So far as she knew, Isobel Syme was Judy's only sister, and they knew for sure Thomas wasn't there.

'Er, of course,' Stracey amplified, '"aunt" can mean a great many things to a child. In this case, I believe it's a close friend of Mrs Baker's.'

Mrs Campbell, thought Liz at once, and her face darkened.

'Aunts are comforting figures,' Mr Stainton remarked. 'Possibly Thomas will be better off with her than with Judy Baker.'

Stracey looked uncomfortable. 'Well, there is that. Of course, it must normally be best for a child to ... the parent/child bond is such a major influence on development, even though Mrs Baker had had her troubles ...'

'She is separated from her husband, I believe.'

But Stracey did not mean that. Marital breakdown was clearly a touchy issue, but reading between the lines Liz gathered that it would not be diplomatic, in a school like The Pines where so many parents *were* separated, divorced or in the process of changing partners, to categorize separation as 'trouble'. No doubt The Pines' prospectus contained fine rolling sentences about inculcating moral values and principles (in unspoken contradistinction to the assumed moral vacuum of state education); but fine words butter no parsnips when it comes to paying school fees.

No, Judy Baker's 'difficulties' were at once more nebulous and more serious. Drink might have come into it; or some similar vice—it was difficult to tell, given Stracey's elusive hints—or mental instability. But Liz had the feeling that in the main it was simply that Judy did not quite belong. The words 'not one of us' were not used, perhaps out of consideration for Liz; but they hovered unspoken in the air none the less.

CAMEX? More evidence that poor Mrs Baker's judgement was doubtful. Few Pines' mums, it appeared, would have been found chained to the fence at Greenham Common. If Pines' parents signed petitions, it was to save whales, demand by-passes and protest against plans for housing estates.

'Would you send your kid to a place like this, sir?' Liz asked depressedly as they walked to the car; and then wished she hadn't: all too possibly he would. He had almost certainly attended something similar in his own youth.

Alec turned his head and smiled at her. 'You didn't think much of our Lionel Stracey?'

'Well, but I'd think twice. I mean, there's more to education than white plimsolls.'

Alec was still smiling as he unlocked the car. 'I'll remind you of that when you're explaining that you'd love to send little Emma to a state school, but in her own best interests you really can't let her suffer for your principles.'

Liz scowled. Bet you have one before I do, she said silently. Aloud, she asked, 'Well, now we know where little Thomas is. What is it about me, sir, that makes everyone leap to pull the wool over my eyes? That woman, she knew where Judy was all the time!'

'I should say,' Alec remarked, 'that Judy was very probably in the house even as you talked.' Alec turned out into the main road and accelerated away, as if he too was only too happy to put The Pines behind him. 'Well, we know where she is now. If need be, I'll go and have a word with our precious Mrs Campbell; but we've wasted enough time on this particular red herring. It's about time we concentrated on finding who killed Kate Randall instead.'

*

Sophy Blake felt the money burning a hole in her pocket. It had come in five twenty-pound notes, whereas she had vaguely expected pound coins or at worst fivers. But the large greeny-brown notes clearly said twenty pounds; and how was she ever to dispose of them?

She tried giving one to Hannah during break; but Hannah looked at her with hot, suspicious eyes; you didn't give money away like that. Fifty pences, pound coins and the occasional fiver were the stuff of real life: twenty-pound notes like 18-rated films were more talked-of than actually seen. She looked at Sophy and asked the inevitable question.

'Where did you get it, then?'

'From my mum,' Sophy said. Well, it was *almost* true. 'Swear you won't tell,' she added urgently.

Hannah looked at her scornfully. 'Parents who give you too much money never give you anything else,' she said pointedly.

'You only say that because yours haven't got any money to give you,' Sophy replied in her misery.

'Oh, Sophy Blake, you cat!'

There was no giving them away; you couldn't tear them up because what could you do with the pieces? Sophy went to the lavatory and tried to flush one of the notes away, but it rose soggily to the surface again and it wasn't till the third try that it disappeared round the bend. And that still left four.

In the end she took them home with her, folded inside her bra, her face hot every time someone looked her way, sure that they must be able to see her secret. Still, she told herself, as she cut them into small squares with her nail scissors, ran the tap and fed them into the waste-disposer, thank heaven they were gone!

Next day she visited five different cashpoints. Three of them gave her a hundred pounds each. The fourth told her she had used up her limit. The fifth, to her relief, swallowed the card. She had been wondering how to get rid of it.

*

Alec expected to find Clive Morris at home; but he rang
and made an appointment none the less. When he and DC
Johnson called, the schoolteacher stood on the doorstep,
blocking the way indoors, sullen. Only when Alec pressed
were they able to move inside. Alec felt mean about that
little exercise of authority, and the more so as Morris
crumpled so easily before it.

Inside was all the evidence anyone needed of the man's
present condition, even had his dishevelled clothing and
badly-shaved jowls not given clues in advance. The house
stank, of dirt and unwashed bodies and closed windows. It
struck cold. In the living-room there were old newspapers;
dirty plates. The television was on. A chess set with an open
book of problems beside it suggested Morris had tried hard
to retain some mental activity. Boxes of CAMEX leaflets
stood on the floor, and some had been sorted into bundles
held together by elastic bands. Morris himself stood mutely
in the doorway as Alec moved a shoe aside and took a seat,
and beneath the stubble looked pale and unhealthy. His
hair was unwashed.

'I'm sorry your wife's left you,' Alec said directly.

Morris began to cry; sniffing, brushing at his face with
his cuff, seeming to sag; he nodded. 'She's taken my girls,'
he said at last.

Who could blame her, Alec thought: girls of nine and
twelve, and knowing her own husband had molested just
such . . . If she hadn't removed them from the house, no
doubt the social services would. How Betty Morris must
have agonized, wondering whether they, more than any,
had suffered his attentions. The four words which were all
Morris had spoken showed plainly that it was the girls, not
Betty, whose loss had reduced him to his present state.
Glover's case; court; a jury's verdict; newspaper vilification;
they would all be by the way now for Morris. What else
had he to lose?

'I haven't come about your own troubles, Mr Morris,'
Alec said, when the man had sniffed hard and had himself
once more in hand. 'I'm afraid it's about Kate Randall. I

want to find who killed her; I'm hoping you can help me.'

Morris seemed to sag again, as if expecting further accusations and innuendoes. Alec kept his voice firm, trying to build Morris up by treating him as a member of the public whose help he sought, not a pathetic child-molester under investigation, and gradually it seemed to have its effect. As Morris took himself in hand Alec could sense Johnson's surprise as his intelligence—and even a certain authority, suggesting that he was at least in one respect well fitted for schoolmastering—became more apparent.

'The way I see it at present is this,' Alec said. 'A CAMEX connection—sounds like the title of a thriller, doesn't it?—seems likely in Kate's killing. But to judge its probability, we need to know more about how CAMEX works, and the threat it poses to individuals, or interests. I've a detective-sergeant and a detective-constable going through every piece of paper we found at Kate's flat or in the car or on her person. But I'm chiefly interested this morning in what *didn't* get written down.'

Morris nodded. 'Kate was very thorough, though. Admin was definitely her talent. She kept all the paperwork personally, and it was very efficiently kept, too. For example: I know after every meeting she wrote up the minutes the same evening, before she went to bed. She wanted them to be right, or they had no value.'

'Who's looking after that sort of thing now, Mr Morris? In fact, who's running CAMEX?' Alec glanced across at the boxes of leaflets. 'Are you?'

'What can I do?' Morris asked bitterly. 'My name'd be the final kiss of death.'

'But you're . . .'

'Well, I suppose we none of us want to see it fold.' Morris looked suddenly belligerent, and as if defying Alec to laugh, said, 'Kate would have wanted us to keep it going. In a way,' he added more thoughtfully, 'I suppose it's the only thing we can do to make her death other than a complete waste. If we give in, they've won, haven't they?'

'They?'

He shrugged. 'Whoever. If it's connected.'

'Do you think it is?'

Morris hesitated. 'Kate thought so. I mean, she'd thought of the possibility of physical attacks on some of us. We talked about it, sure. You see, there wasn't just the . . . the letters, about . . . me, you see; there was something similar which cost Kate her job; and then this malpractice suit against Ginnie Kemp, which so far as we can see the claimants were, shall we say, *encouraged* to bring; and someone had been getting at Judy Baker over her son. Oh, and little things, you know; tyres slashed, hate mail.'

Alec said: 'She had something of that sort—hate mail, I mean—on her when she was found.'

'Did she?' Morris replied. 'I can't say it surprises me. She didn't mention it; but then, Kate wouldn't.'

Alec experienced a little glow of satisfaction at having his hunch so negligently confirmed. But all he said was, 'I should think *you've* about had enough of that.'

Morris gave a little mirthless smile. 'You could say that.'

'But . . . it's a big step from that sort of thing to physical violence,' Alec suggested.

'I know. Kate thought we ought to be aware of the possibility, all the same. Some of the rest of us were sceptical.' He shrugged. 'Seems her judgement was right.'

Yet Morris, and the other CAMEX members, were prepared to go right on with their campaign. What could one call that, if not courage?

'No,' Morris resumed, his eyes straying to the leaflets, 'I keep a low profile, but there's a fair amount of donkey work I can do. I tell you what,' he added forcefully, 'it's opened our eyes to what Kate used to do! She worked full time for CAMEX, and now we're beginning to realize just what that meant!'

'It'll soon be over,' Alec remarked.

'Yes; though CAMEX won't fold, whatever way the vote goes. There'll still be the need for a pressure group like ours, to keep the heat on.'

'You think your campaign will fail to stop the vote in favour of allowing experimentation?'

'There's too much ranged against us. Having said that, there's what happened to the Sunday Trading bill: that took the government by surprise, and that was largely as a result of intelligent campaigning, mobilizing latent support.'

'What constitutes intelligent campaigning?' Alec asked quietly.

Morris turned to him with a penetrating look. He smelt unwashed; but he was talking rationally and forcefully, and Alec knew they were reaching to the kernel of what he himself had called the CAMEX connection.

'Shock,' said Morris. 'Not terror. We are people of principle.'

Alec allowed a faint smile to play across his mouth. 'So are the PLO; the IRA; the Basque separatists; the Islamic Jehad. The Animal Liberation Front; the Sons of Glyndwr. So were Robin Hood, and the Inquisition.' There was a long silence. It was Alec who broke it. 'There was a can of petrol in the boot of Kate Randall's car the night she died,' he said.

This time Morris's smile was one of genuine, though wry, amusement. 'Knowing Kate, there was probably a tow-rope too, but I don't imagine you suspect her of planning to strangle anyone. No, Chief Inspector. No arson: it's counterproductive. Even when, *especially* when, it's laboratories you burn and not people. Attacks on people are unfortunate; but threaten private property and you put yourself beyond the pale, you know. Leaflets, yes. Photographs of foetuses to MPs, yes. Rallies and protest marches and poster campaigns, yes. Picketing, disrupting ministerial visits, nuns in sit-ins . . . But no arson; and no letter bombs or assassinations. Haven't you realized? It's human life we're campaigning about. Where would be the sense in showing we hold it in contempt?'

'But you discussed it?'

'Yes; everything was discussed. I'm sure the minutes of

our meetings will show that the subject came up from time to time.'

'And there was the CAMEX memorandum, as the newspapers called it.'

Morris's face darkened. 'A fake. A smear, and like the others to date, a bloody good one.'

'Because, like the others, it was founded on fact,' Alec suggested quietly.

'No. Oh no. No, that memorandum was a fabrication from start to finish. Look—' Morris stared round at the room as if seeing its squalor for the first time—'like some coffee? It's a bit of a tip, I'm afraid, but the milk's still delivered and I don't suppose I can poison you with instant coffee and boiling water.'

Alec glanced at Johnson, and accepted for them both, and Morris went out, taking a handful of used mugs and dishes with him. 'Well, he's certainly perked up,' Johnson offered. He sniffed pointedly. 'Place could do with a clear-out. You know,' he added, surprise in his tone, 'he really cares about this campaign, doesn't he?'

'Mm.' Alec's own understanding of CAMEX had undergone something of a change since Kate Randall's death, and he was uncomfortably coming to the conclusion that there was a good deal more dedication and single-mindedness about its adherents than he had assumed— and more than was really convenient, from the point of view of a policeman examining an unlawful death.

It was disturbing to have to admit to himself that there were distinct advantages in the 'everyone's guilty of something' approach—and in his ten years in the police force that approach had subtly insinuated itself into his mind. Goodness was inconvenient, from an investigating officer's point of view, and much harder to deal with than villainy. But then, not everyone would regard support for CAMEX as evidence of goodness. Say idealism, then; but that was most dangerous of all.

'Hope you don't take sugar,' Morris apologized as he came back into the room bearing a tray on which were

three steaming mugs and a plate of biscuits, 'I'm afraid I'm
. . . rather disorganized.'

'So,' Alec said as he took the mug of coffee and accepted
a gingernut, 'this is where Kate Randall had been, the night
she died.'

Morris looked up in surprise. 'Of course. Didn't you
know that?'

'You never mentioned it to Sergeant Nelson,' Alec explained.

'Didn't I? Maybe he never asked me.'

Maybe he hadn't, at that, Alec thought gloomily. Aloud,
he asked, 'Who came?'

'Just Kate and Andrew. Mackenzie.'

So: if idealism was too often used to justify atrocity, it
could be pretty cavalier with morality at a lesser level, too.
Mackenzie's name had certainly been on the list of
CAMEX members to be interviewed in the early stages of
the inquiry, and Alec recalled no mention that he had been
with Kate Randall on the night of her death. Where one
uncovered one piece of falsehood, who knew how many
more might be waiting to be dug up?

'CAMEX business, I presume?' he queried.

'Kate didn't have any other sort,' Morris said drily.
'Until the bill came up before Parliament she was as free
from outside distractions as a human fairly can be. That
other chap who came from your place, I don't think he
grasped that idea one little bit. I gather Charlie Poole
upped sticks?'

'That's right.'

'Well, don't you see? If he did, it was precisely because
until the campaign wound down, Kate was leaving him out
in the cold; plus, of course, he'd be windy about your interest in us, I mean after that fake memo. In her own small
way Kate was CAMEX's Joan of Arc; and I don't imagine
it was much fun being Joan of Arc's boyfriend.'

Morris had the ready empathy with other people's
emotional lives Alec had seen before in those whose own
emotions were unnaturally strained. He wondered how

reliable Morris's judgement was, none the less. Yet, looking back to his own meeting with Kate Randall in the restaurant at Brasted, Alec acknowledged that he had been aware of being in the company of a woman of exceptional force and self-discipline.

'Did Kate Randall and this Mackenzie come together?'

Morris looked thoughtful. When his intelligence was engaged, his whole manner was different, more attractive. Alec could not tell how women would respond to Morris, but he had sensed Johnson's antipathy to the man when he first opened the door, and shared it. It was salutary to have Morris's acuity demonstrated, as a reminder that people did not always lie quietly in the categories they were placed in. For that matter, the reference to Joan of Arc hinted that Kate Randall had not been simple to categorize either: perhaps Morris was unconsciously suggesting that her selfless dedication to CAMEX had had something ruthless about it.

'Couldn't tell you,' Morris replied, recalling Alec to his own question. 'They arrived together, and they left together. I thought I recalled seeing them drive away, but thinking about it, I realize that was a deduction from the fact that they left simultaneously, and it may be false. As I recall, I waved from the front door, then heard the car drive away after I'd come back inside.'

'But one car?'

'I think so. But perhaps there was only one parking space outside, and one of them had parked further up the street.'

'What sort of time would this be?'

'Not late. Before ten, more like half nine. There were only three of us, and meetings where Kate's in the chair don't hang about.'

So what was she doing up on the common after eleven? It wasn't even on her route home to her flat.

'How did Kate seem?'

'Strained. Tired. More than that one never knew with Kate. She was—she was an extraordinary person, Chief

Inspector. I don't know whether you've realized that, as you've learned more about her.'

'And what was the *reason* they came, Mr Morris?'

'The reason? Why . . . to, er, to sort out what effect recent . . . well, you know, my . . . what effect it would all have, and plan a strategy for damage limitation and to make sure the work wasn't set back.'

'Just the three of you?'

'Ginnie Kemp would have come too, but she was tied up,' Morris said off-handedly.

'The CAMEX top brass,' Alec suggested with a smile.

Morris denied it awkwardly. 'There was only one top brass in CAMEX,' he said after a pause. 'And now she's dead.'

As they left, Morris seemed to sag, like a balloon forgotten after a party. Staleness pressed forward to resume possession of the room, and the old newspapers, discarded clothes and dirty crockery thrust themselves once more into the foreground. In the folds of the previous week's *Sunday Times* Alec noticed the corner of a magazine which looked too glossy for a colour supplement, and realized with disappointment that it was a men's magazine. They took the shabbiness away with them like a disease caught by proximity, and in the car both men instinctively wound the window down.

As they turned on to the main road, Alec prompted, 'Just turn into this garage here.'

Johnson parked on the forecourt, and the two men walked over to the shop-cum-cashier's office. Displays held key rings, radiator sealant, cans of de-icer, pot plants. A tub of cut flowers stood ready to provide a last-minute gift to mark a wedding anniversary or flatter a hostess.

Petrol cans were on a shelf next to tow-ropes and first-aid kits. They were red, of moulded plastic.

'What sort did Randall have in the back of her car?' Johnson asked interestedly.

'You'll have to check with Mr Fletcher.' Alec frowned, remembering the receipt for the gin in the door-pocket, and wondering about receipts in general. They went out again, and contemplated the sign which proclaimed that the garage was open twenty-four hours. Long shots. Coincidences. What had the caucus really decided about their future strategy that night? Had Kate Randall had a different reason altogether for driving out over the common? Or did she simply, being the foresighted person she was, judge it prudent always to travel with a can of petrol against the possibility of a stranding?

'Check it,' repeated Alec briefly.

They climbed into the car and drove away.

CHAPTER 18

Alec was rather fond of the habit he had got into, of using Frances Walker as a source of ideas and inspiration, as well as company, and since breaking to her the news of Kate Randall's murder he had been promising himself that he would call round to talk it through with her and hear her calm, strong voice weighing up the arguments on his behalf.

He was conscious, however, that he would have to mend some fences first. Neither of them had behaved well when they met at the estate agents' opening, and their only encounter since then had been at the Brasted restaurant where Alec had been introduced to Kate Randall. Alec accepted philosophically that he must be the one to make the approach. No doubt they had both been in the wrong; but he would not cavil at acknowledging his own error first, in order to bring them back into their old comfortable relationship. It did not occur to him that to Frances that relationship was not comfortable at all, and that she might decide that she could not afford to go back to it.

The year was definitely on the up. It was barely the middle of February, yet already a green haze blurred the branches of the trees as Alec drove up through Hever and Four Elms.

The fields had lost the muddy look of winter, and were emerald with new grass. There were lambs running to and fro, and with the window down their thin cries and their mothers' anxious bleatings were improbably loud. For the first time in months the road was dry, the sun strong enough to burn off the perpetual sheen of moisture which had lain there since last October. The fallen leaves which had rotted for months in the gutter had dried too, and the passing of the cars lifted them and swept them aside. It would have been hard to find a more propitious day for embarking on an expedition of apology and renewed friendship.

Alec's pleasurable anticipation was rather dashed when he turned into Frances' drive and saw a white Ford, all wings and stripes, parked by the front door, and belatedly it occurred to him that he might have been precipitate in assuming that Frances was just waiting for him to call or ring.

Tucking the Bristol behind the white car and climbing out, Alec cocked an ear. The rasp of a chain-saw, which since the Great Storm three years earlier had become as natural a sound of the countryside as the calling of the cuckoo, came from not too far away: in fact, Alec was pretty sure, from Frances' orchard.

He locked the car, and turned round the side of the house between the huddle of outbuildings, where the nose of Frances' magenta TVR peeked out of a timber cart-shed, and took the flagged path along the edge of the lawn towards the orchard where the recurrent noise and a little spiral of exhaust smoke told him work was going on.

It was not, to his surprise, Frances who was wielding the chain-saw. He could see her walking to and fro between the trees carrying logs to a neat stack against the old brick wall. Lucy, to one side, watched without helping, her hands thrust in the pockets of her Barbour. Seeing her fine head and fair hair in profile Alec found himself reminded of Millais's *Princes in the Tower*. Her eyes were of the same unlikely blue, and their apprehensive expression completed the resemblance.

By a tangle of branches a stocky man, his face hidden, was bent over the saw; Alec could see the bar flash dully in the spring sun. The engine note rose, and then slowed as the saw struggled at its work. The pile of debris seemed to sag a little further, and the man stood back and let the saw slow down to an idle.

It was Lucy who saw Alec first, and she came over to meet him. He grinned at her absently but knew better than to try and ruffle her hair or hold out a hand to her.

'Your mum got someone in to help her this time?' he asked.

'That's Mr Wetherby,' Lucy said with transparent distaste.

'Oh, is it?' Alec replied sourly, and raised his head to watch as over by the fallen tree the saw whined again and the stocky man bent to his task.

'He's going to hurt himself,' Lucy said casually.

'Mm?'

'Mr Wetherby. He's not wearing the safety things. He doesn't know how to use the saw.' Frances had been on a two-day forestry course and had bought boots, gloves, helmet and eyeshield.

'No?'

'No. He's only doing it because he wants to show off to Mum. Some men,' Lucy concluded devastatingly, 'just can't stand by and see a woman doing something they think is a man's job.'

As if to prove her right, at that point the limb which Wetherby was cutting sagged and the note of the saw abruptly dropped an octave. Alec knew what had happened; Wetherby had cut against the tension of the fallen tree and the saw-cut had closed up, jamming the chain. Now Wetherby was tugging ineffectually backwards. At any moment, he might succeed in freeing the saw, which would race once more, while he himself lost his balance. It had been the last act of many a chain-saw amateur.

Alec crossed the tussocky grass until he was next to the still-heaving Wetherby and before the other man had registered his presence reached out and flicked the red ignition switch off. In the sudden silence Alec leant forward and took the weight of the fallen limb so that the cut reopened and the saw came free.

'What the devil!'

'Hello, Alec,' Frances said pleasantly, coming up. 'What a surprise!'

'You realize you could have caused a nasty accident, creeping up like that?' Wetherby exclaimed angrily. 'Chain-saws are dangerous things, you know!'

'Yes,' retorted Alec, 'and if you don't know how to use one, you should leave it to someone like Frances, who does. Good morning, Mr Wetherby, I believe we've met before.'

In the little uncomfortable silence that followed Lucy, unfortunately, giggled. Wetherby's face crimsoned.

'Well, it's time we stopped for coffee, anyway,' Frances interposed. Her tone was noticeably distant, as if bickering men did not delight her. 'I'm exhausted with humping all those logs. Alec, this is Miles Wetherby—oh! you've met before, of course. Miles, you remember Alec Stainton, a friend of mine.' She turned away from the two men. 'Ready for something to drink, Lucy?' she invited, and began to lead the way towards the house.

Alec drove home the short way by the motorway, in that careful manner which stems from a filthy temper. He was annoyed with Wetherby; he was annoyed with Frances for treating him coolly; but most of all he was annoyed with himself.

Switching off the saw had been a silly gesture, of course; a way of imposing himself on one who, it seemed, had gathered sufficient standing at Frances' house to be not merely present when she set about household tasks, but taking a leading role. Wetherby cutting wood with Frances' chain-saw had had an unpleasantly proprietorial air about him, and it was that, Alec reprimanded himself tartly, which had led him into a silly attempt to establish his own position. Like schoolchildren in the playground, he thought with a curl of the lip, claiming to be better 'best friends'.

There was little transport on the M25 this Saturday after-noon, and Alec deliberately drove in the inside lane, main-taining a steady sixty-five and letting the rest of the traffic pass him in the outside two lanes nose-to-tail in the usual seventy-mile-an-hour game of catch-as-catch-can. When he peeled off on to the M23 Alec had still not resolved the question of whether he should warn Frances that in-volvement with Wetherby might be involvement with a murderer.

No: that was ludicrous, the sort of impetuous building on trifles he still sometimes had to reprove Liz Pink for. But the knowledge that Wetherby was, after all, Judy Baker's husband, and this morning's reminder that he drove a white Ford, were tempting, in his present mood of wanting to find fault with the man. But no, the last thing he must do would be to issue an 'official' warning to Frances of all people!

Almost as bad, Alec decided as he indicated for his exit, would be to become embroiled in some sort of contest. Lucy had spent the morning angling for his support against Wetherby, whom she had obviously taken against. It would be demeaning and ridiculous to play such a part, and Alec had no intention of demeaning himself, or appearing ridicu-lous in his own eyes or those of Frances Walker.

It was uncomfortable to have to admit that it had been a mistake to go over there today; he would make sure that it would be a good time before he went again.

But Wetherby: looking at the matter with total dispas-sion, Wetherby certainly merited further investigation.

'Got Poole, sir!' Nelson fell into step with Alec as he walked along the corridor. Liz, emerging from the Ladies' as the two men passed, tagged on after them, scowling. They turned into the incident room.

'Good. What's he got to say?' Alec picked up a message sheet and scanned it.

'Well, I don't know how far it really gets us. See, I got on to the Health Authority, and got them to look up . . .'

Alec interrupted him with a query to Johnson. 'When did this come in?'

Johnson looked up from his desk. ''Bout an hour since.'

'Why isn't the time on it?' Alec demanded. Johnson began some excuse; Nelson tried for an opening to go on telling how he had tracked Poole relentlessly.

'Come into my office,' Alec instructed him briefly, and the two men left.

Liz lingered. She was unhappy about the instruction to give up on Judy Baker. Nelson's having found Charlie Poole irked her, for although she had effectively located Thomas Baker, she was not as convinced as Mr Stainton seemed to be that Judy was sitting in a chair at Heather Campbell's house waiting to be interviewed when required.

More importantly, Liz was not satisfied that Judy had not had a part in her friend's death. *Why* had she run? Surely not simply because Nelson had been rough with her in the interview room, treating her as if she were a suspect. For pity's sake, she *was* a suspect. Until Liz had satisfied herself as to Judy Baker's every move on the night Kate Randall died, and as to the nature of her relations with Kate Randall, she refused to cross her off the list.

The messenger came in with a sheaf of papers from the typing pool. Johnson held out a hand for them, but Liz intercepted them and shuffled through them dispiritedly.

The last proved to be the transcript of Nelson's notes, which he had made after his interview with Isobel and Donald Syme, all about Judy Baker: back-burner stuff; red herrings; time not to be wasted on . . . Liz caught herself with a jerk, and re-read the paragraph.

'Stupid berk,' she muttered; then looked down at Johnson's uncomprehending face. 'Not you, sunshine,' she said. 'Not me, for once.' She shuffled off the desk. 'If anyone wants me,' she said, 'I'll be in the boss's room.' She waved the sheet of paper. 'You can have this back when he's read it.'

*

Alec sipped his coffee, eyeing Nelson over the rim of the mug. 'Pity we didn't see the possibilities of this earlier,' he said.

Nelson was defensive. 'You said we'd given up on Baker, sir.'

So I did, Alec thought. But he was in no mood to let Nelson off the hook. He lifted the report from the desk. 'This rather changes the picture, though, doesn't it? Why on earth didn't you give me a verbal report?'

'I don't know how much we can trust it, anyway,' Nelson replied sullenly. 'The Symes can't abide Baker.'

'Let's get this straight. Judy's an alcoholic?'

Nelson shrugged. 'She's been a one for the booze pretty well since she was a teenager, and on the bottle properly more or less since she left Wetherby.'

Alec considered this for a moment. 'And the child?'

'A poor mite, innocently condemned to being brought up by a single parent and never know who his father was. I quote. There's a good deal of *envy* in some ways,' Nelson said more reasonably. 'You know: Isobel was always the goody-goody, and she resents the fact that Judy had all the fun.'

'Hmm. If the Symes are to be believed, fun is not exactly what Judy Baker has had. And never the twain shall meet?'

'Mrs Syme is the sort who would say, like, never darken my door again, you know what I mean, sir? You know, shunning the black sheep.'

'And Baker left all his money in trust for Judy,' Alec mused.

'Right! Source of further hostility. Dutiful daughter Isobel is miffed because scapegrace Judy came in for lots of loot. Mind, I wouldn't say Isobel's on her uppers, but we always want more, don't we?'

'Food for thought. So we're back to the same question: how much of what Isobel Syme told you do we discount?'

'Sure; but most of what I learnt came from Syme, when the woman was out of the room. Like about Judy smashing the house up when she was drunk. And,' Nelson added, 'the last nugget. When Isobel was showing me out, she'd gone on ahead to open the front door, and he came up behind me, still in the living-room, and sort of mumbled it. Silly twit.' He leant forward, reaching for the report. 'It's on the second page, sir; somewhere near the middle.'

'Judy Baker has tried to kill herself.' Alec nodded resignedly.

'More than once, sir. According to Donald Syme, she damn near succeeded.'

That was all they needed.

When Nelson had gone, Alec telephoned the police doctor, Peter Lyall, and caught him at his GP surgery.

'I'm struggling with the computer,' Lyall said. 'Even a telephone call is welcome.'

Alec commiserated, then asked: 'Peter, I want some help. I want to know about patterns in suicide.'

There was a cautious pause. 'You can ask,' Lyall said eventually. 'But a GP doesn't really see that many suicides, thank God. You really ought to speak to a psychiatrist.'

'I don't have one on tap. Let me tell you anyway.'

When he had finished, Lyall said, 'This is the missing woman in the Kate Randall case, I take it. You think she's killed herself?'

'Not yet,' Alec said drily. 'But . . . Would it fit, psychologically?' He outlined what they knew of Judy Baker's history, and Nelson's impressions that she was dangerously on the edge.

'Well, it's often the pattern, as I understand it,' Lyall said cautiously, 'that while everything's black, suicide's too much of an effort. It's only when things start to improve that the patient starts to see their position with more clarity, and at the same time their mental resources are greater, so that they start taking decisions again.'

'Mm. I was a bit afraid it might be something like that. It forces my hand.'

'Like me to ask around? I can give one of my friends a ring; there's one I can think of in particular who might help.'

'Please. You can ask what he'd recommend for a depressed and discouraged policeman at the same time.'

'He'd probably say the symptoms will pass remarkably quickly when you find who killed Kate Randall.'

'I hope they will,' Alec said, 'I hope they will.'

There was another matter Alec had to tackle which could not be put off. He rang through to the sergeants' room and summoned Liz. It gave him no pleasure to see her cheery face switch to apprehension as she saw his own stern expression. She stood formally before him and stared at a spot somewhere above his right shoulder as he delivered himself of the reprimand.

'It's no good, Liz,' Alec said directly. 'I'm not going to argue the rights and wrongs of it. Nelson is senior to you and the fact that you think you will probably soon overtake him does not justify you in treating him as you have done. All the more reason, in fact,' he added quietly, 'for you to have shown him extra consideration.'

'I did show him consideration, sir!' Liz protested.

'Did you?' he responded relentlessly. 'Or did you simply see an opportunity to bring another of his mistakes to my attention?' He cursed himself for that revealing 'another', but it was too late now. 'Anyway, that's not the issue. Nelson hasn't made a complaint: but I'm giving you a warning. Behave so childishly again and I'll have you taken off the case and ask Chief Superintendent Blackett to have you assigned elsewhere. You can go to a divisional CID; there'll be no harm to your career in the long term.'

'But I . . .'

To his consternation Alec saw that Liz Pink had begun to cry. Her face crumpled and blotched, and her voice broke as she stumbled out the beginnings of a protest. If Blackett had announced he was gay, or Nelson that he was going to be baptized, Alec could not have been more taken aback. Somehow with Liz the tears which, in principle, one ought to allow for in any man or woman on the receiving end of a dressing-down, were a reaction he had totally failed to anticipate. For a moment he was so flabbergasted at the sight of her standing weeping that he said nothing and simply stared angrily.

Liz herself was no less incredulous to feel the hot wetness on her cheeks, and embarrassment and anger fought for the upper hand. How could she explain that she had tried so hard to fit herself to Nelson's ways; or bent over backwards to give him the chance to share the glory; or that to remove her from the murder team would be a punishment out of all proportion to the actual nature of the offence? Only working with this team on this and previous cases had it gradually dawned on her that she was good at her job, and realized how much she enjoyed it. Above all, she certainly would not attempt to explain how much it counted to work with Detective Chief Inspector Stainton: counted in the force generally, and counted to her personally. Rightly or wrongly, it was to Mr Stainton that she ascribed her success so far and her happiness in the job, because he treated her as an equal notwithstanding her rank or her sex, caring only about competence. And he was not, as some thought, the cold, impersonal, repressed man he had at first seemed. She prided herself on the fact that she knew him well enough to know that.

And now her treacherous glands were revealing her as precisely the kind of droopy female he would least respect. Abruptly, she stiffened. 'Yes, sir,' she said, as firmly as she could manage; and turned and left the room quickly.

Liz walked the few yards back to her room in a daze of misery. Nelson, thank God, was out. The room looked bare and cold, but there was a blue glass ornament on her desk which she loved and used as a paperweight; with a sea-shell suspended delicately in the middle.

She took it in her hand, and flung it suddenly at the wall. It shattered with a disappointingly feeble tinkle, and lay in pieces on the floor.

'But it's unfair, sir!' boys wailed at school, soldiers in the army. 'Life's unfair,' the answer had always come directly, with all the assurance of the one meting out the unfairness. It certainly was.

CHAPTER 19

Alec was still cursing his two sergeants as he drove out to the Campbells' farm that same afternoon; making Nelson and Liz the scapegoats for his ill-temper and his dissatisfaction with himself. He, Alec, was every bit as leaden-footed as Nelson; every bit as tactless as Liz; but he made his mistakes in his private life.

He turned to consider the content of Nelson's interviews with the Symes and with Charlie Poole. It was the value one gave to information which made it important, not the information itself. Alec was not greatly concerned with the fact that Judy Baker could be violent—so can we all—but the context seemed to him very much to the point. At that moment, it seemed to him that the battering of Kate Randall with a broken branch could well have been done by the same person who in a drunken rage would systematically smash every breakable item in a room, as he knew Judy Baker had done in the past.

That was why he had never taken seriously the possibility that Charlie Poole might have been the killer, and Nelson's interview with the boy had confirmed him in his opinion. His mind's instinctive use of the word 'boy' was itself significant, for all that Poole was thirty-one. Even Nelson's unimaginative reportage conveyed the immaturity of Poole's outlook. Poole emerged as nearly colourless as a grown man can be, anxious only to keep out of trouble and stay alive and in possession of his health service post long enough to collect his pension.

The completeness of Poole's desire to dissociate himself from Kate Randall's CAMEX involvement and her death had something indecent about it, and though that in itself made some of Poole's replies to Nelson's questions suspect, it was quite plain that the boy's instincts when trouble loomed were to flee, not to kill. Nor was there much scope for doubting his alibi. By the time Kate Randall died, Poole was painting emulsion on to the walls of his newly-rented flat in Reigate; helping him do it at the critical hour had been the plain only daughter of a High Court judge.

It puzzled Alec that Kate Randall should have bothered herself about Poole at all. He had no redeeming strength of character that Alec could descry in Nelson's account of the interview. It was a while before the depressing thought occurred to him that a man of Poole's stamp might be all that was available to a woman like Kate Randall.

Strength of character, organizational efficiency, idealistic determination and firmness of principle are not the most favourable attributes for a woman who wishes to be lucky in love.

Alec parked his car beside a battered Land-Rover. There was no reply to his ringing of the doorbell, and barely waiting for one, he marched off round the side of the house towards the kennels.

The woman washing down the concrete with a hose could only be Heather Campbell. The sight of her, casual and untroubled, angered him, so that when she turned slightly and saw him, her head jerked up at his black expression. Alec saw her reaction, the momentary fear which crossed her bold features, and it pleased him, as fully according with what she ought to feel.

As he approached her, she turned away, walking over to the tap to turn the hose off. In the distance, the whine of an aircraft's engines on the Gatwick tarmac keened.

He followed her over, and flipped open his warrant card. 'Detective Chief Inspector Stainton,' he said shortly. She glanced at the card nervously. His surmise was correct: she had already guessed his business.

'Judy Baker: she's here, isn't she?' he said. 'Why didn't you tell my policewoman the truth?'

'She's not, as a matter of fact,' Heather Campbell replied with unconvincing nonchalance. 'And what gives you the divine right to know everything, anyway?'

'Didn't it occur to you that we might be trying to find her to *protect* her? Is that friendship, to hinder us like that?'

'Maybe.'

They stood full face to each other, not a yard apart, forgetful of everything except their antagonism. Now for the first time Heather Campbell met his eye tentatively.

The distant keening turned to a roar as the aircraft began its take-off run. Heather said abruptly, 'Come inside.'

He followed her into the kitchen and watched as she gathered the wherewithal for coffee, banging the mugs down on the worktop, her every move taut with emotion.

Heather Campbell kept her back to him while she waited for the kettle to boil. She stirred the coffee and milk into the mugs, brought them over, sat opposite him and pushed one of the mugs towards him.

'Judy doesn't need bad friends,' she said. 'She's had enough of those. She was here,' she admitted more soberly. 'She's not now, poor kid.'

Alec looked up sharply, and she withstood his scrutiny. 'She was here,' she repeated. 'I gave her shelter, after. To hear that her friend had been killed was devastating for her. And the *way* she heard it: frogmarched off to the police station and virtually accused of murdering Kate Randall herself: can you imagine what effect that had on Judy?'

'Anyone would find it unpleasant,' Alec said. 'And policemen sometimes react badly themselves when a murder is in question, and start believing the shortest route to solving the killing is the best, irrespective.'

'Judy Baker isn't *anyone*,' Heather said, looking down at the mug of coffee she circled with her hands. 'That's why the way she was treated was crucial. And that's why I— well, I didn't *lie* to that policewoman, but I know I did mislead her. I didn't want to be obstructive, Inspector. I just *don't* see that investigating one thing about a person gives you the right, or the need, to have that person stripped bare for you. I told your woman all I could which had a bearing on Kate Randall's death. I really did.'

Alec shook his head. 'You can't know. You can't know what might have a bearing. I'm not trying to be obscurantist; it's not some sort of police myth, that we're the experts, the only judges. Suppose one of your dogs was ill. Suppose the vet asked you to tell him everything about the way the dog had been in the past. Would you make your own selection? Not if you were sensible.'

'Doesn't everyone do that anyway? Unconsciously?'

'Yes; and that's a big problem for us; as no doubt it is for vets—' he got the small smile of acknowledgement he had been looking for—'but it's a hundred times worse if you add a conscious level of selection on top of that. You must tell me everything.'

'Must?' she echoed mutinously.

'Yes, if you care for Judy as you say; as I believe you do.'

'And has it occurred to you,' she said, 'that that might be a reason why I kept things back? I want the best for Judy, Inspector. That's more important to me even than your finding the killer of Kate Randall. I'm sorry. That's the way it is.'

Alec replied seriously, 'You know, we don't believe Judy Baker was responsible for Kate Randall's death. But that doesn't mean it's not important we find her. She was probably the dead woman's closest friend. Without her, we are working with our hands behind our backs.'

'Why should I believe you?'

'But even if we thought Judy *had* killed Kate Randall, do you think you could protect her by saying nothing?'

Heather Campbell sagged back in her chair. 'I don't know whether I believe it or not. All I believe is that you will hound Judy when you find her; and you will listen to lies from her enemies, and make clever deductions, and you may well find by the end of it that she is innocent, but on the way you'll have wrecked her life.'

'I think,' he said, 'you'd better tell me why Judy isn't just anyone. I know she has tried suicide a couple of times;

I know she's been an alcoholic, if she isn't still. Where is she?' he asked quietly. 'In hospital?'

Heather Campbell nodded. She sat slumped in her chair, her face slack. Animated, she was a woman of attraction, even though she had no beauty, because character made up for the want of delicacy in her strong features. Now, looking what must be her worst, unkempt and dirty from work, her hair rat-tailed from the rain, her patched check shirt and darned jersey hanging in folds over her drooped figure as she sat back with her forearms on the table, Alec warmed to her; and he waited patiently and almost compassionately for the help she would give him.

'I knew Judy from school,' she said in the end. She smiled briefly. 'You could say she is my oldest friend; my best friend, too. Or was, until she married.'

She looked up, as if to inquire whether Alec wanted to be told of the marriage. He said, 'Tell me about Judy first.'

She nodded, and looked down at her hands, tracing the knots in the pine table-top. 'She was a star, was Judy. We were thick as thieves as girls, and I mean thieves. What we didn't get up to! A little innocent-looking thing, she was. Butter wouldn't melt in her mouth. Me, people always mistrusted from the start; all knees and elbows and a face like a horse. But Judy in her neat frocks and ankle-socks could get away with anything. And she knew it. Her father was the Baker of Baker's Biscuits, did you know that? Pots of money. Ted Baker—he was a queer fish. And not *too* keen on his daughter spending so much time with that tomboy Heather Miller, though you'd have thought Millers and Bakers would go well together, wouldn't you? We did; thought our names a great joke.

'I was always getting the blame for everything. I lost count of the times Judy was forbidden to see me any more. She always got round them before long. He must have had something about him, Ted Baker, to run a successful business and make all that money, but he really didn't know much about kids. We ran rings round him. Judy had a sister, Isobel, very prim, always telling tales to her mum and dad; we called her Pissybel. But though she tried to curry favour with her father, it was Judy he was obsessed by, as though she both bewitched him and infuriated him at the same time. Poor Isobel! For all her toadying, she was out in the cold.'

She thought a moment. 'Judy wasn't nasty as a child; but she was wild,' she said judicially, as if it was important to her to set the record perfectly straight. 'Wait,' she said suddenly, starting up, 'I've got some pictures. Stay there!'

Alec found himself left alone. The perpetual noise of aircraft was a muted drone. The cat, on the range, whickered in its sleep and stretched a paw out.

'Here we are.' The photo album was gaudy and battered, and decorated with flowers and ban-the-bomb signs. Memories of Dansettes and scandals and waif-like models in Mary Quant smocks drifted to the surface of Alec's mind like flotsam.

Heather, glancing up as she flipped through the pages, said acutely, 'It's all ancient history, so just don't die laughing at what terrible frights we made ourselves look. You looked no better in your own day, I can assure you. Here: this is us on a school outing to London. Trafalgar Square.'

A dozen girls, demurely lined up in front of one of Landseer's lions, with a woman in long dark habit and close-fitting white coif. 'Judy and I went to a convent school, as you see.'

Alec smiled, having no illusions about convent schools. 'Which one's Judy?' he asked.

'In the Alice band, looking as if butter wouldn't melt in her mouth.' Heather's short-nailed finger dabbed at the black-and-white photograph.

'And you?'

'I was taking the photo; with my Brownie. This one's got us both on,' she said, turning the page.

Alec spotted the young Heather at once, a tall girl outgrowing her gymslip in the middle of the group in front of Westminster Abbey.

'Bursting out all over,' she agreed ruefully. 'I was thirteen then; or fourteen, maybe, I don't remember. And Judy, of course. Sister Beatrice was in the Abbey at the time, I think.'

Judy stood precociously posed next to her friend: shoulder raised, head turned sideways, one strap of her gymslip slid down to the elbow, skirt hitched up at one side: vamping. Alec smiled, but in truth there was something sad and a little disturbing about the pert little face pouting out of the picture, something too close to the uniformed callgirl, and Alec had the impression that Judy, unlike Heather, and despite the gymslips and knee-socks, had already at thirteen left girlhood behind.

'We gave Sister Beatrice the slip later; when we were supposed to be in the National Gallery we trekked round Soho. It was just a name to me, but Judy had looked it all up on the map. Beak Street, Frith Street, Greek Street, Wheeler's, the French, Shaftesbury Avenue, Piccadilly Circus, she wanted to see it all. We walked our little legs off. In fact, we were virtually running, because we wanted to see it all and get back to St James's Park for lunch. We didn't want to miss out on anything. And Judy, until she'd been whistled at by an Italian ponce in Dean Street she considered the day wasted.'

Alec turned the pages fascinated. Yellowed newspaper cuttings chronicled the major events of the time, as seen through teenage eyes: the Rolling Stones' drug trial, the Little Red Book and the Oz schoolkids' issue.

'We went up to Heathrow,' Heather said, looking over Alec's shoulder at a clip about the Stones' US tour. 'Judy wanted to see these men in the flesh. What we didn't know about Mars bars wasn't worth knowing.'

Alec smiled, remembering; and then Heather Campbell wiped his smile away.

'Ted Baker beat her for that,' Heather said bluntly. 'And he beat her again after we went to one of their concerts. And again for going to the Isle of Wight pop festival.'

'I see.'

'She showed me the marks the first two times,' Heather

said. 'The first time he just hit her with his hand. When we came back from the Stones' concert he used something else. There was a silly souvenir hanging up on the wall in their kitchen—you've seen the sort of thing, perhaps. A length of wood, with a picture painted on of a schoolboy bending over. "Board of Correction" it had written on it, and Minehead, where someone had bought it. I'd seen it every time I went to their house. Ted Baker beat Judy with that.'

'Yes,' Alec said again, 'I see.'

'You see,' she explained, 'we did what every girl did at a pop concert, and threw things at the stage. Handkerchiefs; notes; underwear. It wasn't exactly spontaneous: it was part of the reason you went; the delight of hysteria. Her dad was waiting for us when we got in; she had no time to go upstairs. He grabbed her and threw her over his knee to beat her. That was how he found out she was wearing nothing under her skirt: she'd thrown her knickers on to the stage at the concert. Actually, I remember they travelled about five rows and fell on the head of a boy with red hair who looked most disgruntled. So Ted took the Board of Correction off the wall and beat her with that, for disobedience in going to the concert, and for being a slut. On her naked bottom. And when she bit his hand he beat her some more. I think he got a taste for it after that,' she said flatly. 'Judy stopped showing me the marks and I decided she was too ashamed of having a father who got pleasure from . . . from doing that. He was a big man; she couldn't resist.' She shivered. 'To tell the truth, I thought he was going to launch into me in exactly the same way. I almost wet myself waiting for it.

'It made her more rebellious, not less, of course. She'd do things despite the risk, knowing he would beat her when he found out, but she had to do it none the less, to defy him, to show he hadn't beaten her *spirit*. When I went to their house—not often, after that, but sometimes they would let her invite me—I couldn't keep my eyes off that damned piece of wood with the silly writing on it. His wife never stopped him.'

'I'm sorry.'

'Yes; not much one say say, is there? He never beat
Isobel. It never occurred to me to wonder about it then,
but now I . . .'

The telephone rang then, and Heather moved across to
answer it. Alec flicked through the pages of the photograph
album; the pictures were interspersed with pressed flowers,
handwritten poems, a menu from a Chinese restaurant.
Then came a couple more pages of snapshots of mountains
and seaside. In one a tent was pitched beside a tarn; Judy
in shorts and halter top sat cross-legged in front of it, smiling. It was difficult to tell her age: her small neat face was
still that of a girl of twelve. She had her arm round a
longhaired but unhappy-looking boy of eighteen or nineteen, but he didn't figure in any of the other shots. Heather
herself was in only one, which presumably Judy had offered
to take; a coltish young woman in a generously-cut bikini,
knee-high in the sea, with more mountains behind.

Heather came back as Alec turned the page. The last
picture in the book was of Judy too, also in the sea.

'She wanted to see if the chemists would print that one;
they were always supposed to refuse to do the ones that were
indecent.' Alec smiled dutifully. The picture was poorly
focused, and the figure rather small and faraway, and he
couldn't help thinking that the chemists would have had to
be very sharp-eyed and determined to spot the vague blur
of pubic hair which showed Judy was naked. 'We took a
holiday together in Arran; just before Judy went up to
Keele. 1973. It was a wonderful summer. The end of an
era.'

No more photos, Alec thought. The end of a friendship?

'Who was the boy?' He showed Heather the earlier
picture.

'I don't remember. Someone we met. "Shall we got into
so-and-so and find ourselves a couple of fellas?" we used to
say. It usually meant that she found one, and I was left to
tag along.'

'You were sure enough of yourself that you didn't need

to prove anything,' Alec said courteously. He turned back, staring at the close-up of Judy Baker with the boy she had picked up on holiday. Her features were small and lively, and she had the same delicate frame that Kate Randall had. Indeed, they had the same air of intense energy within a fragile compass, although facially they were very different, and Judy's hair was short and tightly curled and looked dark. Alec tried to espy in her grinning face signs of her unhappy home and traumatic emotional history, and fancied there was a certain forced air to her gaiety.

Heather Campbell took the photo album from him and glanced at it. 'She hasn't changed much.'

'I've never met her,' he said with heavy irony.

She began to turn the pages absently as if they didn't have much to do with her. 'Sharp, aren't you?' she said, unsmiling.

'Judy's family were Catholics?' Alec mused.

Heather took the two empty mugs and clattered them into the sink. 'Yes; hers and mine both. Of course, that meant nothing to us. It was just like saying they were white, or well-off. It wasn't till we left school that we found that the rest of the world weren't necessarily; and of course we had always been used to the fact that even within our own families there were those who didn't believe, as well as those who did. But don't hold Ted Baker against the Catholics, Inspector.'

'Did you? Believe?'

Heather looked up. 'No; not then.'

'And now?'

The other woman shrugged, as if embarrassed to admit it. 'Maybe I always had underneath. Which is probably why I settled down so easily once I'd got it out of my system. I'm sorry to sound so upright and moral; Tim would laugh his head off if he heard me. Most of our friends think I'm bats anyway. But by about the time we went on that holiday I made my mind up that there were more important things to life than purple hearts, free love and hard rock. In fact, I was jolly glad that I'd been a timid little thing—don't laugh—when I was younger, and never gone too far overboard, because that sort of thing's not always easy to go back from. Remembering, one thinks of it as all super and good fun. Sometimes it was; sometimes it was all just a bit too desperate for comfort. I saw Judy; that was all the warning I needed.

'I'm lucky: I've had a bloody happy life, by and large. Judy made an unfortunate marriage, she was miserable for a while, but she's come through it, and in the last couple of years we've teamed up again. It's been good. My apologies for wittering on like this, and will you stay for lunch?'

Alec shook his head. He was not here for mateyness. Instead, he broached the subject of Judy's marriage.

Heather moved to a worktop and began to assemble the ingredients for sandwiches. 'She married a bit of a drip called Les when she was twenty-two,' she said, taking cheese from the refrigerator 'We'd always been going to be each other's bridesmaids, you know the sort of thing. Well, I actually was hers—towering over the bride and groom, poor lambs—but by the time Tim and I got round to it Judy's marriage wasn't so happy, it seemed a bit tactless to ask her to do for me, so we settled for Tim's nieces instead all tricked out in Laura Ashley . . . All right, I'm coming back to the point. Well, this Les was some sort of lecturer at Keele. Judy wasn't stupid; by no means. She was a clever little thing; and whatever else she got up to at Keele, she won a first class degree, and stayed on to do a PhD; but she got married instead.'

'PhD in what?' Alec interjected.

'Sociology, economics . . . something typically nineteen-seventies. Anyway. It was the usual boring story of sit-ins, arguments over student representation on various governing bodies, et cetera, et cetera. Les was at the forefront of the troops, so far as I could gather, waving a banner bearing a strange device and throwing himself into the breach with thoughtless heroism . . . Wore fatigues à la Castro but couldn't afford the cigars. Showed he was on the side of youth and against the establishment by screwing spotty

girls from Purley and New Malden who thought he was
Lord Byron in a Zapata moustache. Have you read a book
called *The History Man*?'

'Mm.'

'Howard Kirk, but without the charm, that was Les.
Calls himself Miles now, and has his beady eyes on
Parliament, Tim says.' She sawed vigorously at the completed sandwiches and apologized for her forthrightness.
'Tim's friends compete to wind me up in the hope that
one day I'll say something irreparably slanderous and be
clapped in the Tower.

'Judy was too bright not to see through him; and being
her, it was inevitable that in the end she would leave him.
When she did, she found she was pregnant with Thomas.
She went downhill fast after she left Les,' Heather said,
piling the sandwiches on a plate and sitting down opposite
Alec again. 'Long before she came here she was a drunk,
and a . . . a slut. I don't know what the right word is these
days. She'd tried most things. She was a drunk because
she'd always been too sensible to use drugs, and after all,
everyone drinks, don't they?—so she could tell herself it
wasn't doing her any harm, until she got so far in that she
was an alcoholic, and then she couldn't stop.

'There had been men, of course. Initially I think she
had proper relationships; one, at least, which might have
developed into something long term—at least, that was
how she remembered it. But the relationships got shorter
and shorter, and I suppose Judy came to seem less attractive. I mean, the sort of men who might have done her some
good steer clear of women who drink. And of course, there
was Trooper, and I suppose men fight shy of taking on that
sort of burden.'

'Trooper?'

'Thomas. Judy's boy.'

'I did wonder,' Alec suggested, 'how Judy managed to
keep Thomas.'

Heather said, 'By lying and cheating and deceiving; and
I helped her. Trooper was the one fixed point in Judy's life.

I honestly think she would have killed anyone who tried to take him away. Guilt over Trooper ate her up; but it was never quite strong enough to lift her out of the life into which she was sinking. Anyway, the men became more frequent, because they lasted shorter and shorter times; and soon they weren't . . . they weren't men like you and Tim, Inspector. They were men who knocked her about; stole her money, brought other women to the house. One of them beat her unconscious because she wouldn't become a whore: he wanted to live off her earnings. That was the first time she tried to kill herself. She swallowed a bottle of pills.'

'Yet Thomas was left with her?' Alec asked, shocked.

'The Social Services never knew.'

'They must have done. When she was admitted to hospital . . .'

'She wasn't.'

'But . . .'

Heather drew in a long, slow breath. 'Thomas had a phone number to ring. Judy made him learn it, and it was tacked above the phone, when they had one. He came home from school—he was five, poor little sod—and found his mummy lying on the floor snoring. He couldn't wake her. So he did what his mummy had told him to do if ever there was real trouble, and rang that number. It was ours.'

Alec nodded. Outside, a world away, he could faintly hear one of the dogs barking, but Heather Campbell seemed not to notice the sound.

'We weren't living here then; Tim was just a middle-ranker, commuting from Norbury, I had a part-time job at Battersea. Thank God, it was my afternoon off when Thomas rang.

'I went over and Thomas let me in. I'm not a great one for kids as you may have gathered, but I tell you, Inspector, my heart went out to the little bugger. He'd been alone for an hour and a half there, with Judy lying on the floor. He'd been physically sick with terror, but he'd done what he'd promised, he'd rung me and then waited trustingly for me

to arrive. Before that he was Thomas; after, he was
Trooper. He'd earned the name.

'As it happened, I had all I needed in the car. I put a
tube down Judy's throat and washed out her stomach. I
shudder now at the risk I took, but the procedure's much
the same for dogs as it is for humans.' She smiled sourly.
'Ever done it?'

'I've seen it done.'

'Well, then. No need to say more.'

'But you just kept quiet about it? No doctor? No social
worker? For Judy, yes, but what about Thomas?'

'Thomas was all she lived for. All!'

'Yet she'd been willing to let him find her body!' Alec
protested.

'I know; I know.' Heather Campbell sighed. 'I was young
and naïve. Instead of middle-aged and naïve like I am now,'
she added with a flicker of her old form. 'Judy persuaded
me it was right; and I persuaded myself. And I persuaded
Tim. It wasn't quite so straightforward, anyway, because
by that time she'd had her twenty-fifth birthday, and that's
when she began to have access to the trust money.'

'Ah!'

Heather Campbell shook her head at Alec's knowing
look. 'In the end that money was her salvation,' she said
quietly. 'Oh, not at first; not all at once. At first she didn't
even bother to move out of the squalid pigsty she was living
in. Well, Tim and I persuaded her that instead of being a
drunk in one room in Brixton she might as well be a drunk
in three rooms in Cheam. Believe me, that was an improve-
ment. Judy didn't move into luxury; she had a starter home
on a new estate. Of course, money meant she could drink
more, and she did. But there was the beginning of a motive
for her to change, if she wanted to, because it was the
sort of place where she would be noticed if she fell over in
Sainsbury's.'

'How much was it?' he wondered. 'The legacy.'

'I never knew. Any more than I know how much is left.
She wasn't rich, you understand, but provided for. She was

glad of it; not just for what it would buy, but because it . . . sort of redeemed her father for her. I think he left almost all of it in trust for Judy, with just a few thousand for Isobel. Guilt offering, I suppose; I think he really did love her, in his way. After that, Judy began to use his name, and call herself Mrs Baker. "Mrs" as a sort of defence mechanism. She was glad too not to be beholden any more to Miles. Her mother was dead by then; and Donald and Isobel had never lifted a finger for her.'

'And Thomas?'

'And Thomas could go to a better school; and he wasn't at risk as he walked home; and he could grow up with the idea that you pay for things in shops, not steal them. And if the worst came to the worst, we weren't far away.'

'Your telephone number was still pinned up on the wall?'

She smiled faintly. 'That's about it.'

'But it didn't work.'

'It was a start.' She pushed the empty plate away from her.

'So what did happen?'

She got to her feet, and took the plate over to the sink. 'Nothing, unfortunately; which meant she had time—too much time—to look about her and see what she was doing. See how empty her life was. She was on a new estate, she knew no one—and anyway everybody else was out all day at work—and Thomas was safely at school. There was nothing to do but drink and get depressed, and drink to counter the depression. Hence suicide attempt number two. This time it was to be the gas. Being natural gas I don't suppose it would have killed her anyway, but she didn't know that, poor darling. Everything was arranged so that a neighbour would find her before Thomas got in from school. She put a cushion on the floor, shut all the doors and windows, turned on the gas hob.'

'What happened?'

Heather giggled a little nervously. 'You're not going to believe this,' she warned. 'But . . . the doorbell rang. You can't ignore something like that, can you?'

'And?'

'It was the man come to read the meter. True! I said you wouldn't believe it. It's true. Judy kicked the cushion out of sight, but the man smelt the gas, of course, thought there must be a leak and turned it off at the main and sealed it so she couldn't turn it back on. She rang me; we'd put an answerphone in by then, just in case; she left a message in which you couldn't tell whether she was laughing or crying. It appealed to her sense of humour. I went over that evening, of course.'

'Where was Wetherby at this time?'

'Not on the scene. No one was, so far as I could make out, not in that sense. She'd pick up men in pubs from time to time; but they don't do things quite that way in Cheam; she was afraid to take them home because of Trooper, and perhaps Cheam's short of back alleys. That was what she had been down to, you see, back alleys and back seats of cars.'

She looked at him keenly. 'I'm boring you, aren't I?'

'Hardly.'

'All this can't really be important, can it?'

'I can't discount it. Tell me more about Judy.'

'There isn't much more. Tim by then, bless him, was raking in enough of the stuff to buy this place, so that I could indulge my silly whims and keep off the streets. The two cottages came with it, let, of course; but I knew one of the tenants was not long for this world, and Tim knew I wanted Judy to have it. There was only one way if Judy was going to survive, and that was for her to crack the drink completely. I bullied her into it. For Thomas's sake, I said. No booze. No more men, not in that way. I was as nasty as I could be,' she said, 'playing on every nerve. Did she want Trooper to grow up ashamed of his mum? Did she want him to have to face other kids at school who said his mum was a dipso and a slag? I laid it on about what Tim and I had done—which was little enough, God help me—and was this how she was going to repay us? I kept at her until I'd got her in tears, poor love, and then I made her put that grotty starter-home on the market, and Tim hired a van and took it up there, and we moved all her stuff. We didn't quite drug her and drive her senseless down here, but pretty near.

'Since then,' she said, 'things have been different. I really believed—and Judy believed, too—that the past could be put behind her. She had bouts, of depression, or when she hit the bottle, but this last year . . .' She shook her head, as if it had been naïve to believe in happy endings.

'Until the night Kate Randall died.'

'Yes.'

'Your telephone number was still pinned up on the wall in her cottage. You were still the person she ran to.'

'Yes,' she mouthed.

After a while, Alec asked, 'Where is she now?'

Heather Campbell gave him the name of the psychiatric hospital; he made a note of the ward.

It seemed this time Heather Campbell hadn't been able to cope; maybe her resilience was worn down; maybe the involvement of Kate Randall's death put the whole business on a different plane. Judy for her part remained sunk in depression, not eating, bursting out in violence, neglecting her appearance.

When she hit Trooper, Heather's husband insisted that this time they had to go for help. The GP visited, and within the day Judy Baker was compulsorily admitted to the psychiatric hospital.

Mrs Campbell shook her head helplessly. 'I've never seen her like . . . I thought I knew everything, Inspector, about what happens when she . . .'

'She'll get treatment,' Alec reassured. 'You probably should have done it long ago. It's very rarely forever, these days.'

Mrs Campbell nodded, and her own fingers were weaving nervous cats'-cradles. 'I'd never seen her like . . . perhaps that's the problem; I never really have seen her, not for days on end . . . we just rushed in, Tim and I, doing our rescuing. With no concept what it was like for her day after day. She wouldn't move, she hardly spoke, she didn't eat . . . All I knew was it was beyond anything a few kind

words and a hot meal could cure. Kate Randall's death . . .
Inspector, I found I was even wondering whether Judy
couldn't somehow have done it . . . killed her, I mean.
That's a horrible . . . you don't know what a horrible thing
that is to have to think! Kate's death has tipped her over
the edge. Trooper . . .'

'Yes, what's happened to Trooper?' Alec asked.

'We've . . . I took him to his grandfather's yesterday. I'd
have kept him here, but I'm no good with kids . . . And
Daniel Wetherby dotes on the kid, whatever he thinks of
Judy, and Carro will see him right . . .'

'I'll go and see Judy when the doctor reckons she's up to
it,' Alec said thoughtfully. 'I'm sure she's peripheral to
Kate Randall's death, no more. But—' suddenly his carefully guarded anger burst out—'I wish you'd had the
bloody sense to play straight with us from the start instead
of leading us up the garden path. If you'd—' He stopped
and shrugged with a rueful smile. He couldn't find it in him
to be angry with the woman opposite, whose diamond-
tipped accent contrasted with the head bowed over the table
and the work-stained hands folded submissively together
on the table-top before her strong body in its quilted jacket.

'So where was Judy, that night Kate Randall died?' he
asked.

She looked at him strangely. 'She went to see Dan. Didn't
you know?'

'Her father-in-law? I thought they didn't . . .'

'They don't. Well, to Dan Wetherby, no one's good
enough to be Thomas's mother; and Judy and Carro, of
course, are chalk and cheese: if Judy enters the room, Carro
walks out. But Judy's always been very careful to let
Thomas keep in contact with his father's side of the family.
In fact, I understood it was about Thomas that Dan rang
Judy and asked her to go over. At least,' she added, 'that's
how I understood it. If you've heard different, you're probably right, because Judy only mentioned it.'

'No,' Alec said, puzzled, 'no, I'm afraid that's news to
me.'

CHAPTER 20

Coming out of the washroom where she had been bathing her eyes and glancing out of the window by the stairs, Liz saw that the morning had brightened up. Voices wafted from the incident room, and they were happy voices: Sally Field and Johnson joking together, underoccupied while Nelson and Mr Stainton were out of the building. Liz was not in a mood to enjoy other people's light-heartedness. Thinking that they would have to invest in an office cat, for the kicking of, Liz clattered down the stairs and along the corridor to her room, grabbed her jacket, and two minutes later was letting herself into her car and opening the window to the sweet-smelling February sunlight.

There were daffodils in bud on the verges, and in sheltered corners one or two blooms were already opening yellow trumpets to the sun. Liz drove slowly, partly to savour the mild freshness of the day but also because she was none too sure just how she meant to proceed. In the end, she decided that there was definite hope of profit from a renewed attempt to rout out Judy Baker's next-door neighbour. Neighbours, after all, can observe a good deal, and elderly neighbours especially.

In the event there was no need to rout him out; he was in the garden when Liz drew her car up by the roadside, forking over his vegetable plot in the thin spring sunshine. Seeing her, he bent back to his work, and didn't lift his head until she had opened the garden gate and walked down the path to within a few yards of him.

'Excuse me.'

He straightened up, so far, it seemed, as old age and rheumatism would permit: a sparely built man with leathery face and watery blue eyes the irises of which were ringed with paleness. He wore corduroy trousers and heavy leather boots, and a tattered tweed jacket over two jerseys, and the expression on his childlike face was placid, so that Liz wondered whether he might be a little senile and her journey a waste of time. Disconcertingly, he said nothing but merely stood patiently waiting, so that Liz was obliged to play all her cards at the outset.

'I wanted to have a word about Judy Baker, who lives next door. I'm a police officer.'

'Oh, yer?'

'Yes. Mrs Baker from next door. I just wanted to ask one or two questions about her. You know?' God, Liz thought, I sound as if I'm the witless one.

Harry Weeding's faded blue eyes travelled slowly and happily over Liz's body. Bundled up as she was in boots and denim skirt and Fair Isle jersey, she might have been Venus rising from the waves for all the sense of being covered they afforded her. If he tells me I remind him of the way women used to look when he was a lad, Liz told herself, I swear I'll belt him.

To her incredulous exasperation he then turned back to his fork; but it seemed he only wanted to clean it, which he did at length with a piece of broken slate, before carrying it down the path along the side of the house and putting it away in a wooden shed. He nodded to Liz, where she stood trying to contain her impatience, and she followed him round to the back of the house, where there was a lean-to wooden porch.

The kitchen was small and warm. What she had seen of the corresponding room in Judy's cottage, peering through the window in the rain that day, had been the mirror-image of this, but modernized and tidied and made bright with fitted units and carpeting. Liz doubted whether this room had changed much since the cottages were built.

Harry Weeding picked his path around it with the negligent accuracy of long practice. There was clean newspaper on the quarry tiled floor, and looking round her, Liz realized the whole room was actually very clean, though it

seemed cramped and dark. A plain deal table occupied
most of one end of the room, with two bentwood chairs.
The other end of the room offered two armchairs, set at an
angle to the Rayburn which filled the chimney alcove, and
was the source of the sense of warmth and comfort which
Liz had noticed as soon as they came in. Simple cotton
curtains hung at the window, and a matching flounce round
the mantelpiece. A black kettle sat on the range, and Weeding, stumping over in stockinged feet, lifted the cover from
a hotplate and slid the kettle over.

He gestured to the chairs, and Liz sat in the one which
was obviously not his. She could see how the other was
placed within arm-reach of kettle, tea-caddy, matches,
tobacco-pouch and the riddling-arm of the range. The chair
was low, but comfortable. The kitchen smelt a little musty,
but in a clean way, which Liz thought might be the way
cottages had smelt fifty years ago.

'Cupper tea!' Weeding pronounced, and Liz, unsure
whether it was an offer or a statement, played safe with
'Thank you.' He moved sturdily though not fast. It was not
so much that he seemed weakened by age, as that he had
an economy and patience consistent with a very large number of years spent in the world, and no great desire to hurry
himself out of it.

He assembled everything within reach of his chair, and
then lowered himself into it and turned his translucent blue
eyes on Liz. She fancied his gaze was appreciative, but it
was shrewd too and by no means as vacant as she had first
believed. Even if she wished to deceive this old man, she
had little likelihood of succeeding.

'It's a bad do,' he said firmly.

'I'm sorry?'

The kettle began to sing, and Weeding stretched out a
hand and swung it over to pour water into the pot. 'This
murder, then, thass' what you're here about, I reckon? If
that ain't a bad do, I don't know what is!'

Liz nodded, smoothing her skirt absently over her knees.
A ragged tortoiseshell cat materialized from nowhere and

sprang easily into her lap, where it nosed and paddled for a while before flopping down for a snooze. Liz felt vaguely trapped, as if the cat were a trick Weeding had pulled on her unfairly.

'We're worried about Mrs Baker,' Liz said. 'She knew Kate Randall quite well, didn't she?'

Weeding shook his head reprovingly. 'You don't wanter be thinking Mrs Baker ain't done it,' he said.

'Well, I'm not sure we actually . . .'

'Fer whoy? 'Cos she ain't got many friends, thass' whoy, so she ain't abouter goo killing those she *has* got.'

'I'm afraid that isn't proof,' Liz muttered.

The old man laughed suddenly and joyously. Liz wondered again if he were a little cracked. 'No it ain't!' he exclaimed, as if Liz had made a telling point. 'No it ain't.' Disconcertingly, he leant forward. 'You are a police officer, then?' he asked with a keen gleam.

Liz was glad she did not have to try to deceive those shrewd pale eyes. 'Yes; I really am.'

'Lessee your doo-dah. Your card.' Liz brought out her warrant card and he scrutinized it, and nodded and handed it back. 'Cupper tea? Should be brewed by now, I reckon.'

It was. It was the colour of varnished oak. But by some black art, it tasted sharp and fine, and few cups of coffee had ever clarified Liz's mind so.

'Well then,' Weeding resumed after he had poured out and topped up the pot, 'I'll tell you for whoy liddle Judy ain't killed that gel.'

'Go on.'

'Judy, she went out that night. Night of the storm, weren't it? Now, Judy, she got herself a new car, see, and I hears her drive orf in it as I'm having my tea, and a mite later I'm fetching in a bucketer coal fer the stove and there she comes back, and the nipper with her, and a girl, a young girl, like, might be fifteen or sixteen, and she's been before. Going to babysit, see? So that's how I knows Judy's going out fer the evening.

'Yes, but that doesn't prove . . .'

'Yew just wait,' he reproved her sternly. 'I ain't done yet. So. 'Bout ten minutes later, Judy, she goes out. Now, she don't come back. Not by midnight; not by one, neither.'

'Were you awake?' Liz asked curiously.

'Not awake; nor not asleep neither.' Weeding looked at her sorrowfully, and then grinned. 'You'll understand! One day! Well. I'm just thinking as something's the matter, d'you see, and what's to be done? That babysitter girl, she did oughter be going home; but maybe Judy's asked her to stay the night, see? Then I hears a car, and I gets up and I looks out, and there's that big tank of a car of Mrs Campbell. Mrs Campbell, she owns the cottages, see. I live here, because I've always lived here; it's my home, like!' he said simply, as if the law of landlord and tenant had never been invented. 'But liddle Judy, she lives next door because she and Mrs Campbell, they're mates, see? So when I sees that car of Mrs Campbell's, I know something's up, and that gel, she's called Mrs Campbell.'

Liz listened patiently, in case the old man was going to say something more to the purpose. This all proved nothing. Indeed, as a means of demonstrating that Judy Baker could have been up on the common between eleven and two murdering Kate Randall it was hardly to be improved on.

Weeding caught the look of scepticism on her face, and leant forward again. 'I ain't done! You don' wanter be thinking people're fools, even if they is old enough to be your father twice over. Now, listen! Mrs Campbell's old car is in the lane; and I'm just deciding whether to go back to bed or go down and see what's what, when there comes another vehicle; and it's one of them trucks; and on the back of it, there's Judy's liddle car, see, plain as a pikestaff. And up comes the truck and stops, and down jumps Judy, and dashes indoors as if she'd been kicked in by fifty donkeys.'

It had been a hard lesson in curbing her impatience, but Liz was beginning to think it might have been worth it. She had no doubts about the old man's faculties now.

'Judy, she'd been over Uckfield way, see? Set off home, 'bout eleven, stopped for petrol, see, because she's low. Now she knows the garage, and she knows id'll still be open, but what she don't know is, since she been in there last, they've gone and put in new pumps. Before you can say knife, she's gone and poured ten gallons of diesel into her liddle car.'

Liz mentally tested Weeding's story against her sense of truth; it rang sweet as a bell.

''Course,' concluded Weeding, 'Judy, she starts up and drives off, like, on what's in the carburetter, because thass' petrol, ain't it? Then there's what's in the fuel pipe . . . so she's got as far as the middler nowhere before her liddle car conks out, ain't she. See?'

By the time Judy Baker had trudged back to the garage—and a car travels a long way in a few minutes—it was shuttered and dark. The storm was nearing its height then, and there was little traffic on the roads—next to none on the short cut Judy was using which skirted the towns, twisting and diving in tree-beetled gulleys. Liz had enough imagination to picture a little of Judy Baker's desperation, when she found herself in a moment no longer a woman in charge of her immediate destiny, with the means of reaching home in a few minutes, but one reduced to human scale, alone on a wild night, her motor-car inanimate and useless, with only her two legs for transport, and her only other resources the contents of her handbag and the car's glove compartment.

Judy had set out to walk to the next village in the hope of finding a telephone-box. She decided early on that she could not risk flagging down a car, even if one were to pass: on such a night, and in such a spot, the mildest-looking of men might feel tempted to try their hand. Liz experienced a fleeting scorn as this part of the tale was related; but she had to admit that most people would judge Judy prudent, and nobody needed extra corpses at the moment. It was getting on for half past eleven by the time Judy found a telephone and had rung the RAC. An hour later a recovery truck appeared, and just after one Judy was running up the cottage path to put her arms round a stolid but pale-faced Trooper and apologize to a tearful Sophy, whom Mrs Campbell was just bundling into her coat preparatory to driving her back to her parents' house.

Weeding poured himself a second cup of tea, holding the pot aloft interrogatively. Liz shook her head. It was plain that the only source for such a circumstantial account of what had happened must have been Judy herself; but it *was* circumstantial, and easily checked from the RAC's call-out records and the till receipts of the garage where Judy had bought the diesel. The buying of the diesel was the key time: Liz was mindful that Ransome had estimated the time of death at later than eleven so that Judy could not have killed Kate Randall without some hypothesis involving the faking of the alibi. Liz was disinclined to construct fantastic explanations of the murder when there were still so many straightforward possibilities unexplored.

She looked up, and realized from Weeding's expression that she must have been frowning.

'See,' Weeding explained gently, 'when yer mates come and tell liddle Judy her friend's been killed, and ask Judy ter goo back ter the police station with them, she'd already had a hard night. That was the last straw, see.'

Liz nodded. In the face of this pacific old man's gentleness it was difficult to see police methods in quite the light she normally did. 'You saw her after she got back—from the police station, I mean?'

Weeding shook his head. 'All I've told you, Judy told me after breakfast. See, when I saw she was up, I dropped round, like. Garridge, they called to fix her car; then your mate turns up, don't he? Judy came back an' put the nipper straight in the car and they took off in it. Coulder gone anywhere, couldn't they? Far's I know, they ain't been back.'

Liz sighed, and levered herself out of the armchair with reluctance. The cat jumped down huffily, and even as Liz was fishing in her bag for a pen, sprang up and took her place, curling economically into the warm dent left by Liz's bottom.

'If Judy comes back,' Liz said, 'would you ring me, please? This is the number.'

'Ain't got no telephone,' Weeding replied with maddening equanimity.

'We want to be sure she's safe. Look, there's a phone in the village. Can't you walk down there? I'd appreciate it, and you'd be doing Judy a kindness too.' Liz smiled winningly as she pushed the piece of paper with the telephone number across the table; but it occurred to her that he didn't seem to need much guidance where kindnesses were concerned. So long as they were at one on where his duty lay!

Weeding creaked to his feet and leaned out to watch her from the porch as she walked back up the garden path. At the gate she sketched a wave, and he nodded.

Well, she told herself as she drove through the somnolent village and forked left by the chapel, taking the road which passed the Campbells' farm, that's cleared that up. I'm surprised he doesn't know where Judy is, though. If she's at the Campbells' . . .

'Shit!'

She had just recalled the words Weeding had used when he described Judy and her son driving away after her interview with Nelson. 'Coulder gone anywhere, couldn't they?' he had said.

The old blighter! Damn his innocent, truthful blue eyes! He knew all the time! No wonder he watched me walk up his garden path with such a seraphic smile!

She instinctively slowed as she passed the farm, and looked up the drive. A parked car caught her eye, and she stopped and reversed and turned in. The car was Mr Stainton's. It was about time they compared notes.

'Here!'

Liz took the plate, and the paper-napkin-wrapped cutlery, and set them before her happily. Mr Stainton was treating her as if this morning's reprimand was done and dusted, and she was naturally a woman who enjoys her food. She had long ago realized that there are more sorts of beauty than fashion-plate skinniness. Plenty of men found her generous figure enticing, and having to worry about diets the whole time would have been a bore. Today she felt she had earned her lunch, but she was not to be allowed to get at it yet awhile.

Alec said, taking his seat and unwrapping his cutlery, 'You'd better tell me what you learnt from the old man.'

When she had done so he sat thoughtfully for a while. Liz was glad of the opportunity to stop talking and start eating before her pie got too cold; he had almost finished, and she had barely started, and for a while she got her head down and made serious inroads into her meal.

'First, the story: it seems to fit together pretty well. Granting that there could easily have been some collusion between Heather Campbell and your Mr Weeding, nevertheless it sounds plausible.'

Liz nodded, and swallowed. 'I thought so. So far as Weeding's personal involvement is concerned, I'd say he was telling the plain truth. It's the rest of it which is open to question, isn't it? Until we talk to Judy Baker, it's only hearsay.'

'We can get on to the RAC and have them check their records,' Alec reminded her. 'Anyway, both Mrs Campbell and old Weeding have a pretty strong instinct to protect Judy,' he mused. 'But would it go as far as conniving in covering up a murder?' He pushed his plate aside and cupped his hands round the glass of his drink. Liz munched on. 'We've no motive for Judy,' he continued; 'but on the other hand we've no way of telling what sort of relationship theirs was—again, until we actually talk to her. We know she could be violent enough on occasion.'

'Talking to her's going to be pretty difficult, isn't it, sir?' Liz remarked gloomily.

'I don't know. I don't know how volatile her mental

condition is; and how much it will affect her capacity to undergo a rational interview.'

'Volatile enough,' Liz pondered, 'to make her kill?'

'Ah! I doubt it, from what little I understand of these things. Look, we'll follow both lines. Go over and see Daniel Wetherby and try and establish just what time Judy was there that night, and put Johnson or Field on to getting hold of the RAC's record of the call-out; and in the meantime I'll speak to whoever's looking after Judy's case at the hospital and see if she'd be in any condition to see one of us.' He paused doubtfully. 'That probably ought to be you again, Liz.' The unspoken awareness of Nelson's unsuitability hovered between them; but it was not a task Alec would want to allocate to one of the DCs. 'I hope,' he said, 'we'll then be able to rule Judy Baker out of the picture altogether.'

Liz put her knife and fork together, and drained her glass. She held it up interrogatively. 'Another, sir? Something soft?'

While she was at the bar, Alec considered just who was left once Judy Baker was eliminated as a suspect. It was a pity Charlie Poole could not be made to look much like a murderer: he had been one of the few people to know Kate with any degree of intimacy—but he had fled the scene when things first got hot for Kate.

The other lead which had looked promising until followed up was Andrew Mackenzie's suspicious omission to mention that he had been with Kate Randall the night she died. Johnson, despatched to locate the record of Mackenzie's initial interview, came back long-faced. The local bobby who had called at the Mackenzies' house had never in fact interviewed Andrew Mackenzie at all. Alec had not remembered Mackenzie mentioning the CAMEX meeting because he never had mentioned it—or anything else. Arriving home from the meeting when the storm was at its height, Andrew Mackenzie had found a heavy conifer in a stone tub blown over across his driveway. Unable to get his car into the garage, he had climbed out and gone to

move the fallen tree. Within the hour Andrew was occupy-
ing a bed in Crawley Hospital, a very frightened man,
recovering from a minor heart attack.

Alec sent Johnson to see Mackenzie, recuperating at
home. All he could confirm was that he had dropped Kate
Randall near her flat on the night of the storm, at about
ten past ten. Asked about her state of mind, he said she
had been very quiet, and seemed tired. Things, Mackenzie
said vaguely, had not been going very well for CAMEX.
She had not mentioned any letter; nor any plan to go out
again after Mackenzie left her.

Alec watched Liz Pink walk carefully back from the bar,
a full glass in each hand, and decided that in a way it was
comforting to think that they were steadily eliminating the
CAMEX connection; but when you had said that, you had
said everything, for it left the field wide open. If Kate's death
was one of those depressing crimes of opportunity which
speak so profoundly of human sinfulness—the abduction of
young children who happen to be walking along an empty
road, the mugging of pensioners in the shadows between
streetlights, the rape of women whose cars have broken down
at the roadside—then the chances of ever finding her killer
were thin. Alec looked that fact squarely in the face, and
accepted it. In three or four weeks' time when the inquiry
ground to a halt for lack of clues, personnel would begin to
be reassigned, resources slimmed down, telephones be dis-
connected, and he himself forced to concentrate his efforts on
crimes more likely of solution. Kate Randall's murder file
would not be closed, but it would be reduced to a pile of dead
bones waiting for the miracle of a fortuitous clue to breathe
life into them once more.

'I don't know what you think of this idea, sir,' Liz said,
putting their fresh drinks down and sliding back into her
seat, 'but I was just wondering: if Judy Baker isn't tied up
in this case as the killer, what about the possibility that she
was meant for the victim?'

Alec smiled. 'I was wondering when you would get
there.'

Understanding dawned in Liz's face. 'That's why you were more interested in finding where Judy was than in actually going to see her?'

He nodded. Ever since he learnt that the Renault was Judy Baker's, lent first occasionally and then on long-term loan to Kate Randall, Alec had known that there was a possibility that the wrong woman had been killed.

They finished their drinks in silence, Liz facing up to, and Alec reassessing, the implications of this new avenue. If the two women were together . . . or if the killer knew his victim only from a photograph, or from a distance . . . In the dark, and in Judy's car: would not Kate Randall look very like Judy Baker to a waiting observer? Mentally Alec had more than once held their snapshots side by side. Kate had had her long hair tucked up under a woolly hat: in the dark the effect would be not unlike Judy Baker's close curls; and the slight figure, the narrow shoulders were very similar. Of course when Kate Randall's body was found, the possibility of mistaken identity did not at first seem very likely because it was Kate whom they knew to have enemies; but they had learnt a good deal about Judy Baker since then—and who knew what enemies she might have acquired over the years?

Assume that the killer had tracked Judy's car unaware that she had lent it to someone else; had followed it to the common and struck down the driver with a stump of wood while she squatted, preoccupied; before she could turn, or cry out; and he had done so, ruthlessly, while the wind howled in protest at his brutal act. But then assume he had realized his mistake! Perhaps the moon had revealed the dying girl's staring features, or maybe it was the coil of fair hair dislodged from its pins by the violence of the blow that glinted in the moonlight; so he had muddied the waters by disordering more of the clothing. And after that?

Maybe Judy herself had realized, as soon as she heard of the murder, that she herself was the intended victim. No wonder she had run and hid—and no wonder the knowledge had tipped her out of her precarious balance and into mental

instability! If that was the case, talking to her became even
more desperately urgent than it had been before.

There was one further thought which Alec strove to thrust
from his mind. That evening, deliberately putting specu-
lation behind him, he settled down in a chair with *The New
Men* by way of clearing the mental palate and for two hours
succeeded in becoming absorbed into Snow's apolaustic
prose. But when he got up to walk round the flat putting
off the lights his mind insisted on nagging again at a further
hypothesis, like a tune which is stuck on the brain.

It stemmed from the same argument. If Judy Baker was
meant to be the victim of the killing, who most obviously
stood to gain from her death? Who would, in the absence
of special arrangements to the contrary, come in for her
substantial estate? Whose upward career was hampered by
the presence of a discarded, mentally unstable wife? And
who, just by coincidence, drove a white Ford Sierra?

Miles Wetherby.

CHAPTER 21

Alec sent Nelson and DC Johnson up to talk to Wetherby.
He was aware that if he went himself the antipathy between
them would affect the outcome of the meeting, and though
he was tempted to try his manipulative skills accordingly,
a moment's thought decided him that he could not risk
coming out the loser. Nelson was a better choice: phleg-
matic, unimpressed by status or affectation, and with a
tendency to rudeness which might just be what was
required to needle a budding politician. Moreover, sending
Nelson was a declaration of his continued trust in him. In
any event, Alec himself had squandered time on Heather
Campbell, and the price was evident in the mountain of
paperwork awaiting his attention in the office.

Sally Field was still taking the occasional call from members of the public, but none had been to any purpose: Paul Russell's sighting of a pale-coloured Ford remained the only clue to the way the murderer might have approached or left the scene. Sally had dutifully printed out details of all pale-coloured Ford Sierras registered in the area, and found herself all but buried under the avalanche of computer listing paper which resulted; and who was to say that it was a local car anyway? Liz set her to sift through it, and tried not to envy Nelson his task.

Wetherby had left Keele University the year after Judy left him. Somewhere in the intervening years Les Wetherby, left-wing sociology lecturer, had become Miles Wetherby, Labour councillor and parliamentary aspirant. Nelson showed Alec the address he had found for him: in Wandsworth, South London. It could be less than an hour's drive from South London to the common on a stormy January night which had swept the streets clear of traffic.

Alec glanced at the address. 'Mind how you go,' he warned. 'Don't be needled. Don't force a confrontation. Bend over backwards to be polite and grateful for his help.'

Nelson nodded curtly. He had been a policeman longer than Alec had. It was frustrating not to be able to take his resentments out on senior colleagues, but he knew better than to try to take them out on such as Miles Wetherby. Some men have 'trouble' written on their dossiers before ever you meet them. Wetherby was one.

'Right, Sergeant.' Miles Wetherby nodded, his eyes smiling with vulpine amiability, handing back Nelson's warrant card. 'You'd better begin. By the way, who's your senior officer on this case?'

'Chief Superintendent Blackett, sir,' Nelson replied helpfully.

'Blackett . . .' Wetherby repeated, writing the name in a small notebook with a gold propelling pencil. 'It's as well to know, just in case . . . Not Mr, what's his name, Stainton?'

'Chief Inspector Stainton's my immediate boss, yes, sir. I thought you meant the head of—'

'Stainton,' Wetherby said slowly, writing that down too. Nelson licked his lips. So Wetherby intended to play rough, and was already giving notice of his intention to complain if Nelson overstepped the mark. Johnson sat to one side, eyes prudently lowered, his notebook open. Wetherby reached into a drawer and placed a Sony Professional on the desk. The little red light on the microphone blinked complicitly as Wetherby switched it on. He smiled the smile of a man for whom policemen hold no terrors. Nelson had spoken to a mate at the local nick. Wetherby was on the Police Committee of the local force. It transpired that it was every policeman's dearest wish to be able to stop him for speeding and find him drunk into the bargain. He made a profession of championing the right of the man in the street to be free of police intimidation and brutality and kept a copy of the Police and Criminal Evidence Act by the mobile phone in his car.

Nelson began obliquely: they had hoped to learn something of Kate Randall from Judy, who was her friend, but Judy was unwell; he apologized for troubling Wetherby, knowing he and Judy were separated, but had Judy spoken to him of Kate?

Wetherby weighed each question as if to decide whether or not to answer, but was blandly cooperative. Nelson, listening with respectful mien to the replies, decided he had caught Wetherby just in time. The man was as yet still on the political foothills and as such not yet fully accomplished at evasion. Nelson began to insert supplementary questions into his main line of inquiry, and a picture began to emerge.

It had never been possible that Miles Wetherby's marriage to Judy would endure. Wetherby required a wife who could fulfil a very definite role. He spoke of Judy's need for her own career; of feminine independence; of the tyranny of the Judaeo-Christian marriage ethic.

Bullshit.

What you want, Nelson thought, is a little wifey who

makes a career out of supporting *you*. You want a woman who will entertain the right people, accompany you to the right functions, exemplify the right outlook, sleep with the right colleagues. A rising politician, like a barrister aspiring to a judgeship or an army officer looking for a battalion or a priest seeking a deanery, requires a wife as official helpmate; and all your talk of independent careers is so much smokescreen. I know what you did: you decided that no wife was better than the wrong wife; and out Judy went. But now there she is, uncomfortably still linked to you, and off her head into the bargain. Perhaps now you need a wife again?—and until Judy is out of the way, you're stumped.

The word 'divorce' was mentioned. Temporarily Wetherby clammed up, warning Nelson that he had overstepped the mark, that to go further would be categorized as harassment; but a moment later Wetherby was returning to the subject himself, unable to leave it without justifying himself.

Initially it had been compassion which had prevented Wetherby instituting proceedings for a divorce. 'Poor Judy, as you know, Sergeant, she's unfortunate enough to have various personality disorders. At the time she left me, she was in a very volatile state. I judged it positively dangerous to subject her to further stress. Besides, naturally I hoped it would prove to be only a temporary separation.'

Naturally; just as naturally you were unwilling to cut yourself off from the prospect of the money she would inherit on her twenty-fifth birthday, Nelson thought cynically. Then had come Wetherby's election to the council and his steady rise in 'profile'. A divorce then would have been inopportune. No doubt Wetherby now wished he had not procrastinated, for it might now be even more inopportune, given Judy's present position. The financial arrangements? Judy had intimated her wish to be independent when she came into the trust money, and Wetherby had acceded to her request; no more maintenance payments had been made thereafter. Nelson introduced Thomas's name into the conversation. If anything happened to Judy, Thomas would of course be well provided for . . . ?

The nonchalance with which Wetherby remarked that he really did not know what would happen to Judy's money in those circumstances struck Nelson as rather studied. Nelson observed that Thomas's name aroused Wetherby to no great protestations of emotion or concern.

The tape began to make a little squealing sound, and the button clicked off. Wetherby looked at it, but didn't bother to turn it over. Nelson made a play of consulting his notes.

'Where were *you*, the night of January the twenty-ninth?' he shot abruptly.

To his disgust a slow smile spread over Wetherby's face. 'I've been waiting for you to ask me that since you walked through the door, Sergeant. I was at a friend's house. Her name's Walker, Dr Frances Walker.' He chuckled maliciously. 'Tell *that* to your Chief Inspector Stainton.'

Thirty miles away, Liz Pink was interviewing another Wetherby.

Miles's father, Judy's father-in-law, Daniel Wetherby lived on a new estate three-quarters of a mile from the town centre in Uckfield, with the second wife he had married after retiring from his engineering business. The house was pleasantly cottagey; sand-faced bricks and stained window-frames testified to the developers' awareness of the value of character, and Liz, looking round as she waited on the doorstep at the relatively silvan scene, and a small child pedalling her tricycle happily up and down a driveway, decided that she was prepared to overlook the developers' motives, if the result was so pleasant.

Liz was prepared to find Carro Wetherby younger than her husband; on the telephone her voice had been active and lively; and the door was opened by a woman who could not be that much older than forty.

'Mrs Wetherby?' she inquired, and received a nod and a social smile in reply.

'You must be the policewoman who rang,' Carro Wetherby said; 'come on in.'

She held the door for Liz: a strongly-made woman, dressed in a denim skirt and designer sweatshirt which proclaimed comfortable financial circumstances, but sat rather uneasily on her. The effect was of a woman anxious to hold tight to her youthfulness in the face of increasingly disturbing evidence that it was already slipping from her grasp. In the small lobby the two women executed one of those little self-conscious dances people do when they want to avoid body-contact as Carro squeezed by to lead the way into the living-room. The hall was heavily beamed, with dark timbers not only across the ceiling, but up the walls too. Through an open door, Liz could see that a framework of timbers separated the kitchen from a breakfast area, as if an old cottage had been renovated and lath and plaster stripped away to reveal the structural bones. Surreptitiously, she let her knuckles knock against one of the uprights as she followed her hostess through the hall; it rang reassuringly hollow. Liz would have hated to find it was genuine.

Daniel Wetherby half-rose from his chair as the two women came in. A large man, he could not disguise his age, which Liz placed at about seventy, and seeing him it was easy to understand why Carro was so keen to claim her place in a younger age-group. His face was deeply seamed, and its colour was only partly the tan of a recent holiday; beneath, the brown of age vied with a ruddier tinge which hinted at whisky, or blood pressure. Liz noticed that the chair he sat in was not part of the low, soft suite, but harder and almost orthopædic in shape, and guessed blood pressure. She was almost sure he was wearing a hairpiece.

It took Liz a moment to realize that there was another occupier of the room. Over at the far end, by the television set, a boy of eight or nine was kneeling on the floor, assembling a jigsaw on a large tray. He glanced up as he felt her gaze resting on him, with a brief stare from blue eyes in a small, girlish face, then dropped his head again. He didn't seem to fit in this neat, too-orderly room, where the carpets were such a vulnerable pale cream that Liz had to restrain an urge to look down at her own feet, to check they were clean.

'You'd like some tea,' I expect,' Carro Wetherby suggested.

'Thanks; that would be very nice.'

'Come and help me make tea, Tom. Shall we take the jigsaw through into the kitchen, and you can do it on the breakfast table.'

Liz stood awkwardly while the child scrambled to his feet and placed the box on the part-completed puzzle on the tray, and picked both up.

'Show me how much you've done, Thomas,' Wetherby invited as the boy started for the door. He turned the tray so that he could see, while the boy stood reservedly. 'You're half way through, aren't you? Clever boy! You'll soon have it finished and we'll have to buy you another one.'

The compliment was stilted, and Liz, watching the boy's closed face, felt the tension between him and the old man. Yet Wetherby's face was soft as he gave vent to his extravagant praises, and Liz thought he did not sense how little they were wanted.

When Thomas had followed Carro out and the door shut behind them, Liz took a seat across from the big old man. 'I'm sorry to have to disturb you,' she said. 'I've got to ask you some questions about Judy. And you must be worried about her.'

Wetherby shifted his weight in his chair, touching his hair in an unconscious gesture which confirmed Liz in her guess that it was not his own. 'It's a nasty business,' he agreed; which was not quite the same thing, Liz thought, as admitting he cared about Judy's state for her own sake.

'She came to see you last month,' Liz said directly. 'Why did she do that, when she and your son are separated?'

'It was about Thomas,' Wetherby replied. 'I don't see as it's any of your business, but it was about Thomas's schooling. I'm not much taken with that namby-pamby place she sends him to; if the lad's going to get to a decent school in a year or two's time he needs the best he can get now, and the place she sends him to is too arty-farty by half.'

'The Pines?'

'Ay; that place. I offered to pay for Thomas to go to a decent prep school that'd get him properly prepared for this Common Entrance examination.'

He spoke as if he was by no means at home in the world of prep and public schools, but was determined Thomas should have the best money could buy. Liz, to whom public schools were just so many expensive spawning grounds for Hooray Henrys, pictured him sitting in the evenings poring over prospectuses like a novice ordering expensive wine with his finger on the list of vintages to remind him of the names.

'So she came over to talk it out.'

'That's about it. Stubborn, of course but,' he said, with grudging admiration, 'I suppose it's something that she came.'

'She kept in contact, then, after the separation from your son?'

'She brought Thomas over to see me from time to time,' Wetherby admitted. 'Judy didn't really want to have much to do with us, but she brought him over. It's only right a boy should see his grandfather. We used to go on outings in the holidays, too, him and me. I didn't mind taking him, you see, to the Science Museum, or Beaulieu, or somewhere; and his father was always saying he couldn't find time.'

'And now you're looking after Thomas while she's in hospital,' Liz said conversationally.

'He's a good lad, that boy,' Wetherby replied at once, as if Liz had been attacking Trooper's integrity. 'He's got a good nature. You could see that for yourself. There's nothing nasty about him. Kids these days, some of them are downright nasty. Spiteful, couldn't care, rude. Thomas is a right good lad.'

Carro came in, wheeling a tea-trolley before her, and glanced solicitously at her husband. Liz glimpsed flowery plates, paper napkins and bone-handled knives. Carro smiled at Liz.

'Where's Thomas?' Wetherby inquired.

'In the kitchen; he's quite all right. He's quite happy with his jigsaw.' She soothed her husband patiently, and Liz wondered about their relationship: the strong, energetic Carro with a body which looked, or at least was dressed, as if it demanded action, and the old man, powerful still but fretted by age, feeling his hairpiece and fussing over his grandson.

'How's poor Judy?' Carro asked.

'I don't really know,' Liz said. 'I hope to be able to see her in a day or two.'

'I'm sure there's no connection with that awful murder,' Carro said. 'The dead woman was driving Judy's car, wasn't she? Poor Judy! She should never have lent it to her; never! Just the sort of silly, impulsive gesture . . .' Carro Wetherby broke off in a dying fall as if impulsive gestures always were foolish, and inexplicable into the bargain.

'What time did she leave here, that night?'

''Bout half past ten,' Wetherby answered shortly, with a corroborative glance at his wife.

Carro nodded. 'Yes . . . yes, or thereabouts.' She laughed. 'Of course, one doesn't look at the clock to record everything one does, but you locked up after her, didn't you, darling, and I seem to recall we went to bed about ten to eleven. And she ran out of petrol or something on her way home, or so we heard! Just the sort of thing that Judy *would* do, of course.' There it was again: that jag of disharmony; but then she recovered herself and added, 'It was an awful night, though; it must have been very frightening for her. I remember thinking, I hope she gets home all right.'

Liz sipped her tea and nibbled at a home-made biscuit. Of course it was possible that the Wetherbys were covering up for Judy and she had actually left later. The fixed time was her collection by the RAC at half past midnight. Before that time, if Judy was the murderer, she had to have driven as far as the common, killed Kate, then driven back to where the RAC found her five miles away. However, there was also the buying of the diesel from the service station just before it closed, and the telephone call to the RAC, which had been logged at eleven twenty-three.

Ah, but suppose she had not rung the RAC from where she said she had? That would give her more time to play with, since she could surely have counted on them taking twenty minutes at least to get a recovery truck out to her, and more like the hour it had actually taken. That would allow her to kill Kate within the pathologist's parameters, certainly. But then she still had the alibi to set up, which involved stranding herself five miles away with diesel in the petrol tank of her car. After eleven o'clock the service station wouould have been closed (but check that!), and Liz was almost certain there was not another before Haywards Heath; which surely was way outside the distance Judy's car could have run on the fuel which was in the carburetter.

On the other hand . . . Liz looked up, but the Wetherbys were occupied with their tea. On the other hand, how much fuel had actually been put in that tank? Johnson had spoken to the patrol-man who was called out to help Judy, and Liz had read the report. On hearing the symptoms, the patrolman had taken the petrol filler cap off and sniffed the contents of the tank. Registering the distinctive odour of diesel fuel, he had offered Judy the option of draining the tank and refilling it with petrol (the recovery vehicle carried a gallon or two for just such emergencies) or putting the car on the recovery truck and taking it and Judy home, where the messy business could be done by the local garage the next morning. Judy had seemed very much on edge, and kept mentioning her son, and the need to get home as soon as possible; moreover, the patrolman had himself thought they were best getting out of the wooded area as soon as possible on such a stormy night—and, Liz guessed, had not much relished lying on his back under Judy's car to receive a stream of dirty fuel in his face.

So: had there ever been more than say a gallon of diesel in the tank of Judy's car?—an amount she could easily have carried with her in a can in the boot, subsequently getting rid of the empty can by hiding it deep in the under-growth.

All of which meant that Judy could have killed Kate Randall within the pathologist's stated times, rung the res-cue service from any convenient telephone-box, and still have had plenty of time to 'strand' herself at a spot several miles away from the murder site well before half past twelve when the RAC recovery truck reached her.

This time when Liz looked up, she found both her hosts watching her steadily.

On an impulse, she asked, 'What did you make of Judy's involvement in this CAMEX organization?'

Wetherby snorted, but Carro cut in before he could com-ment, saying, 'We were pleased when she became involved with that. I thought it would do her good to have a real interest, an issue to take her out of herself.' Liz noted the change of pronoun, and took a sandwich from the plate Carro proffered. She bit into it, hoping the others would go on talking. 'We felt a bit sorry for Judy,' Carro continued obligingly. 'I wish we could have seen her more often. She needed someone to look after her.'

'She did that all right,' Wetherby said grimly.

'No, I meant to take an interest. She hadn't many friends. Oh dear!' Carro realized, 'I'm talking as if she was dead.'

'She'd tried to take her own life once or twice before,' Liz prompted.

'It's good to know,' said Carro, 'that where she is now, they will presumably be able to prevent her if she feels driven to try again.'

'Just seeking attention,' Wetherby snorted. 'If she'd meant it, she'd have made a success of it first time round. It was just a silly way of getting people to take notice of her.'

'Darling, don't get worked up. Have another sandwich. We find it so difficult,' Carro explained to Liz, 'never having been in that position, to know what it's like for someone like Judy, don't you agree?'

Liz said, 'What about enemies? Is there any chance that Kate Randall might have been killed by someone who was really after Judy? Because she was in her car, I mean.'

'Sounds a damn silly idea to me,' Wetherby observed. He was barely bothering to hide his impatience now. She wondered how different it would be if it were Thomas, not Judy, who was involved.

Carro took the teapot out to top it up, and Liz snatched the opportunity to confront Wetherby directly. 'You don't agree that Judy couldn't have had anything to do with Kate Randall's death, do you?' she asked.

'Unfortunately,' Wetherby said with heavy sarcasm, 'I know my son's wife rather better than Carro does. Nothing she did would surprise me. It's been the same story since she and Les went their separate ways. Always alcohol, and drugs, and sex, sex, sex. And this CAMEX was just the same,' he said with his own impenetrable logic.

His bitterness against Judy was so strong that for a moment Liz toyed with the idea that he himself had done the murder; but there was no way she could bend fact or probability to make that horse run. Wetherby had plenty of opportunity to kill Judy, if she had visited him that night; but there was no way Liz could convince herself that the outcome would be the death of the wrong woman.

Reluctant to return at once to the office, where she seemed to have been pent up all winter, Liz drove from the Wetherbys' to the service station near Chailey where Judy was supposed to have filled her petrol tank with diesel; but a different attendant was on duty, and she had to content herself with making a note of the manager's name and phone number, and taking away a receipt from the wastebin; she was interested to see that it recorded date, time and the pump number. One theory—that Judy had indeed visited the service station, but buying a small quantity of *petrol*, which she then used up driving to the common and back—fell by the wayside.

Liz climbed into her car and strapped herself in. She was relaxed and still disinclined to drive straight back. It wasn't hard to persuade herself that there was some value in tracing the route Judy should have followed that fateful night, and having a nose around at the spot where the RAC recovery truck had found her, and she drove slowly, turning her theories over in her mind and wondering how much store she could set on anything Dan and Carro Wetherby said about Judy Baker.

The place where the RAC patrolman had found Judy's car broken down was a gateway a few hundred yards after a small junction. Liz pulled in with a sense of disappointment, for it was immediately apparent that the road here was bordered by fields, not by the expanse of bracken and scrub birch and bramble thicket which she had counted on. The only place a fuel can might be concealed was in the hedgerow itself, and Liz nosed around dispiritedly, kicking at the tussocky grass with her boots and trying to avoid snagging her leather jacket. The pale feathers of the new season's leaves were already reaching out of the sharp buds. A pheasant squawked; and a hundred yards away a rabbit leapt from its hiding place and scampered away across the field. It was hard to accept that it was still only February.

Liz straightened up, and looked around. A car rushed past, the white blur of the driver's face turning briefly towards her. On the far side of the field was a small copse. An empty can could be anywhere; only a fool would jeopardize the alibi by pushing it into the nearest clump of grass; and if Judy's tale *was* a cleverly contrived alibi, she was not a fool. QED, Liz murmured frustratedly.

Another car passed, and then slowed to a halt and reversed alongside her. A window whirred down; a male face was thrust forward. 'Problems, darling?'

'No, thanks.'

'I can give you a lift, if . . .'

'That's all right. I just stopped to look at the view,' Liz said firmly. There was no view.

'Oh! Suit yourself!' The window whirred up and the car took off with unnecessary wheelspin. Liz brushed grit from her skirt and stumped back to her car. The sun smiled serenely down.

'What have you got to be so pleased about?' Liz muttered, and drove rapidly away.

CHAPTER 22

Alec listened to Nelson's report impassively. When Nelson got to Miles Wetherby's final needling remark, Alec frowned, then nodded. 'All right; that's easily checked.'

'I, um, asked what time he left, sir. Well, I had to, didn't I?'

'And?'

'He, er, didn't stay all night. I mean, he could still have been on the common bashing Randall.'

Alec made a face. He felt like the person required to believe one impossible thing every day before breakfast. The news of Wetherby's whereabouts that night had shocked him; but he *shouldn't* have been shocked, he told himself. It was always a possibility. And the idea that the revelation implied deceit on Frances' part he set aside at once: she could not know that Wetherby was a suspect—indeed, Wetherby barely *was* a suspect.

Nevertheless, he would have been glad to hear that Wetherby had spent the evening somewhere else.

Sophy Blake waited impatiently for her crime to be unmasked and the storm to break. She was not afraid; indeed, she was very much looking forward to it, because she longed for the clearer air which she believed must follow. It would give her the opportunity to voice her anxieties. Her mother would say something like, 'Sophy, I know you've been using my cash-card. What is it you're anxious about?' and Sophy would tell her, and her mother would listen gravely as she used to once and then nod and tell her why she could not possibly have had anything to do with Kate Randall's death. Sophy would say, 'By the way, Mum, the money's in my treasure chest' (which was the little jewel case where as a small girl she had kept her trinkets), 'only I'm afraid I spoilt some of it.' And there would be trouble about that, but not very much.

But the end of the week came and nothing had been said. What could she do now?

On Saturday evening Miles Wetherby called to take Frances out. Lucy was upstairs when he arrived, and stayed there. They didn't come back until after Lucy was in bed, but not asleep. She heard the car, and voices, and listened tensely to hear if her mother was going to invite Wetherby in; but there were cheery farewells, and an ominous silence quite long enough for a kiss, and then a car door slammed and the car drove away.

Ten minutes later Frances' footsteps came past the bedroom door, paused and returned, and Lucy turned her head to see her mother edging the door open.

Seeing Lucy was awake, Frances came into the darkened room. She smelt of cigarette smoke, alien and hateful, as she bent over her daughter to kiss her.

'Had a nice evening, Mum?' Lucy murmured.

It was one of Frances' virtues in Lucy's eyes that when you asked her something she thought about her reply and didn't just respond automatically.

'I'm not sure, darling. Have you?'

'Yes, thank you. Why aren't you sure?'

Frances looked down at her daughter's earnest face. 'I don't know that either. Silly, isn't it?'

'No.'

Frances said gently, 'Go to sleep now. We'll talk about it in the morning.'

Lucy rolled over suddenly. 'He only wants you for your body!' she cried; and instantly regretted the words. Adults

said these things, but when you said them yourself they just
laughed and dismissed you as an amusing child. But it was
not shock or amusement which she heard in her mother's
response, but puzzled reflection.

'No; that's the funny thing, Lucy. Not very flattering,
really; I don't think he does.'

'Money?' suggested Lucy, emboldened.

'I wish I knew,' said Frances quietly. 'I wish I knew.'

March came in as if determined to live up to its reputation.
On the day Liz Pink and Heather Campbell travelled to
the psychiatric hospital to visit Judy Baker, those buds
which had begun to unfold so early were clinging precariously to twigs and branches whipped by a gusty south-west
wind.

The hospital was majestic in Victorian Gothic, as if it
had been ordered from a firm specializing in railway termini
and casually plonked down in three hundred acres of Surrey
green belt. Liz sat in the echoing reception hall while Mrs
Campbell went in search of Judy.

The three women had the grounds pretty much to themselves. They followed the broad paths through woodlands
and formal gardens, not so much sauntering as marching
to keep their balance against the bullying wind. Down in a
dell they found themselves by a little gazebo, and accepted
its shelter gratefully.

Liz was treading carefully, feeling the weight of the
responsibility Mr Stainton had placed on her. Liz approved
of this gentle approach to the scarred and vulnerable Judy,
instead of hauling her in unceremoniously to answer questions in a bleak interview room; but she was keenly aware
that Mr Stainton depended on her to make it work. She
had spoken on the telephone to the registrar treating Judy,
trying to forearm herself to meet the girl's mental state and
likely response to Liz's presence.

'Tell me about Trooper,' she encouraged. 'He sounds a
nice boy. You must love him very much.'

'I do,' Judy Baker replied, staring out at the greening

prospect, and the grass rippling in the blustery wind.

'I expect he's having fun at his grandfather's. I expect they're spoiling him rotten,' Liz said. Judy nodded. 'Still,' Liz continued gamely, 'you'll be glad to have him back, I know.'

Still Judy did not reply, and Liz felt the increasing strain of trying to keep the semblance of a conversation going one-handed. The doctor had suggested Judy might not be long in the hospital, or Liz would not have risked the remark about Trooper. Perhaps they had not told Judy herself. 'I saw him a few days ago,' Liz said lamely. 'He seemed very happy.'

'So you've decided you haven't found Kate's murderer after all,' Judy said.

'What do you mean?'

'Me. Wasn't I chief suspect? My car; and I ran away . . .'

'Perhaps we ought to get back to the cars before it rains,' Heather said, looking at the sky. They got to their feet and walked on.

'The RAC logged your call at eleven twenty-three,' Liz said carefully. 'We had them trace their records. I spoke to the garage attendant yesterday. She remembers you stopping for fuel just before she locked the pumps, which means just before eleven; and your own garage told me they drained at least six gallons of diesel out of your car's tank. Your father-in-law says it was half past ten at least before you left them.' Judy nodded. 'You tell me how you managed it, bearing in mind that Kate died five miles away!'

'Maybe I wasn't where I said I was when I rang the RAC,' Judy said slyly.

'All right,' said Liz, deliberately losing patience, 'so you're telling me you killed Kate, are you? Good. Just give me a few details and we'll be only too glad to charge you. How did you know she was going to be in that car park?'

Judy hung her head. 'It just seems sometimes every-body's after me,' she muttered defensively.

The wind slackened abruptly and it began to rain in big

drops, but slowly, as if experimentally. The three women lengthened their stride. The path wasn't wide enough; Heather lagged a step or two behind, and Liz felt a frustrating sympathy and intimacy with the woman who walked beside her, shoulders hunched, staring at the ground. It was an effort to remember that she herself was the younger.

'In a way, there are advantages in the present situation,' Liz said tentatively.

'Such as?'

Liz said awkwardly, 'We're just a bit anxious about you going back to your cottage until we've found the person who killed Kate Randall.'

'Now you think it was me that was meant to die,' Judy said.

'I don't suppose the idea comes as a great shock to you. It was your car . . . and in the dark, you and Kate Randall would be much alike, wouldn't you?'

'Her hair's long,' Judy said.

'She had it tucked up under a black woolly cap.'

The end of the path came in sight, where it debouched on to the gravel forecourt of the hospital. The rain had given up, as if the time for falling was not quite right, and instinctively the three women turned away into a side-path.

Heather said to Judy, 'Well, there's no problem. You stay with us, and Thomas comes too. The shrinks'll have sorted you out and I'll be on hand to make sure you don't flush your pills down the loo. You can give Dan a ring when you're discharged, and we'll go over and collect Thomas straightaway, if you like.'

Judy turned to Liz. 'What if it's Trooper? What if it's him that gets . . .'

'There's no reason why it should be,' Liz said firmly. 'The most likely killer of Kate Randall is still some bloke who just happened to chance on her. The other possibilities are outsiders, and they none of them involve Trooper.'

'Bonkers,' Nelson said dismissively. 'I knew it.'

'God, you astound me sometimes! The fuss you made six

months ago over having your wisdom teeth out, I'd have thought you might have had a bit more sympathy.'

'Yeah, but that hurt; I mean, it's not the same, is it? I mean, she's not ill, not in that sense, not like if you have a heart attack or cancer or something. She's just off her rocker.'

Liz stared at him in distaste. 'You'll be saying next that Judy Baker must have killed Kate Randall because only mad people commit murder.'

'Well, why not? You just said she's been certified. You've got to be round the bend to kill someone, haven't you?'

'All murderers are mad; Judy Baker is mad, therefore Judy Baker is a murderer,' Liz muttered incredulously. Aloud, she added: 'I *said* she'd been admitted for treatment for a depressive illness.'

Nelson shrugged. 'Same difference.'

Liz shot him a glance of pure scorn, and turned away to make a note for Chief Inspector Stainton. At least he might appreciate the difference between being admitted to hospital for treatment of depression under the Mental Health Acts and being committed to Broadmoor as a psychopathic criminal. In the circumstances, depressive illness sounded pretty mild and reasonable, Liz thought. If it were me, I'd have gone straight home and turned the gas on.

She initialled the report and set it to one side. There was something else she had been meaning to do, and the quickest way was to slip upstairs to the incident room.

Sally Field was sitting disconsolately at her desk, and looked up eagerly at the prospect of company.

'How's it going?' Liz asked.

'It isn't. The phone hasn't rung at all today. I thought everyone had solved the case and gone home and forgotten to tell me.'

'Cheer up! All be over in a week.'

'Yes?' Sally looked sceptical.

'Wait and see. The boss is just about to pull the rabbit out of the hat.'

'How can you tell?'

'Experience,' Liz replied absently, leafing through papers. 'Sal, you didn't throw out the printout on Ford Sierras, did you?'

The WPC got up and crossed to the filing cabinet, glad to be able to be active and look efficient. Wordlessly, she pulled out the wad of listing paper.

Liz turned over the sheets and ran her finger down the column of surnames. Wetherby, Miles Leslie she expected to find; but it was not totally unexpected when she read on the same sheet, Wetherby, Albert Daniel. She sat back, letting the sheets fall closed.

'What have you found?' Sally asked.

'I don't know,' Liz answered thoughtfully. 'A coincidence, I think. Or an impossibility.'

'All right,' Alec said, 'where does that get us?'

'Still just the one sighting, sir, the kid, Russell. I've seen him again, tried to jog his memory, didn't get any further,' Nelson said. 'Pale colour Ford Sierra; pulled a few yards off the road where a track comes out; can't tell us where, and there are a hundred places on that stretch of road where it could have been. But it looks as if Baker's out. With the till receipt, and the attendant identifying her photograph, her story's unbreakable.'

'Could she have put the diesel into a can, sir, rather than into the tank?' Johnson asked.

'Seven gallons of it?' Nelson asked witheringly. 'No, DS Pink thought of that one, son, and you're both wrong. Like I said, Baker's out. Morris is out. Mackenzie *isn't* out. His story is, he dropped Randall at her flat at ten or just after. Only person who could back that up's Randall, and she isn't here to do it.'

'His wife says he was back home by half ten,' Johnson reminded him, unabashed.

'Well, she would, wouldn't she?'

'You're thinking that they travelled to Morris's in Kate

Randall's car after all, and took the scenic route home?' Liz clarified sceptically.

'Picking up a bottle at the off-licence on the way,' Nelson agreed. 'Cold night; bit of something to keep the chill out.'

'Warmer in Randall's flat,' Johnson remarked.

'OK, and Randall was a virgin too, which is against it. But did Mackenzie know that? Say he wants a heart-to-heart, my wife doesn't understand me, that sort of thing; then he starts to chance his arm, loses his rag when she turns him down, like I said at the start.'

'Won't work,' Liz pronounced. 'On your showing, Mackenzie left his own car at Kate Randall's flat. How did he get back there after the killing? Anyway, we've got his time of admission to Crawley Hospital. Couldn't be done!'

'Who says? All right, it would be tight, but—'

'Go on, Nelson,' Alec instructed.

'Right, sir, where was I? Blake and Darby: Blake's out, Darby isn't. Nor,' added Nelson, looking sly, 'is *Mrs* Blake, is she? Don't forget the other things: anonymous letters, fake memos. That looks like a woman's mind at work, to me. So where was *she*, that night, eh? Who's to say she hadn't made an appointment to meet Randall up on the common?'

Alec nodded and made a note. 'I'd like some further investigation there. Start with Darby; we'll keep Mrs Blake in reserve. Then?'

'Then both Wetherbys have Sierras, but Miles is out because he was, er, he's got an alibi and Dan's out unless he fancies himself as Stirling Moss and leapt into his car to follow Judy home, but if he had, even he's not such an old duffer as to clobber the wrong woman.'

The sun streaming in through the generous window was trapped between the cream-painted walls. Here indoors it was hot though Liz, by half-turning her head, could see passers-by butting into the fresh breeze in the street below and the branches of a plane tree waving. Nelson's voice died away to a disregarded hum in the background. Life seemed good to Liz. It must be the effect of the season, for nothing else had changed, yet she was conscious of a rare contentment.

She tried to imagine herself inside the skins of these other women: Kate Randall; Judy Baker; Heather Campbell; Carro Wetherby. She supposed that, like her own, their spirits dipped and soared along with their hormones and the trivial events of the day and whether it rained or shone. On the other hand, her own spirits had never dipped so far that life itself seemed an oppression, nor soared in religious ecstasy and selfless dedication. Perhaps some people lacked the normal mundane middle ground and had only the artificial peaks as an alternative to the deadly troughs; and others, like herself, inhabited a happy unremarkable world where the graph stayed more or less level.

Suddenly the idea of there being choice in the matter, which appeared so improbable at first, clicked together and made a sort of sense. It was Mrs Campbell who seemed to have made such a choice most obviously—and ended up the enjoyably sane, lively woman she clearly was. But Kate Randall, too, *chose* the principles of her beliefs over idle pleasure, even to the extent of denying herself lovers and working unpaid for a selfless cause. Carro Wetherby, Liz supposed, had *chosen* marriage to Dan, financial security and a comfortable home above the struggle and pleasure of bringing up a family. Judy Baker, though: the hypothesis broke down with Judy, for she had chosen, with great effort and painful deliberation, one life—and ended up with another very different, committed for her own safety to a psychiatric hospital, to the numbing routine of institutional existence. Liz could not find it in her to believe that Judy's plight followed inevitably from other choices she had made, maybe years before.

And I—have I chosen, Liz wondered? When I have put it down in the past to happenstance and serendipity? She drifted into reverie, musing on events in this new light. How far, she wondered, could you take this anyway? If she wasn't careful, she'd be elevating it into a Philosophy for

Life. But if you *could* choose to be content . . . optimistic
. . . resilient . . .

'Do you agree, Liz?'

'Sorry, sir?' Mr Stainton was looking at her with the
beginnings of a smile on his lips and with her new percipi-
ence she was quite sure he had guessed the content of her
day-dream.

'In a world of her own,' Nelson said grumpily, breaking
the spell; and the sun went in, and the beautiful theories
collapsed.

'I'll tell you what happened,' Liz said abruptly. 'Kate
Randall drove up on to the common alone. Mackenzie
dropped her at her empty flat, and suddenly she just
couldn't face it. Everything had collapsed. She'd found out
what sort of people her troops were. She had hate mail in
her bag. Her boyfriend had run like a rabbit. She got her
car out, bought a bottle of gin, and drove off to find somewhere lonely to drink it. That's what I'd have done. Everyone tells us how strong she was, how single-minded; how
she put everything into the campaign. What happens, when
a person like that suddenly can't face things any more?'

Nelson's mouth was opened to scoff, but Liz saw Mr
Stainton was looking at her queerly, almost with respect,
as people look at someone manifesting a sixth sense. 'So
who killed her?' he said. 'Nelson's right: it's the casual
passer-by; is that what you're saying? Because nobody
could possibly have known she was going to be there?'

'I don't know,' she said sadly. 'I'm afraid I can't see that
far.'

CHAPTER 23

Alec and Frances met by arrangement that Friday evening.

Activity had died down on the trading estate where
Frances had her business. Though lights were on in most
of the buildings, the car parks were all but empty. Nature,

efficiently excluded at ground level, nevertheless imposed its influence from above, dropping a steady soft rain so that articulated trailers abandoned by the side of the road glistened like beached whales.

Frances was sitting with her briefcase open on the desk in front of her when he found his way to her office. Looking up, she nodded a welcome, and he took a chair to wait for her to be done. After a while beeps and burps came from the briefcase, which was revealed to be a lap-top computer, as Frances shut it down. She folded it into its casing and set it on the floor beside her, then rested her arms on the desktop and looked at Alec gravely.

'You're looking tired,' she said. She was warmly clad, in polo-necked jersey, a single row of artificial pearls—were they artificial?—gleaming on the russet wool. The fine material revealed Frances' figure. She was the one woman, he realized, that he could never regard merely in the light of a colleague. Beneath the desk he glimpsed soft leather boots and a long suede skirt. He felt stale and ordinary, and he found himself reluctant to speak, for fear that his voice would betray resentment at his disadvantage.

Frances surveyed him with what might have been sympathetic appraisal, or could just have been weary exasperation. 'Let's go for a drink,' she said.

Frances locked the office and Alec, with misgivings, followed the tail-lights of Frances' red sports car through the murk to Bletchingley. The evenings were drawing out, but on a night like this it was difficult to credit it, and the balmy spring weather which they had enjoyed earlier in the week seemed like a brief aberration. In the pub, the bar was almost empty, and confident of being able to talk unheeded they took a table by the fire, where hurricane-fallen wood from three years earlier burnt with a lazy, deceptive strength.

'How are you getting on?' Frances asked.

Alec pulled himself together. 'Slowly, but . . .' He told her of Liz Pink's speculative reconstruction of Kate's last evening: the dejection, the hopelessness, the lonely bottle of gin and the solitary drive through the windswept countryside; and as he did so he felt again how elusive Kate Randall was.

'You know,' he concluded, 'you probably knew her as well as anyone. I mean in understanding what was inside her. There can't be many women of her age who are so . . . self-contained.'

Frances nodded thoughtfully. 'Self-contained is probably right. When you describe it, it sounds like a weakness; in a way maybe it was, but not in the obvious way. I feel I've only really begun to understand Kate a little since her death; and I'm beginning to wonder whether she wasn't one of the most remarkable people I've ever known. You say self-contained, and that's right; but it's the sort of self-containment and . . . *completeness* which produces remarkable people: I mean the Mother Teresas, the, I don't know, the Catherine the Greats, the Florence Nightingales, the Julian of Norwiches.'

The Frances Walkers, he wondered? In the fireplace a log subsided with a little sigh, and a stream of tiny sparks climbed into the broad, uneven chimney.

'Your Liz Pink may be right,' Frances said after a while. 'Poor Kate must have been very low, that night, when she got back from Clive Morris's. You can understand her going straight out again to tramp over the common in the storm, or hug her bottle of gin to herself. If I understand her at all, I can imagine her doing that.'

'Yes,' Alec agreed. 'So can I.'

'She wasn't the girl to look for shoulders to cry on, or want to bend a friend's ear, or drive her depression away at a party. She'd look it straight in the face, Alec, and endure it; and I'll bet by next morning anyone who met her would have had no inkling it had ever overtaken her.'

She toyed with her almost-empty glass. 'I checked back as far as I could with Allied International, you know, about this business which led to me sacking Kate.' This was the ostensible reason for their meeting tonight. She looked Alec in the eye, and smiled. 'I made them sit up and take notice.

When they realized they weren't going to get rid of me until I was satisfied, I started to get somewhere.'

She looked down again at her fingers. 'I should have done that at the time. I wish I had.'

'I don't suppose it would have made any difference. In the long run.'

She made a face, as if she didn't agree. 'It did go back to Medisearch. Someone there—I couldn't find out just who—rang a chap in Allied Inter called Fowles. As far as I can make out—there was nothing written down—this mysterious someone hinted that there was a possibility of conflict of interest, or security leakage, if Kate Randall, active in CAMEX, was employed in a company with links with Allied Inter, which had a stake in Medisearch and received copies of its reports and projections.

'Fowles took a nod as being as good as a wink and went full steam ahead. He bent the ear of John Slater, who wrote to me, and Bob's your uncle.'

'But you said there was an actual document, a specific . . .'

'It turns out,' Frances said drily, 'that there were after all other paths by which it might have ended up where it did.'

'Oh!'

'Quite.'

'Slater admitted all this?'

'No. I was talking to Holland by this time, to head office. Reinhart Meer, who is the UK overlord, did. Cost me a fortune in international calls. I told you I stirred them up.'

'You'll have made yourself enemies.'

She shook her head. 'They come out of this business with egg on their faces. Slater gets his knuckles rapped because my intelligence system turns out to have been better than theirs. Meer is infuriated because he's had to apologize to me for a piece of underhandedness he never even knew about, but that's all turned inward. Fowles's head rolled into the basket, and the guillotine will no doubt be left poised over Slater's neck for a few weeks, just to remind

him to mind his p's and q's. To me, everyone's grovelling
for a while.'

Sometimes the business world seemed much on a par
with Chicago gangland. The thought must have shown in
Alec's face, for Frances remarked, 'Office politics, Alec.
Don't pretend it isn't just the same in your place.'

Alec took a deep breath. 'I have to ask you . . . to confirm
what time Miles left you that night.' He looked at her,
willing her to understand the necessity of the question.

She gazed steadily back. One eye had a tiny red streak
in the white. Alec could see little reflections of the fire flickering in each green iris. The expression was fathomless. 'I
see . . . So Miles is a suspect.'

Alec said, 'There could have been a case of mistaken
identity. It has to be cleared up.'

'I see,' she replied again. 'The answer to your question
is . . . about half past eleven. But . . . Miles rang me, at
about twelve-thirty. I asked him to do so, because it was
such a wild night; so that I knew he had reached home
safely.'

They were both speaking matter-of-factly, as though
there were no personal implications to the information
Frances was giving. Alec said, 'The latest Kate could have
died seems to be about two; but what you say rules Miles
out anyway. I refuse to believe he drove back to the common for no reason at all and just happened to see Judy's
car by chance.'

'He might not have been at home. He has a car-phone,'
Frances said slowly.

'He would,' said Alec, who had thought of that possibility
as soon as the telephone call was mentioned. He hastily
smiled the sting out of the remark. 'It's not feasible. Forget
it. I had to just check.' He looked round. 'Shall we eat?
There seems to be a bar menu.'

When they had ordered, and replenished their glasses,
they chatted sporadically while they waited for their food.
Alec did not deceive himself that it was just like old times.
To divert them both from such thoughts, and keep clear of

the subject of Miles Wetherby, Alec asked Frances about her hobby. She was a gifted amateur military historian: indeed, it was only because she had a more lucrative conventional job running Delta Communications that her hobby could be called a hobby at all. She had had more than one book published; the latest, based on the researches of a dead colleague into volunteers from the Dominions who joined the RAF in the Second World War, had just received its first reviews. Frances talked happily about the prospects for sales.

Their food was a long while coming, and when finally it did, Alec glanced surreptitiously at his watch. It was unusual for Frances to let herself be involved in anything unscheduled after work; she was meticulous in her responsibilities as a mother to Lucy, to the point of obsession Alec sometimes thought. Now, surely, she would be on tenterhooks to rush away, was already regretting, probably, having agreed to stay to eat.

Frances caught the direction of his glance and read his thoughts in his face. Her animation vanished as if a tap had been turned, and she said abruptly, 'I'm worried about Lucy, Alec.'

There was, on the face of it, nothing epiphanic about Frances' remark: yet later, looking back with dazzled fascination, Alec knew that those five words altered everything irrevocably. Floodwater in a dyke rises stealthily and with no bally-hoo; but when the first trickle seeps over the top of the bank no power on earth can stop what follows. The eye is too slow to register the crumbling of the soil and the opening of a crack, a gap, a breach. With the suddenness of an explosion water rushes through in a torrent, sweeping the confining banks away and flooding the landscape as far as the eye can see. So Alec found himself inundated by love.

Frances' head was bent, her features slack, as Alec hadn't seen them before. Her remark about Lucy had been thrown out would-be casually, for him to pick up or not; but he was not deceived as to just how much she needed him to pick it up. And he remembered his blithe assumption that this was a woman who neither needed nor wanted protection or comfort. Tonight, he could believe that she could cry.

'Tell me about Lucy,' he said quietly.

If his moment of revelation had brought any change into his voice, she didn't notice. She shook her head, her face immediately alert and reserved as usual. 'Oh, nothing,' she said.

Alec reached out a hand, and placed it over hers, which lay on the table, her forefinger tracing and retracing the line of a crack in the polished wood. The knife and fork lay wrapped in their paper napkin; her plate of food untouched. She glanced up at him in surprise and as if sceptical searched his eyes; then smiled wanly, and reached for her cutlery.

Herself again, she began to speak.

It was more than Alec could do, driving home, to consider the ins and outs of Kate Randall's sacking, and Miles Wetherby's whereabouts on the night of her death, and all the myriad details of the investigation of the murder. His mind was too disordered by the revelation of his own feelings.

It was as if at thirty-six he had ceased to be tone deaf, or colour-blind. He had always registered the crude rhythms of emotion to which men and women were subject: now he saw that there were subtleties of tone he had never dreamed existed, and what had been noise became music. In particular, Frances was a symphony he wanted to hear over and over, a painting he could not look at too often. And a small insistent voice whispered: how much better a policeman he could now be, understanding the heart as an initiate!

Fate's timing was impeccable, he told himself, swinging from elation to depression; and typically cruel. He and Frances had spent countless evenings together, and yet tonight's brief time had overturned the status quo just when it was certain that his revelation had come too late.

A disinterested observer, he told himself bitterly, would

have been completely baffled by the nature of their relationship and its failure to progress on the usual lines. They had been colleagues; they had enjoyed each other's company; they had shared plays and concerts and country walks and meals; but no more. He had allocated Frances a place in his life which was bounded and fenced on all sides; and had assumed that that was the place she desired to occupy. It had taken until tonight—and even then, he thought, it had almost not happened—before chance had opened a breach in his defences. What had been held back might rush boiling away in a short, seething torrent, powerful but soon over; or might spread and rise and fill the whole dry valley. For good or evil it had happened. He might be in for a lot of pain; if so, he could not now prevent it. If it were not too late, he might also have been on the verge of something which would enhance and enliven every dry and dusty corner of his life.

Much later in the evening Alec, sitting in his armchair in the silent flat, let his mind drift back to the Kate Randall case.

So she had been right: at least one of the chain of 'coincidences' which had plagued CAMEX traced directly back to the Medisearch laboratory. It looked as if John Blake had been acting a part when he derided the value of smear campaigns and claimed CAMEX was beneath notice.

Alec frowned. The crassness of it niggled, because bully-boy tactics could only lead back to Medisearch. And yet, he reminded himself, the result *had* been to eliminate CAMEX as an effective opposition to the embryo legislation. On that level it had been an effective campaign. Key workers had been removed: Morris; Ginnie Kemp. Kate Randall's might have started out as such a case—but her sacking had had the effect, not of breaking her spirit, but of enabling her to work for CAMEX full time.

Then had come the CAMEX memorandum, a clever leak or an inspired forgery, but either way effective; give a dog a bad name and other people will be only too ready to do the hanging for you.

The last link in the chain was the one he balked at. Thus far, the anti-CAMEX campaign had been a matter of words and innuendo. Would the perpetrators really have crossed the line into direct action?

For the idea of Kate Randall's death being connected with CAMEX was the fact that the blow which smashed Kate Randall's head had also brought death to CAMEX. Without her, and whatever Morris and the others tried to believe to the contrary, the organization was dead. But against that was the fact that CAMEX had already been patently dying. Killing Kate Randall was a work of super- erogation. Only a fool would try to forward Medisearch's future by such an excessive and unsound move; and Blake was not a fool. On the contrary, he was a man of undoubted intellectual brilliance, and such people are not fools—are they?

Alec glanced at his watch; it was late, and he began to tidy papers away, lock doors, switch off lights, aware tonight of his solitariness as of a phenomenon which had not necessarily been inevitable.

His thoughts drifted away from CAMEX and the murder and back to Frances Walker, sleeping peacefully, he hoped, in her bed in the old house in the clearing twenty miles away; and Lucy: growing up, and awkward with the prob- lems of impending womanhood, and the weight of her and Frances' mutual responsibility. What Frances had wanted to talk about had not been anything serious; and Alec sus- pected that she had not mentioned it all, because some of it had to do with Lucy's reactions to Miles Wetherby; but she had needed to talk, and he had realized for the first time that she must be lonely, and long to unburden herself of her load for a while at least.

He could not help a spurt of hope flickering up within him: she had chosen *him* to share her burden—not Wetherby. But then, he reminded himself, *he* had been on the spot; Wetherby had not.

If things had been different, now, Alec might have shared some of Frances' burden about Lucy on a permanent basis—and lifted Lucy's burden about her mother, too. There were cruel strains in any family where one parent and one child had only each other to depend on.

With a silent click, the gearwheels meshed in his mind. There were indeed strains—great strains—in a situation where two people were so exclusively interdependent: conflicting urges to break free; to preserve at all costs; to establish separate identity; to safeguard the future.

Alec had considered Frances as verging on the obsessive and yet she was in other respects perhaps the sanest and most rational person he knew. But if she, if it came to it, would stop at nothing where her child was concerned (would she kill for Lucy's sake?)— what might not a less sane person do?

Alec jotted down his thoughts in the notebook he kept in his briefcase: he knew otherwise he would revolve them in his head all night. Then he looked at his watch again, decided it was not too late, sat down by the telephone and dialled his sister's number.

Tonight, at last, he knew that if she wanted to unburden herself he would be able to speak her language.

CHAPTER 24

'Hey!' Tony Darby protested angrily; then he looked at Tina quizzically. 'What's brought this on?'

'Why the hell did you have to *say* I was here with you?' she cried.

'Are you crazy?' He laughed incredulously. 'D'you think they're going to be taken in by a pair of amateurs like us?'

'You *wanted* John to know. You *wanted* to end it!'

'I don't want to end it,' he replied roughly, 'but I'm not lying to the police. And for God's sake, what does our little affair mean compared to finding out who killed that poor girl? If John's found out about us in consequence, that can't be helped. It stands pretty low in the scale of things, I should have thought. John's not blind, you know!'

Tina gave up miserably and turned away, thinking how feeble it would sound if she told him the truth, which was that it was she who wanted to bring it all to an end. She was weary of Darby: but for the first time she was truly weary of herself, too, and sickened by the futility of her ways. How had she got here: here to this squalid affair, and here to all the rest of the muddle—the mess at home, the guilt which dogged her steps over Kate Randall's death, Sophy . . . ? She felt guilty now about the prospect of revealing to Darby—casual, good-humoured, lazy Tony Darby—that she had had enough of him and all he represented, and so she engineered the bickering, the falling out, which gave her the excuse to finish it all. Yet she felt a tug to disburden herself to someone, and it was only the thought of Darby's amused smile as he listened which prevented her pouring out the whole incoherent muddle in her heart to him.

'I'm sorry,' she said, looking back but not quite meeting his eyes. She turned away, rummaging in her bag, and began to repair her make-up at the mirror.

'OK.' He shrugged. 'By the way, Tina, I suppose you *did* go straight home when you left me that night?'

'Yes, I did, for your information! And how do I know that *you* didn't go out on to the common? It's not far!'

He looked at her without favour. 'You'd better go.'

She nodded, hating him for falling in so readily with the ending of the affair. She knew she must make the break clean, now she had started it; but why could he not, even if only for pity's sake, take those few steps towards her to kiss her, to slip a hand beneath her blouse.

Driving home, Tina felt no sense of virtue or release, and asked herself derisively what she had expected. Did smokers feel better the day they gave up? Did drug addicts? Did alcoholics view the tempting bottle with equanimity when they had decided to go on the wagon? Or did not rather every nerve shriek that all they could expect was hell for as far as the future stretched?

It was growing late, but the mysterious traffic which always seems to flow along main roads even in the dead of night was there, a succession of white double moons which grew and dazzled, then changed magically to red in her mirror, and receded. On an impulse Tina turned off, leaving the caterpillar headlights behind, and letting her own lights pick up the steep earthen banks of the sunken lane. A signpost flickered past, and she glimpsed the name of a village. The lane would take her in more or less the right direction; and who was there to care if she was late home one last time?

She did not deceive herself that breaking with Darby would instantly bring Sophy back to her in daughterly love (indeed, if she had not convinced herself that Sophy knew nothing of her adventures, she could never have entered on them in the first place), or resurrect the simple trust and companionship there had been between her and John when they were first married. Her own gesture towards virtue would not increase her daughter's or her husband's love for her by one drop. But she knew, as certainly as if it had been sprayed on the windscreen in front of her, that someone had to make the first step. Maybe things had gone too far for retrieval; but until at least the most blatant of her drugs had been repudiated, she could not even make the attempt. Her virtue gave her bitter amusement, and her lip curled as she drove. It wouldn't last, she told herself.

Twenty miles away another relationship, less advanced, physically at any rate, had come to a more dramatic end.

Frances was disturbed to find how upset she was by having to admit to Alec the details of her evening with Miles Wetherby. She felt shabby guilt, as if Lucy had caught her masturbating. It had not escaped her notice that when she had uttered her ambiguous plea for help Alec had understood and offered comfort. Perhaps she had been mistaken, and Alec could offer intimacy, if she herself were only able to receive it?

Now that she had reached this point, it began to seem incredible that she should ever have committed herself in any way to Wetherby, and Frances was aghast that she should have let herself travel so far with him down a path, the inevitable end of which must have been disaster. Looking back, she was hard put to it to understand what she could have been thinking of. Wetherby was so very alien in outlook, behaviour, philosophy: they hardly seemed to have a thing in common. She did not think he had killed Kate Randall—but he was a man of whom thinking it was conceivable, and that horrified her. Yet she had quite readily spent large parts of her free time with him, had contemplated sleeping with him although always instinctively deferred the occasion, had defended him to others, had slighted her friends for his sake.

I did it deliberately, she thought. Primarily to spite Alec Stainton, but also to hoodwink myself about the passing of time. If it now seems like lunacy, I shall have to live with that. Her anxiety lay in whether she could resurrect what she had sacrificed for Miles Wetherby's sake: not Alec Stainton's friendship, perhaps; that had probably been lost for good; but definitely Lucy's trust.

Earlier in the evening, over hors d'oeuvre at the riverside restaurant near Tonbridge, Miles had hinted at the possibility of them living together. Frances' reaction had been puzzlement: indeed, it was a while before she realized that was what he was driving at, because she could not believe that he had overlooked such a vast obstacle to his plan.

'But you've got a wife,' she said stupidly. 'What about Judy?'

Wetherby had gestured dismissively and opened his mouth to reply; but the waiter came up to clear their plates, and another wheeled up a trolley on which in a dish was a whole roast duck, which he began to debone with deft flicks of the wrist. The interruption had given Frances time to gather her wits, and she was surprised to find that she liked

Miles's proposition a good deal less than she had assumed she would. She was also annoyed that the suggestion should have come like a bolt from the blue. What mindless cloud had she been floating on? His next words, however, had chilled her, and as she prepared for bed now she was inclined to consider that that was the moment when her eyes were opened to the fatal flaws in Miles Wetherby which she should never have allowed herself to overlook, and which his charm and ambition could not outweigh.

After the duck flesh was disposed on plates and vegetables served, Wetherby had leant forward. 'She's in hospital, as you know. It wouldn't be too hard to make out a case for keeping her there. I'd divorce her, but that's the sort of thing the papers would seize on—heartlessness, and so on. No, much better for all concerned that Judy stays where she is, where she can be looked after.'

'And Thomas?' Frances asked.

Wetherby had failed to catch the warning tones in her voice. 'Again, fine where he is! Dad's besotted with him, and he and Carro'll look after him far better than I could. I mean, we could have him with us, of course, but I sort of assumed you'd rather not be bothered.'

'Do you know what you *sound* like?'

'What's the matter? Oh, come on! Let's be businesslike!'

At once Frances had realized that that was it. Miles Wetherby had decided that the next stage in his rise demanded a consort—and she was elected to the part! It would not be expedient to divorce a wife incarcerated in a mental hospital; but one could set up a new and impeccably contemporary menage with a conspicuously successful self-made woman. Frances suddenly saw herself as part of a business deal and anger swept over her like a wave.

She banged her knife and fork down, pushed back the chair, and stood up.

'What the hell, Frances?' Miles asked, looking up and registering for the first time the expression on her face.

She simply walked out, leaving the roast duck on the abandoned plate, the eddies of steam drifting upwards in front of Wetherby's astonished, and then furious, face.

'My coat,' she snapped to a waiter who stepped appre-
hensively forward. 'And . . . get me a taxi.' And because it
was an expensive enough restaurant, where walking out is
not as infrequent as in places where the clientele feel bound
to stay and eat what is being paid for, both were on hand
within minutes. Frances spent those minutes in the bar,
with a double gin, knowing that no one as conscious of bad
publicity as Miles would follow her and risk a scene.

Ten minutes later she sank back into the upholstery of
the cab and felt gin and adrenalin coursing agreeably
through her veins.

I should have done that long ago, she told herself now,
reaching behind her neck for the fastening of her dress. Her
bed felt cool and large and very empty; and tonight she
found great comfort in it.

Sophy Blake lay on the covers of her bed and stared miserably at the ceiling through the pools of tears gathered in
her eye sockets. Shortly she felt their soft wetness spill and
trickle down her cheeks. Jason Donovan and Madonna
gazed dispassionately down at her from posters on the wall,
and her china horses stared glassily at her plight from their
shelf. This room was all she had of home; this, and what
was inside her head. Everywhere else, in this house and out
in the wider world, was hostile territory, all occupied by
those who would destroy her if they could. She had no
friends, she thought with the grief of adolescence, which for
all its melodramatic role-play is real enough to those caught
up by it.

Sophy was a child of her generation; a generation where
the certainties disappeared earlier and earlier: where
parents had ceased to be infallible before you left primary
school; where half her class were habituated to spending
alternate weekends with their mother and her partner, and
their father and his; where there was no time for romance
because you had to hurry on to sex; where television had
ceased to mirror life and come instead to initiate it. Sophy

could cope with parents who were remote; she could cope
with the precarious feeling that they were on the point of
splitting up every time she heard them rowing downstairs.
She could not cope with parents who destroyed the careers
of men like Mr Morris, nor with parents who manipulated
genes with no thought of life or death. She could not cope
with parents who committed murder.

She was as sure that they had done it, as she was sure
that they had got away with it—just as they had got away
with ruining Mr Morris, with smearing Dr Kemp, and with
all the other attacks on CAMEX which Sophy had read of
in the local paper.

Jason Donovan and Madonna offered her no sympathy.
The china horses had nothing to say. Nobody had; nobody
could help her. Nobody could put things right unless she
did herself. The responsibility rested on her.

Tina Blake parked her car in the drive and walked slowly
towards the door, her footsteps ringing on the macadam,
savouring the mild night. Apart from her own footsteps
the night was inexpressibly still. But for her own car, the
driveway was empty. John had been away all day at a
conference at Bristol University: it was not unusual that he
should have been delayed.

Once indoors Tina lingered downstairs, sorting out the
events of the evening and the previous months slowly in her
mind, giving them the form in which they would be filed in
her memory. There was something reassuringly domestic
about padding in stockinged feet round the kitchen, setting
milk to heat for a chocolate drink, and a freedom in knowing
that her relationship with Darby was ended.

At half past twelve Tina at last climbed the carpeted
stairs. It was while cleaning her teeth in the bathroom
attached to her bedroom that she suddenly noticed in the
mirror that the door of the medicine cabinet hung open.

The cabinet was empty.

Dropping the towel Tina ran at once along the passage.
Her daughter's bedroom door stood ajar—as she had

passed it only a few minutes before. Tina flung it open, and
even before she had fumbled for the light-switch the pale
glow of the moon through the uncurtained window was
enough to show her Sophy, half-dressed, face up on the bed.
The overhead light, as her trembling fingers finally found
the switch, revealed the bottles and cartons on the floor by
the bed, the little trickle of vomit at the corner of Sophy's
mouth, and the laboured rise and collapse of her chest, as
if each next breath would be her last.

John Blake, turning into his own driveway fifteen minutes
later, found it inexplicably crowded with vehicles and
strange-coloured lights. It took several seconds before his
mind registered with a sickening lurch that one of them
was an ambulance, doors open, blue lights rotating lazily.
Beyond it was a Volvo with a GP's green revolving light on
the roof, and beyond that Tina's car was just visible on the
edge of the encircling darkness. As he braked to a halt, a
little procession issued from the front door: men in uniform;
a stretcher; two women. He heard the words '. . . plea for
help' carrying clearly in a competent professional voice as
he leapt out and hurried over.

One of the ambulance men climbed out of the vehicle
and began to close the back doors. The two women looked
round at the sound of Blake's cry and he saw Tina's pale,
fearful face, the light from within the ambulance casting
weird shadows over her features.

He saw her register his presence and summon her
reserves of normality.

'Sophy?' he croaked.

The woman with his wife said, in the same calm, forceful
voice he had heard before, 'Sophy's taken some pills. She's
going to be all right, but they're taking her to the hospital
to look after her.'

'But why . . . .'

'John, I'm going with Sophy . . .'

He stared at his wife as at a stranger speaking a foreign
language; and then belatedly his mind clicked into gear.

'I'll stay by the phone,' he said. 'Ring me; ring me as soon as you can!'

Tina breathed out, and reached out her hand. He took it and she squeezed his nervously, and then she turned and climbed into the ambulance. The ambulanceman shut the door behind her and went round to the driver's seat. The ambulance turned on the lawn, rocked back on to the drive, hesitated briefly at the gateway and accelerated swiftly away.

John turned to find the woman watching him; a dumpy, capable-looking woman with an energetic face unmarked by being called out after midnight: not their usual doctor, presumably a locum from a night-deputizing service. 'Will she be all right?' he asked the inevitable question.

The woman nodded, and began to walk over towards the Volvo. 'Should be. Overdosed with her mother's contraceptive pills.' John felt a little stab of pain. It was five years since he had had a vasectomy . . .

'I expect they'll keep her in a couple of days,' the doctor was saying. 'Her mother will be able to stay with her, if that's what she wants. Done this before, has she?'

'No; never!'

'Well. You're going to look after things here?' She turned as she reached the door of her car, her eyes searching John's face, as if to decide whether she might have made a mistake and ought not to leave him in charge of an expensive house. 'You *are* her partner, I take it?' she asked, stressing the unsatisfactory modern euphemism.

'No,' said John firmly. 'I'm her husband.'

After the Volvo's lights had faded away among the trees John Blake stood for a moment on the deserted driveway, mentally catching his breath, waiting for the wave of adrenalin to seep away and letting rational thought take over from the instinctive gut-twisting urgency which had sustained him through the last ten minutes. The night was still and silent. In the last few days the year seemed to have turned for good; and as his senses relaxed he became aware of the smells, released by the previous day's rain, seeping soothingly round him. Damp soil; and crushed grass where the ambulance had turned on the lawn; and a curious, exotic vapour which after some thought he identified as pine resin from a fallen tree.

After a while he turned and walked over to his car which stood, door agape, a little way back up the curve of the drive. As he did so it was suddenly illuminated in the harsh white glare of headlamps turning in off the road, and a police patrol car rolled to a halt behind it.

Tina Blake sat awkwardly on the plastic hospital chair and looked at her daughter propped on the pillows in bed. She saw a stranger. Sophy had been living in the house with her and John, meeting at meals and in the bathroom with fleeting greetings and averted faces. She had her own room, of course; and her own television, and her schoolwork to do and her own social life; but was that the whole reason why Tina had never noticed her daughter growing up, never thought of taking her into account where her own life was concerned?

She saw a pale-faced, tired girl-woman. Sophy's Snoopy nightdress opened wide enough at the neck to reveal the clear smooth skin Tina had once had herself, running in perfect, innocent curves from chin to throat to clearly-swelling breast. Tina wondered emptily what Sophy would see, if she would only turn her head. A dried-up middle-aged stranger, she told herself ruthlessly.

She asked the only question there was. 'Why? Why, Sophy?'

The tired young head rolled on the pillow until the blue eyes met her own, and at once they drifted away, and Tina shivered as she saw her daughter's gaze turn incuriously away from her.

'Oh God, Sophy, I mean, I don't want to . . . I just want to *know*. *Why?*'

'It was the only way I could make you listen,' Sophy said simply.

CHAPTER 25

Alec was running through computer printouts when the telephone rang. He was pretty certain he knew now who had killed Kate Randall, and why. Soon, he would have sifted out the proof. He listened briefly, raising his eyebrows, though not in surprise.

'I'll be down,' was all he said.

Nelson was out on another case; Alec was guiltily glad, and for that reason was abrupt with Liz when he asked her to come with him, and she had to skip to keep up with him as he strode down the corridor past the lift to the stairs.

When they entered the interview room and he saw how Tina Blake's glance leapt at once when she saw he was not alone, and then calmed as she accepted Liz's presence, Alec felt regret. This was the way it was going to be. No one would make the decision, but Nelson would drift off the promotion ladder. People would speak of his mistakes, his failures of judgement, and they would overlook Liz's, because she was going places, and Nelson was going nowhere.

They sat down.

'Well, Mrs Blake, you've come to see me at last.'

She looked him straight in the eye; but he saw hers was moist. 'Yes. I've come to confess.'

'Believe her?'

'Yes.'

'Me too. She's a clever woman; her mind's under-stretched, and so's her time. Mischief was bound to come of it.' They were standing in the corridor. Alec nodded towards his office, and Liz followed him in. He sat on the edge of the desk; she leant against the filing cabinet. Even in the midst of the matter in hand, Liz registered the shift in their working relationship which had taken place.

'It's whether she would have stopped at smears,' Liz said. 'That's the question. If Randall hadn't died . . .'

'Academic. Because Kate Randall *did* die, so Tina knew her little game was at an end. We knew Tina Blake didn't kill Kate.'

'But we do know now Randall's death wasn't the climax of a series of attacks. At least, we know that whoever killed her was not the same person who sent the anonymous letter about Morris, and made up the CAMEX memorandum, and framed Ginnie Kemp, because Tina Blake was responsible for all those things—'

'—But we don't know,' Alec finished for her, 'whether the killer didn't benefit from them to mask the true reason for what he did. Which would posit a killer who thinks—which is also not news.'

Liz gazed intently at the label on the drawer of the cabinet. 'If you take that line, Kate *was* the intended victim. And we're back to the chance encounter.'

'We never left it,' Alec said.

Liz herself was to take Judy Baker over to Uckfield to collect Thomas. Judy seemed to have adopted her as a second Heather Campbell—a second prop and confidant. Liz was flattered, though uncomfortable too. Who were these women, anyway, in their thirties, with marriages and children behind them, that they should see her as one of them? But although Liz was aware of the risk of encouraging dependency, she thought in Judy's case it was unlikely to prove dangerous; after all, she had proved hard enough for Heather to help in the past, which argued for a strongly independent streak.

Judy was due to be discharged in the afternoon a day or two later. Liz arranged half a day's leave—to Nelson's undisguised amazement—and Judy had already spoken to Carro to arrange for Thomas to be ready.

At ten that morning, the telephone rang.

Liz burst into Alec's room like a clap of thunder. He was

on the phone, and waved her to a chair. She walked rest-
lessly up and down instead.

'D'you know what they've done to Judy Baker?' she
demanded before the receiver had touched the cradle at the
end of Alec's call.

'Yes.'

'Some *bloody* social worker has suggested she's unfit to
look after Trooper! She's been told she can't have him back
pending a formal assessment.'

'I know.'

'It's too much! They've been digging everything up;
they've been to that creep of a sister of hers and got her to
tell them how Judy's a drunk and immoral and beats her
son.'

'All true,' Alec said. 'They've done it before. There was
an anonymous accusation that Judy sexually abused
Trooper. It was one of the smears against CAMEX that
Kate Randall told me about.'

That caught her attention at last. 'Tina Blake never mentioned that.'

'No, she didn't, did she?'

Suddenly Liz cottoned on. 'You *knew* all this?'

He nodded. Possibly she expected he was about to
embark on a sermon on the need not to get emotionally
involved, for she faced him mutinously. Instead, he suddenly smiled. 'Take it easy, Liz. It'll all come right. Wait
and see.'

'So it's all sewn up?' Frances inquired, glancing at him as
they walked side by side through the grounds of Sheffield
Park.

'I think so. The motive was the problem; once I cottoned
on to that, the rest was easy.' He shook his head critically.
'I was slow. You'd have been quicker. I'm used to nice
solid material motives, like money. I haven't your acuity
where the emotional life is concerned.'

Frances shook her head as if to deny it. 'Will you make
a good enough case for a conviction?'

'Right to the heart of the problem, as usual! I think we've a fair chance. Once we're in a position to take a few samples of this and that the scientists seem to think they'll be able to prove it one way or the other.'

She smiled. 'I don't know why I'm asking. You wouldn't be you if you hadn't made absolutely sure before saying anything. By the way, I'm flattered to be taken into the great detective's confidence before you've even made an arrest.'

'Shows how much I trust you. We make a good team,' he said lightly.

There was a silence then, apart from the muffled fall of their footsteps as they ambled over the grass. By the lake they instinctively stopped, and Frances turned to him.

'By the way, Miles Wetherby asked me to marry him.'

'Congratulations,' he said eventually, surprised by a hot needle of pain despite having lived this moment over in anticipation a dozen times in the last few days.

'Aren't you going to ask me what I said?'

Alec said nothing. She looked at him as if bewildered by him. In the end, she said, 'God, you're worse than he is. I'll tell you. We had a row. I don't suppose I shall be seeing him again.'

'I'm sorry.'

Momentarily her green eyes glinted as if an unintended double meaning amused her, then the light faded out of them again. He thought she looked tired, and maybe tired of him. It usually happened that he went so far with a woman, and then she wanted more: more of the things he didn't know how to give, like intimacy and trust and vulnerability and dependence. Justice, perhaps, that this time, when at last he should be prepared to give precisely those things, he should be denied the chance; bitter justice.

Misreading his sudden sadness, Frances said, 'I'm sorry. You prefer the efficient, businesslike Dr Walker, I know. That's the trouble with you, Alec. You don't like to be burdened with what people are really like, in case it makes demands on you. Let's walk on.' And she set off towards the half-glimpsed façade of the mansion.

Suddenly he wasn't prepared to let her walk away from what had been said. 'So you didn't turn Miles down on my account,' he wanted to know.

Frances strode on, her strong legs thrusting at the material of her skirt, her hands thrust deep into the pockets of her jacket so that it flared like embryo wings. 'I should be a fool to do so, shouldn't I, quite frankly? I'm fine so long as I fulfil the role of intelligent companion. Probably you'd be content for me to add the role of lover. I'm sure we would be very good at that; very *efficient*. But those two roles aren't the sum of human emotion, Alec. And that's not just your problem as a man; it's your problem as a policeman. That's why someone like your Liz Pink is in the long run going to be a better police officer than you. Maybe not so clever; maybe she'll never be so senior—you'd make an excellent Chief Constable—but a better bloody policeman!'

'Hold on!' he said. 'Stop a minute!' Reluctantly she halted, and turned to him with her calm clear-eyed gaze. 'Marry me,' he said.

Frances' eyes opened wide, very slowly, and her face paled as if he had hit her. Alec waited, not knowing what possible reaction she woud make, any more than he knew whether it was anything rational which had made him utter those words. He only knew that he had had to say them, or regret it for the rest of his life.

'You don't mean that,' she said in the end, sympathetically.

'I've never said anything to you that I meant half as much.'

She gave a half-laugh. 'Lucy always wanted you for her father,' she muttered.

'And you?'

'I'm afraid. Afraid I might say yes. Because I couldn't live with you on your terms, Alec. Compartmented; restrained; always reining in my true feelings, knowing you liked me less when I burdened you with my demands.'

'You couldn't demand anything I wouldn't want to give,' he said, smiling reflectively as he heard himself utter the words.

'Yes, I could,' she said. 'Comfort; and vulnerability; and weakness. You see me as you have known me over the last two years, Alec, and you like what you see. You like the surface Dr Walker, the businesswoman, the colleague, the companion, the comrade, the woman with not at all a bad mind—for a woman—who knows better than to gush; knows better than to impinge. That's *not* me; any more than the rising chief inspector in the smart suit and the regimental tie is you. *Me* is illogical, and unreasonable; moody; cursed by the moon; full of faith, and of doubt; *demanding*, Alec!'

'D'you think I don't know all that?' he said quietly. He took a deep breath, and then looked not at her but around him, at the green banks and brows of parkland, the specimen trees, the placid lake ruffled by the spring breeze. And back into her eyes. 'That's the you I want. And the . . . the me I am offering you is pretty much the same,' he said. Could this be Alec Stainton talking? Frances could be forgiven for doubting it.

After a while she said, 'You are quite prepared for me to take you at your word?'

'Perhaps we should allow a fourteen-day cooling-off period,' he suggested.

Her eyes lit up at that, as if she thought they just might have a future together after all, and she turned so swiftly that her skirt swirled round her calves, and began to stride off up the hill.

'What do you say?' he called.

'Yes!' she shouted back over her shoulder. 'Yes! I think that's a bloody good idea!'

Trooper had nursed the idea for a week. In lessons at school; in bed before he dropped off to sleep; at table while his grandfather and Carro discussed their latest project, the redecoration of the spare bedroom—he savoured the idea of running away, and laid his plans. When his classmates' teasing became too acid, or his grandfather's praise too oppressive, or his mother's absence too agonizing, or the days were simply too long, he took out again the idea of slipping away and leaving it all behind, and felt the tingle of secret knowledge. One day soon he would go and find Mum. He was sure she needed him. Maybe tomorrow. Maybe at the weekend. Soon.

It was not a good weekend. Trooper sensed it at breakfast on Saturday morning, though he had no way of knowing that it had its origin in the moment when Daniel Wetherby, who had woken at five, had decided his wife had slept long enough, rolled pleasurably over and placed his hand on her thigh and she flinched from his touch. Watching his grandfather warily over the rim of his cereal bowl and noting the short, tightlipped interchanges which took the place of their usual conversation, Thomas began to plan his escape.

They went shopping. Carro found she didn't have enough money and had to write a cheque, and Daniel Wetherby told her off in front of the whole check-out queue for her lack of foresight. The car park was overcrowded, and in trying to extract them among the waiting shoppers hovering for their parking place Daniel backed into a supermarket trolley which jammed beneath the bumper so that he had to get out and prise it out. He was wheezing when he climbed back in behind the wheel, and snapped at Carro when she told him to calm down.

Back home, Thomas sat down quietly to watch cartoons on the telly out of the way, but that was no good because Carro wanted to clean in there, and his grandfather kidnapped him to go down to the DIY shop with him for some more curtain rail, and spent the journey complaining about his mother. Trooper wished he wouldn't do that. He didn't do it very often, but Trooper had overheard Daniel and Carro speaking of her denigratingly, and had begun to hate them even before they began to speak of having him there

forever. He did not think he could face living forever with
Dan and Carro.

By lunch-time Trooper's mind was made up, and as soon
as the meal was over he disappeared upstairs 'to play' and
collected his Garfield rucksack stuffed with the few things
he might need on the easy journey back to Judy. When he
slipped silently downstairs his grandfather and Carro were
busy discussing what shade of pink to redecorate the bedroom. Trooper eased open the lobby door, shut it behind
him, then turned the handle on the front door and walked
out to freedom. He hitched his rucksack determinedly on
to his shoulders and trotted down the cul-de-sac towards
the road to town.

'*Cui bono?*' Alec explained. 'It's not a bad principle. It's led
us after a few red herrings on this occasion, but it's brought
us to the truth, in the end.'

'What's the good?' Liz hazarded. Latin had not been an
option at her school and she had never felt the lack of it.

'Not quite; "to whom is the good?—" i.e., who benefits?'
Alec waited for the traffic to clear, turned on to the main
road and accelerated away. 'In this case, who benefits from
the murder? Most obviously, Medisearch; but when you
look more closely, that horse won't run. CAMEX is a
national organization, albeit the local branch was extremely
active and strong. So killing Kate Randall because she was
running CAMEX wouldn't have that much effect on the
debate taking place on medical experimentation and the
use of human embryos.' He glanced at his watch. 'By
the way, the vote is being taken today; remind me to put
the radio on later and we'll see if it's in the news. No, that's
the first red herring. But in a way it's part of a much larger
red herring, because Kate Randall was not meant to die at
all. It was simply her misfortune to be driving Judy's car,
and to look, that evening, more like Judy than Judy was
herself, if you see what I mean.'

The woodlands and fields of the fringe of the Ashdown
Forest pressed close alongside them, the green of the foliage

unreal and dazzling. The sun slanted warmly into the car. Liz fiddled with the sun visor to shade its dazzle.

'So, we take Judy to be the intended victim, and the question *Cui Bono?* begins to take on a different hue. Who benefits by Judy's death?'

'Miles Wetherby,' said Liz promptly.

'Well, yes. In two ways, because he gets her money—and he is not too proud to like the idea of that—and he is free to, er, to marry again, thus providing himself with the one thing lacking to complete his eligibility for a safe parliamentary seat.'

For a few minutes Alec descended into thoughtfulness, so that Liz prompted him. 'But?'

'Sorry! But . . . he has an alibi, and anyway, how likely is it that he, of all people, is going to mistake another woman for his wife? In any case, you're thinking too literally. There was something Judy possessed which she herself would consider far more valuable than any amount of money; that she would hold on to at all costs, come what may, so that only death would separate her from it.'

'Ohh . . . I see!'

'We're dealing with a nutcase, of course,' Alec said grimly, and for a moment Liz thought he meant Judy. But he went on, 'At least, I hope that only a nutcase would think that depriving a young boy of his mother was a virtuous act—however unsatisfactory she was *as* a mother. But then, of course, to this particular nutcase that was only the rationalization: the real motivation was the craving to *get* the boy: a child to pamper, and to look after them in old age.'

They swooped down a side road, and came out shortly on the A22. Alec turned south, and in minutes they were driving through the outskirts of Uckfield. 'The mechanics you can work out for yourself,' Alec said. 'Once we knew the killer, *how* it happened becomes clear, and the element of coincidence, although not totally removed, falls well within everyday bounds. There was one important question we omitted to ask, but in fact we'd been given the information in a different form more than once, and all we needed to do was make the mental connections.' They drove through the town, bumped over the level-crossing by the station and turned off on to a minor road. Half a mile further on Alec indicated left and turned into the estate Liz remembered so well. The same little girl was riding the same tricycle up and down the same driveway. The trees which the developer had shrewdly left standing at the far end of the road cast a rural temper on the cottagey boxes. Alec pulled in, and parked by the kerb.

Daniel Wetherby discovered Thomas's absence at half past two, and the hole in the fence at twenty to four. He had been half an hour walking round the estate, he had taken the car and driven up towards town, he had decided in the end to try once more on foot. He was overdressed for the mild weather and his exertions had worked him into a heat. Now anger darkened his large seamed face into a yet duskier red.

The fence divided one of the estate's internal footpaths from the railway cutting. The footpath made a short cut into town—but Trooper, who had only ever travelled into town by car, didn't know that. To Daniel Wetherby it was very likely that Thomas had come this way, and even more likely that his destination had been this illegal access to the railway line. With difficulty Wetherby squeezed his bulk through the opening, and began to scramble down the side of the cutting. Once he slipped, dropping several feet, his smooth shoes unable to grip, before he was able to grab an elder with his left hand; it stopped him abruptly, and his broad bottom hit the hard mixture of earth and shingle with a cruel bump.

By the time he regained his feet Wetherby was breathing stertorously, and his temper was restrained only by the absence of anything on which it could be vented. Impatiently he turned his large head this way and that, trying to decide which way Thomas would have gone.

Behind him, his simmering brain told him, lay the station. Thomas, then, lay ahead.

As Daniel Wetherby walked steadily along the track—it was awkward, stumbling on the oil-stained ballast, and very wearing—he kept half an eye on the fence which divided the cutting from neighbouring properties. Kids always managed to make a new hole, slipping through out of devilment and provoking angry parents to write to the newspaper asking why British Rail couldn't do something about it. Wetherby's memory slipped back nearly sixty years, to a day long forgotten until now, when he and his brother George had trespassed on to the line near their home at Sharpthorne. It had been an afternoon in high summer, and he almost thought he could smell the seductive mixture of meadow grasses, steam, coal smoke and hot oil.

The silence had long ago grown uncomfortable. Carro Wetherby sat on the sofa opposite Alec biting her lip. Alec was reconciled to waiting, but it had been a long time now. From time to time their eyes met, and Carro's darted away.

'He should be back soon,' she said again, and jumped up, her muscles vigorous beneath her Jaeger skirt, her breasts jigging beneath the fine wool of her jersey, to cross to the window, as if it offered a panorama of the town from which Daniel's whereabouts might have been picked out, instead of only a view across the street to a child's plastic tricycle abandoned in a driveway.

'Perhaps they've stopped to buy sweets.'

'It's not good for Thomas to have sweets,' she said sharply. 'He can't have gone far . . . not without the car. He must have found him by now.'

They froze in their tableau while another five minutes passed. Alec gestured to Liz, and she slipped out to use her radio.

'His heart's not strong, you see.'

'He's getting on in years,' Alec agreed; as if Carro of all people needed reminding. Her neck was barely lined, her

waist distinct, her hips and thighs active beneath the soft
tweed skirt. Liz came back into the room, and took up a
position near the other woman.

'He's . . . not always quite what he seems,' Carro said as
if explaining something. 'He *has* been good to me. He has
a lot of love in him.'

'I can believe it,' Liz said. 'I've seen him with Thomas.'

Carro looked down contritely. 'You have to understand.
He's never had children of his own. Miles was just a tot
when Dan married his mother.' Liz glanced at Alec, who
shook his head fractionally: this was news to both of them.
'And Miles—Dan doesn't talk about it much, but I know
Miles was the cause of a lot of pain to him; as if he invested
so much hope in him, and then he turned out . . . not bad,
but different. He was very involved in, you know, student
sit-ins, that sort of thing; they never have seen eye to eye
politically. Now he invests it all in Thomas. More so, if
anything. I suppose that's because he's older, do you think,
Chief Inspector?'

'I think it's dangerous when anyone invests all their
hopes in another person,' Alec said. 'You start to want to
control . . . and we can't do that. We can't be God even to
our *own* children, Mrs Wetherby.'

She looked at him speculatively. 'No; I suppose not.'

Trooper was weary. The pavement had run out and it was
harder going than he had anticipated, walking on the verge
by the side of the busy road. Cars sped by at cruel speed,
and every so often a lorry passed and the shock-wave buffeted him and tried to snatch him into the roadway. He
walked doggedly, head down, and tried not to think how
far he had to go. Uckfield seemed to have stretched for
miles, and though now at last he had left it behind there
was no sign of the next village which, in the car by his
mother's side, had been but the blink of an eye away.

Once or twice a car seemed to slow a little as it passed,
and he began to hope that someone would stop and offer
him a lift. He had started walking with his mother's warn-

ings against accepting lifts ringing in his ears; but that had been a long, weary, footsore way away, and the warnings echoed a good deal less insistently now.

Over on the far side of the road in a driveway he noticed a flash of colour, and glanced furtively sideways. Two policemen sat in a patrol car, watching the traffic. One of them opened his mouth wide in a yawn; the other was picking his nose. Thomas kept his gaze down and walked on.

Wetherby had walked, or rather stumbled, half a mile when he first saw a flash of colour and movement by the lineside far ahead. He screwed up his old eyes and picked out the small, blurred figure crouched down by the rails: putting a penny on the track, the monkey, to see what the train would do to it, just as he and George used to do so long ago with ha'pennies, when there were ha'pennies, and then see if the shopkeepers would take them for pennies. Wetherby called out, but he was too far away, or the boy too intent, to be heard. He saved his breath and lengthened his stride.

The two-toned horn of the train drifted up the line from the station, and Wetherby suddenly felt apprehension. He could see that the boy had heard it, because he had backed off and was almost invisible behind a linesman's hut, his eyes fixed on whatever it was he had placed on the track. The old man could see it glinting: a tin, or a glass bottle; and as the rails began to hum and the deep burble of the diesel growled up behind him, it winked in the wan sun and rolled off with a distant clink.

Wetherby stumbled clumsily into a run as the boy ran out to replace the bottle and the two-car diesel unit rounded the corner. He heard the clap of the vacuum brakes coming on as the driver saw the child; but even a small train not travelling very fast takes a lot of stopping. Stumbling, wheezing, desperate, Daniel Wetherby tried to run as he had all those years ago when he had been a boy; ran until the pain flooded over his body. The wheels were screeching on the rails as the train slid past him and bore down on the small figure only yards ahead. Wetherby felt the tears in his eyes, and opened his mouth to cry out at the same moment that the child turned its face and he saw it was not Thomas at all; not his beloved grandson, but another, older child, a girl. The relief and the disappointment hit him a great blow in the chest: something inside him seemed to swell up and explode; and merciful blackness descended in front of his eyes.

The train driver, ashen-faced, climbed trembling down from his cab, staggering as he reached the lineside. Unsteadily he walked back to where a girl in dirty jeans and grubby T-shirt stared down at the man's body lying rag doll-like on the stained ballast. The child turned to him and he opened his mouth to sear it with all the anger born of his own fright; and then he saw the terror in her eyes, and the dark stain spreading at the crotch of her jeans, and his anger seemed to deflate.

He looked back at the train, where the guard was climbing down from the last compartment with a sack of warning detonators, then turned back to the unmoving huddle of clothing. The dark, congested face of Daniel Wetherby stared up at him as he rolled the body over. 'You stupid cunt,' the railwayman muttered as he began the futile preparations for artificial respiration. 'You poor sod.'

Carro Wetherby looked down mutely at her husband's heavy face. Death had slackened the elderly sinews even further, so that the flesh hung in ugly folds pulling back the corners of the mouth. He looked very old indeed; but who could tell where Carro fitted in? An onlooker might put her down as a daughter, maybe, or a niece. Only the cut of her clothes and the single strand of pearls on her cashmere jumper hinted that she might be this elderly man's widow. Alec, watching her, wondered what her future would hold. With her dead husband's house, his car, his money, she would be a woman of substance. If he met her in a year, he wondered, would he know her? In a sweatshirt, maybe, and jeans; by the side of a man like her stepson?

'It was all for him. Thomas would have been everything to him.' Carro's voice broke into his reverie.

'I know,' he said wearily, though he didn't believe it.

'We'd have been a *family* then,' she protested.

'I know,' said Alec again. 'I've no doubt it was hard, to see Judy, with Trooper, knowing what sort of woman she had been, how she had brought Trooper up, when you had . . . everything else, but no child.'

Carro Wetherby bowed her head. 'Judy . . .' she began, and faltered.

'Judy; a drunk; a suicide; promiscuous; but she was Thomas's mother, Mrs Wetherby! However hard it was for you to accept that.'

'It was,' she whispered. Then her voice stiffened. '*Why* should she have him? What had she ever done to deserve a boy like that? A little tart; why should he have to stay with her and suffer, when we could give him everything?'

Love kills as often as hate. Husbands kill their wives because they can't bear their marriage to drift down into staleness. Lovers kill because they can't face the fact that love is going, or has betrayed them. We all know of something which would make life perfect, if only we could have it; and it doesn't really seem so awful to help ourselves.

'I didn't really mean anyone any harm,' Carro complained. 'I didn't want that girl to die! It was all a dreadful mistake!'

Alec turned from her in disgust and glanced at Liz, who had her notebook out. 'It's a mistake Kate Randall didn't get a chance to live with,' he said shortly.

Carro Wetherby's legs folded inelegantly as if they had been punctured and she slumped heavily on to the sofa provided for grieving relatives and began to sob.

'Caroline Wetherby,' Alec began, 'I arrest you for the murder of Catherine Denise Randall. I have to warn you . . .'

'You don't have to bother,' Carro said through the tears which were streaking her Elizabeth Arden make-up. 'I did it. And I'd do it again,' she cried defiantly, 'if it meant

saving Thomas from that little shit and having . . .
having . . .'

'A son of your own,' Liz murmured under her breath.
'Oh, you poor cow!'

CHAPTER 26

Frances switched off the little portable radio before the
weather forecast. The medical experimentation bill had
passed its preliminary stages in Parliament: it was unlikely
to be stopped now. It had been the last item on the news.

She looked at Alec ruefully. 'Poor Kate. Somehow, I can't
help feeling that if the bill had been defeated, at least she
wouldn't have died in vain.'

'I don't suppose she did,' Alec replied. 'Her death made
sure the whole debate came out into the open. It's awful to
say it, but dying as she did, she achieved more than ever
she could have otherwise. Do you know CAMEX enrolled
fifty thousand new members nationwide in the four weeks
after her death?'

'I hope wherever she is, she knows that. And I'm glad
her death didn't simply become one more unsolved murder.
It would have, in the end, Alec, wouldn't it?'

He nodded. 'We were slow. I was. We had the information in our hands all the time. We knew Carro couldn't
abide being in the same room as Judy; but we never made
the connection. When Judy came over to see Dan, Carro
always arranged to be out—it was as simple as that. She
was out the night of the storm: at the cinema in Crawley.
Driving back, she found herself passing Judy's car, which
was turning off the road. I still don't know where Kate had
spent the previous hour; she had plenty of choice, if she
wanted a remote spot to drown her sorrows.' He shook his
head in bewilderment. 'Anyway, by eleven or so she had
either turned for home, or was looking for somewhere to
finish off the bottle. She must have been fairly well oiled;

enough to make her a danger on the roads, I should say; certainly enough, anyway, to make her kidneys work overtime. Carro passed the car park just as Judy—as she thought—was turning in. Carro was the opportunist killer we had been looking for all the time, the passer-by with sufficient hate for Judy, and a burning conviction that providence had allocated Trooper to the wrong woman.'

'So will they get a conviction,' Frances asked, clearing away the plates and placing a bowl of strawberry mousse on the table, 'or will Carro be shown to be somehow insane?'

'I don't much care, frankly,' Alec said. 'We've done our part, found poor Kate's killer. The proof is down to Ransome and the scientists. You don't kill someone as Carro Wetherby killed Kate Randall without taking away some traces.'

'I thought it was the criminal who panicked who convicted himself? Carro sounds too cool for that.'

Alec helped himself happily from the bowl. 'Very cool,' he said. 'She behaved just as I imagine you would have done.' He caught her expression and wished he had chosen his words differently. For all her insight, she still believed there was an immutable gulf between those who do, and those who don't commit murder. 'It wasn't until Kate's hair came adrift that Carro realized she had killed the wrong woman. She immediately rucked up the clothing, then resisted the temptation to go any further. She walked to the trees at the edge of the car park—the last thing she wanted was to be fixed in the headlights of anyone who turned in, or to be seen walking along the roadway. Don't forget Kate's body was by now out in the open, very obviously dead.

'Horrible!' Frances said, but her eyes showed she could not free herself of fascination about how it had been done—and perhaps Alec's remark about Carro's similarity to herself held her fascinated, too.

'Mm! This is good! Well, Carro knew her own clothing *must* be stained, even though it was pitch black and she couldn't see. So once in shadow she peels off her gloves—

she's a woman who wears gloves, and it was a cold night, remember, as well as a windy one—and puts them, inside out, in her jacket pocket. Then she takes her *skirt* off, carefully turning it inside out. Then she takes her jacket off, turns that inside out, and ties the skirt inside it. Underneath she's got a dark jersey on, and a black slip. Nice and inconspicuous: could almost have been chosen for their suitability. For this reason she leaves the jersey on, even though it may be marked, reckoning that the jacket has protected those bits which are going to be in contact with the car seat. See how she's thinking?'

'She must have been absolutely wasted all these years,' Frances said, spellbound.

'She makes her way back to her car, climbs in, and drives home, arriving about half past eleven and slipping in unseen by Dan.'

'I'd have taken my shoes off before I got in the car,' Frances said at once.'

'Yes . . . but you're used to driving in bare feet. If you're not, I shouldn't imagine it's easy, and Carro decided to risk it, thinking that the trek across the grass would have cleaned them pretty effectively.'

'So that's how they'll get her.'

'Yes, she'd stepped in poor Kate's blood, and some of it stayed on the heel ridge of her shoe. They've taken enough from the clutch pedal to match it serologically.' He hesitated, then added: 'There was more on the seat, as it happens: a smear that had come off her underskirt. She explained it to Dan by saying she'd had an accident: her period had taken her by surprise.' He said with a grimace, 'Her last period was six months ago. When they stopped, she thought it was because she'd become pregnant at last.'

'Ah!'

'Quite. It was shortly after that, that Carro tried to get custody of Trooper given to Miles.'

'How much of all this did Dan suspect?'

'I think Dan knew. He certainly knew how much Carro hated Judy, and the intensity of her belief that it was unfair that a woman like Judy should have a son, and she not. I think he also found out that Carro had put the social workers on to Judy, to try and get Trooper taken away from her and placed in his father's care—which would have meant, in effect, Carro's and Dan's.'

Frances pushed her dish away and rested one arm, bare but for a simple ruby ring on her third finger, on the linen table-cloth. Alec thought of Tessa: of how even a marriage as basically stable as hers and Christopher's had downs, as well as ups. He felt his emotional muscles, debilitated by long inactivity, stretch themselves, and surprised himself by the eagerness with which he was looking forward to embarking on this new adventure.

'Ironically,' Frances remarked, 'because you suspected Judy, Carro got what she wanted for a while. Who's Trooper going to now, by the way?'

Alec sighed. 'He's in temporary care. The social workers are arguing it out, but it looks likely that he will go to Miles. Judy is considered too unstable, and Trooper still had the bruise where she'd hit him. Carro had achieved her end, as far as that goes; but she won't be around to benefit from it. Along the way she's lost all the family she had, now Dan's dead.'

She nodded. Miles's name seemed to cause her no pain. 'It's time he had a father. But to lose his mother . . .' She sat up suddenly straight. 'Alec, you don't think I'm marrying you just to secure a father for Lucy, do you?'

He looked at her guiltily, aware that he had been prepared to enter marriage on that unsatisfactory basis.

'You *do* think that!' She sprang to her feet, and came round to his side of the table, moving with her characteristic vigour and purpose. '*No!* Not to secure a father for Lucy; not because I want a conventional family; not because, like Carro Wetherby, I feel the urge to prove to myself I am still fertile. There are ways of finding *that* out, for heaven's sake!'

They were both laughing now. Alec felt his heart lighten as she seized and dismissed his apprehensions.

'Why, then?' he asked, genuinely wanting to know.

For answer she merely seized his head and pressed it to her breast, and his arms moved automatically to encircle her strong, slender waist.

'Because I love you, you dope!' she exclaimed exasperatedly.

'That's all right, then,' Alec murmured happily.

Alec dropped the last bulging file on to the heap. 'Take them away,' he said. 'Let's get back to ordinary life. A little decent crime.'

'That it, then?' Sally Field said disappointedly.

'That's it,' Liz confirmed. 'If you're lucky there'll be a nice little shoplifting for you tomorrow. Or I've got half a dozen Neighbourhood Watch visits to catch up on: cup of tea and a chat about the budgerigar and the grandchildren. Here: you take these.' And she dumped a stack of files into Sally's arms, and topped them with a pile of wire trays.

When the WPC had left, Liz said, 'I called on Judy Baker on my way home.'

Alec grunted. It was not on her way home at all, and they both knew it.

'I think it's going to be all right. I think *she's* going to be all right.'

'And the boy?'

'They've been persuaded to let him back to her for a trial period. I think probably his father didn't really want him. Poor Trooper—all the looking after Judy he had to do as a little lad; and then to be shunted from pillar to post. God help him if he ever finds out what it was all about. Poor little sod. Makes you wonder how he'll grow up, doesn't it, sir? But Judy's a good mother, really. If I had half of what either of them have had to go through I'd fold up and give in.'

Alec leant back in his chair and linked his hands behind his neck. 'I doubt it, Liz. People survive. In thirty years' time young Thomas will be indistinguishable from anyone else. Moderately good, moderately bad.'

'But we *aren't* the same, are we, sir?' she said wistfully. 'Only on the surface. The surface is pretty much the same, to make our job difficult, just as Carro Wetherby's surface was as ordinary as any woman's of her age. But underneath . . . these things *do* make a difference.'

'It just depends where you judge by. John Blake thinks nothing of moving genes around like pieces in a game of chess, whereas to Kate Randall that was irresponsible tinkering with nature. You just need a norm, and then you can judge everything else from it.'

'And what is the norm?'

'For all practical purposes you and I are, Liz,' he observed. He grinned. 'Which reminds me: you can put a date in your diary, if you will. May the sixteenth.'

'What's happening then?'

'I shall become a husband; and also, incidentally, a father. You'll come, I hope.'

Liz stared at him for a full minute. 'For crying out loud,' she said at last. 'Here comes the end of the world!'